WHEELS OF DESTRUCTION

MURDER IN PETRA

SEEMS DETECTIVE AGENCY
BOOK 6

GINA CHEYNE

First published in 2025 by Fly Fizzi Ltd
Pyers Croft
Compton, Chichester
West Sussex PO18 9EX
www.flyfizzi.co.uk

www.ginacheyne.com
Cover design by Kari Brownlie

ISBNs

978-1-915138-19-4 Wheels of Destruction ebook

978-1-915138-20-0 Wheels of Destruction paperback

978-1-915138-21-7 Wheels of Destruction hardback

Created with Vellum

To Faisal, Kalipha and all the people I met in Jordan who told me their stories. Thank you.

My lover asks me: What is the difference between me and the sky?
The difference, my love, is that when you laugh, I forget about the sky.

Nizar Qabbani

AUTHOR'S NOTE

Title headings in the book relate to Arab sayings in use in the past or in the present day. Most of them are similar to sayings used in the the English language and are, I believe, self-explanatory.

PROLOGUE

The Mayfair bookseller jumped onto the podium in an athletic manner and raised his arms for silence.

'Ladies and Gentlemen, thank you all for coming this evening. Just a few important points before we get started...'

The risk warnings done, he swept his arm towards the woman to his right and said, 'Now, enough from me. The moment you have all been waiting for: Lady Bumstead, author of *Murder on the Mekong, The True Story*. Please welcome our inspirational authoress.'

As the clapping died down, a slim woman wearing Chanel clambered onto the podium. Athletic she might not be, but inspirational she clearly was, capturing every eye in the room and holding it: at eighty-two years old she still had immaculate black curls and flawless skin.

Lady Bumstead began her speech and Cat, in the back of the audience, sighed. She'd already read a pre-publication copy of the book and knew it was a bundle of baloney. Lady Bumstead had taken the profession of storyteller literally.

She even claimed the CIA tried to push her into a piranha pool because she knew too much.

Cat was one of the detectives who had caught Lady B and got her arrested. The book had made her so angry. Yes, Lady B had been convicted by a judge, but only of "manslaughter when her mind was confused by the prescription drugs she was taking". And, because she was already eighty-two, her punishment had been house arrest. Hardly a punishment when you saw the incredible spread the billionairess lived in. Cat shook her head and tried to remember who it was that had said, "How much justice can you afford?" Was it Benjamin Franklin? Certainly Lady B could afford the best, and her legal team did an incredible job. She let her mind go back to the enticing voice of Lady Bumstead as it slid around the room.

'... and, as you will see when you read it, the whole story was completely different. It was murder! MURDER! Done not by me, but by someone with international power behind him. Someone able to escape the wheels of justice. A travesty. A travesty indeed, making a mockery of our *impartial* justice system. I hope you enjoy the book and learn the *truth* about our laws.'

And then the champagne-soaked crowd was clapping and stamping their feet. Some were yelling: 'Bravo.' 'Shame.' 'String him up!'

Lady B put up her hand for silence. 'Sadly, I do have something to add to this. I am here under special licence just for you, my audience and friends. As you know, I was erroneously found guilty of manslaughter and am sentenced to life in my tiny little house in London.'

The applause started again and Cat gagged. A house so tiny you could fit all three detectives' houses inside and still have space to swing a cat (hopefully not Cat). The house even had a ballroom.

'But I am allowed visits from my doctor and unfortunately, he has diagnosed me with a rare but, I hope, entirely curable form of cancer.' She blinked away tears, dabbing her eyes with her silk handkerchief. 'So, tomorrow I shall be going into The Toppest Hospital where I will be operated on. With luck, all will go well, but anyone wanting to know my condition should contact my darling step-granddaughter, Jade.'

As the clapping and cheering started again, she raised her hand a third time. 'One more thing. All the profits from my book will be going to a charity close to my heart: The Underdogs. The Underdogs is a new foundation administered by my darling Jade. So, buy! Buy! Buy! You are giving to a tremendously worthy cause.'

She blew kisses to a young woman in the audience, who walked forward and waved unsmilingly. Cat sucked in her cheeks. Jade was an unlikely granddaughter for Lady B: she was dressed entirely in black leather, had numerous studs in both the leather and her skin, several visible tattoos, and punk-style hair.

If only Miranda, one of her SeeMs Detective Agency colleagues, was here. Miranda would gallop up to Jade, say hello, and quickly find out all about her connections and more. But this was an invitation-only party and Cat was only there because her boyfriend was part of the entertainment and had smuggled her in.

Thing is, thought Cat. *I don't believe any of it. What is Lady B up to?*

When Cat got home there was a handwritten message from Miranda on the kitchen island, propped up against a vase of flowers. Cat looked at it, wondering why she hadn't just sent a text, rather than walk round from her house to leave a note. But that was Miranda. Determinedly anti-tech. How lucky the third member of their team was Stevie, who loved technology. Her only drawback was that as an airline pilot, she was not always available to do things, but, thanks to the mobile world they lived in, she usually had time for research between flights.

Had a mysterious phone call, Miranda had written. *New client in Chelsea wants a visit tomorrow morning. Said he knew it was short notice but he'll make it worth our while. That means Stevie is out; she doesn't fly back from SA until the end of the month. More Zoom calls! Pah! Ugh. Ugh. Call me a.m. Love you. Xx M.*

Interesting, muttered Cat to herself. Lack of detail but exciting. Roll on tomorrow and we'll see what the future holds.

CHAPTER 1
THE TREE BEGINS WITH
A SEED

S andy Blee stared at the email from the literary agent. She'd been so excited to get it. Everyone knew they only replied if they thought you were worth following up, and there'd been several paragraphs of feedback. Lots of praise:

Excellent character description.

Good dialogue.

Really got into the story.

I would buy this if I saw it in a bookshop.

And then.

But sadly not a good fit for me.

Followed by the little sop: *but I will ask around the agency in case anyone else feels differently.*

Ha! She might as well not have bothered. It was still thanks and no thanks.

Sandy had written to every literary agent covering crime. Several who liked thrillers, romance, or fantasy. She entered every competition she could find, from short stories to long, poems and satire, cartoons and children's, and recently she'd started a blog.

But she was still a receptionist and not a published writer.

She thought of moving north. Up north they had agencies who specialised in Up North writers. Or she could take those pills to make herself Black like the model in *Tales of the City*, then she could get an agent who specialised in under-represented authors. Nobody specialised in twenty-something white women living in Surrey. No one.

She bent her pencil crossly. Perhaps she could break it into thousands of pieces and burn it in the fire, cause a huge conflagration, and burn the house down like Mathilda. Trouble was, it wasn't a real fire, so the bits would just slide off, and she wouldn't have a pencil to write with so she'd have to buy another.

Her brother stopped snoring and looked over.

'No good then?'

'No.'

'Not surprised. You're a bit too ordinary to be a writer. You haven't experienced anything. Writers have depth. What you got?'

He laughed and shut his eyes. She wondered whether to stick the pencil in his eye. Would it kill him? That would certainly get her noticed. All her stories would become best-sellers overnight as psychologists, judges, lawyers, and all sorts struggled to find out what compelled her to kill her elder brother. Her only remaining family member. Perhaps they would dig up her mother to see if she killed her, too; although since her mother spent ten years dying of cancer, it seemed unlikely.

He opened an eye. 'If you're taking the dog out, get a newspaper.'

'Thank you,' she murmured sarcastically, 'please.'

He ignored her.

She looked at the dog asleep in its basket. Perhaps if she went to the park she would find a handsome young man who would fall madly in love with her at first sight. Perhaps she would witness a murder. Chase the perpetrator. Rugby tackle him while others around her were too scared.

Her name would then be on everyone's lips, her books would sell in crazy numbers, and agents would be queuing at her door to represent her. It was almost exciting going to the park with this in store.

What a hero.

She dug the dog out of its bed and dragged its unwilling body to the door, where she put on the lead.

In the park, two old men were discussing whether to go to the pub before it closed, and a woman pushed her daughter in a pram. No one looked her way. No thirty-two-year-old billionaire dropped his helicopter into the empty green square and asked her to be his, albeit with lots of weird conditions.

Back home, she gave the newspaper to her brother. He took it without looking up and continued scrolling on his phone. Porn, probably. Or one of the dating sites where no one ever swiped him right. Or was it left? She had never joined one. The thought of who would choose her made her feel sick. It would either be some serial killer who wanted another victim, or some pimply git who couldn't even get a desperate housewife to date him. She wasn't sure which was worse.

Her brother shut his eyes and placed the newspaper over his head.

Should someone else murder him? At first she would be thought guilty. Her books would sell and he would be dead: not entirely an advantage since they shared the rent.

Would she be able to keep paying the rent from prison?

How quickly would the police discover she was another innocent victim?

There was a terrific banging on the door. Sandy jumped and accidentally bit her lip. Tasted blood. Was this her brother's murderer? Or, alternatively, a gorgeous man who had seen her in the newsagent but was too shy to talk to her... No, not that. That was the sort of man she did meet: geeky twits who couldn't look her in the eye, perhaps one of the two who signed up to her blog. No, this man had landed in the square and wanted to charge after her but had to shut down his helicopter first, or maybe he had to fill the Porsche with fuel so they could go off to Marbella or somewhere to expound their passion. Did one expound passion? Better than expend, certainly.

The banging on the door was repeated, louder, and her brother moved the newspaper enough to say, 'Are you going to get that?'

She opened the door. The dog hadn't barked. But then it never did.

Outside was a gorgeous man with the largest bouquet of roses she'd ever seen. 'It's for you,' he cried, 'my darling.'

Well, he would have been handsome thirty or forty years ago. Not that that was any use to her since she wouldn't have been born. And he did have a large box.

'Amazon,' he said. And after quickly taking a picture of her holding the delivery, he withdrew into his Ford Escort.

The parcel was for her brother.

'Oh, yeah, I forgot.' He took it. 'What's for supper?'

She twirled her pencil thoughtfully.

CHAPTER 2

THE LEADER OF THE TRIBE IS
THEIR SERVANT

I n Chelsea, Cat and Miranda entered the cold chill of an undistinguished office block, heading for the UIO (Unbelievable Insurance Offers) suite and their appointment with the new client. Taking one of the many lifts, they found themselves on the fifteenth floor and walking out directly into UIO's offices.

'Thank you for coming,' said the thin man approaching them, his hand extended. He wore an elegant suit. *Made for him*, Cat thought, *and, judging by its cut, probably in Savile Row*. She wondered if Miranda had noticed it, but then fashion wasn't really her thing.

'Would you like coffee, tea, glass of water?' he asked. 'Or shall we get down to it?'

The girls sat, declining refreshments, too fascinated by this potential client who didn't even give his name, to drink coffee.

'I've been reading your files,' he said, 'and I must say I *am* impressed with the work of the SeeMs Detective Agency.' He emphasised this with a head nod and a smile.

'You've done some excellent work, of exactly the kind we need.'

'Thanks,' said Miranda, 'we enjoy what we do.'

He nodded again, less enthusiastically. Perhaps in his world that was a given; enjoy work or die.

'Tell me,' he said, 'why the name SeeMs Detective Agency? It seems,' he allowed himself a discreet laugh, 'almost counterintuitive to call yourself *It Seems to be a Detective Agency.* As though you did spy work.'

Miranda gave a big, bellowing laugh. 'Clever!' she said. 'I like it. But no, it's somewhat different. SeeMs: See – C – is for Cat, M for Miranda and S for Stevie; we're the three principals; plus we're looking behind what *seems* to be true to the reality beneath. And we're all girls: MS. You get it?'

'Yes,' he said drily.

'Great,' said Cat, moving impatiently on her seat. 'And what is it you want us to do?'

He stared at her for a moment. Had she been a bit too hasty? Was he reconsidering his offer?

He looked down at his paper. 'I need you to identify a missing person, someone who has absconded from prison, and prevent them from leaving wherever you find them, long enough for us to get them arrested by the local police. Are you with me so far?'

They said they were, although Cat couldn't help wondering why they had been chosen for this job, which seemed both so simple and nearly impossible. A job more suitable for a local police force or a tracking team.

'You may wonder why I chose you for this job.' He paused and examined them. 'Well, the truth is our absconder is a real Scarlet Pimpernel and it will take an expert, or someone who knows them well, to see through their disguise. You, however, do know the missing person well. And you've brought them to justice before. So, with any luck and a following wind, you should be able to do it. British justice is relying on you,' he said with a sudden hyperbolic skyward sweep of his arms completely at odds with his serious face.

When his arms returned to his side, he continued. 'Have you ever heard of a Second World War spy called Virginia Hall?'

'No,' said Miranda.

'Yes,' said Cat.

'Well, she perfected the art of disguise – anything from a young man to an old woman. And we suspect your target will be even more cleverly underhand than her. Anything is possible, even a sex change. This person is desperate to leave our clutches and start a new life.'

Cat and Miranda exchanged glances. Which of their previous clients had run amuck?

'I'll need you to travel soon. We know the person in question is planning to go on holiday, but we're not sure exactly where they're planning to go. However, there are distinct tourist routes in the world of the rich and this person is very rich. We have information that our villain will be heading for Petra in Jordan.'

'Ooh,' said Miranda, 'will they be looking for Indiana Jones or his treasure?'

'Ha ha, most original. Furthermore, we know that our absconder has used a wheelchair before and most certainly will again.'

'How do you know all this?' said Cat. 'And if you know where they're likely to be, and how they're likely to be disguised, then surely you can alert the local police force yourselves. Why do you need us?'

He looked at her, pursing his lips thoughtfully. 'Yes, I

understand why you're confused. However, when I tell you who the person is and how we know their likely itinerary, you'll understand why we need your help.' He paused a moment. 'The most important thing is that they are with a group who are all in wheelchairs.' He snorted. 'A perfect disguise.'

Cat rubbed her nose. This was getting odder and odder.

'Provided you agree, I can give you more information, which should help identify our client when you get out to Jordan.'

They glanced quickly at each other and nodded.

'Good. Before I give you exact details, I have to tell you, you may be needed to leave at any time, either immediately or not for weeks. Are you ready to go at any time?'

Cat knew she could leave at any time, but Miranda had young children. However, she also had a husband who worked from home. She looked at her. Miranda nodded. 'Yes,' she said, 'we are ready.'

CHAPTER 3
WHAT IS COMING IS BETTER THAN WHAT HAS GONE

Preparing for work the next day, Sandy thought she might do something different. Wear a tight-fitting jumper, perhaps? Stilettos? Straighten her wild curls? Tiny pink skirt? Trouble was, no one saw anything above the waist, rather like a news presenter in the old days. Come to think of it, she was a bit like a news presenter, only the news she gave was the arrival of the next client at Percy's Bifold Doors.

When she got her job, she thought she'd been chosen from hundreds for her Svengali-like personality, a lure for every potential client who saw her sitting at the reception desk in her lacy shirt from Primark. Later, she found out she was the only candidate.

Staff and clients flew in throughout the morning, some saying, 'Morning', or 'Hello, Shirley'.

Shirley was actually the girl who covered middays and weekends, but their names were so similar she could understand the confusion. Others blew her a kiss and said 'still beautiful' or some such rubbish.

The highlight of the day was the post. Not, sadly, the

elderly postman, although he'd already told her he was single and looking.

She sorted through the mail, divided it into where it needed to go, and waited for Shirley – wearing her delivery girl hat – to take it away. There was the usual junk and one particularly optimistic company trying to sell them bifold doors. Sandy wondered whether to mark it URGENT and send it directly to the CEO.

Today, there was a letter for her.

Sandy had her letters delivered to work because if she had them delivered to home, her brother opened and read them. He said it was because he thought they were for him, both having similar names. Although, in truth, he was J. Blee and she was S. Blee. Perhaps his eyesight was going already.

Her letter looked like a circular and she opened it lethargically. It started badly:

Congratulations. You have won an all-expenses-paid holiday!

Yup! She'd had plenty of these before. Sometimes they referred to a previous phone call, email or text, none of which had happened.

She was about to fold it into a dart, ready to throw at the next person who blew her a kiss, when she noticed something different about this letter. It said:

Dear Ms Blee,

Congratulations on winning the Blerglergle Writing Competition sponsored by Wheelchair Warriors Holidays. You won the first prize: a paid working holiday in Jordan.

Please contact Miss Abbey for further details.

She frowned. She didn't want to get too excited. But what if this *was* something genuine? They did address her by name. None of her usual "prizes" did that. Could she have actually won something for once? She vaguely remembered one of her many competitions was indeed titled some ridiculous name like Blerglergle Writing.

She dialled Miss Abbey's number.

CHAPTER 4

WHOEVER RELIES ON OTHER PEOPLE'S SUPPLIES WILL FIND HIS HUNGER LASTS LONGER

Wheelchair Warriors Holidays! Jordan: A Petra Exclusive!
You deserve a break! A holiday for carer and caree!

Experienced pushers. Contact us now!

Declared the poster in bellowing letters. Underneath were the contact details and an explanation that you didn't need to be in a wheelchair to go; guests willing to push other guests would get a half-price holiday and their fares fully paid.

Jade looked at the poster and laughed. Since her gran was refusing to die, she still had little money, so a working holiday it was. She would volunteer as a 'pusher'. She sniggered. The people who made that poster must be dumb fuckers – pusher! Yeah, right. And whoever talked about a caree? Weird.

Many other people passed the poster, including Abbey, or Miss Abbey, as the guests preferred to call her. She too, wrinkled her nose. Guests. Warriors. Pushers. La di da. Who did their advertising? Clearly they were cheap. But Wheelchair Warriors Holidays paid her and she didn't have to push anyone, although she did have to deal with the problems of those inside and out.

They had pretty much filled the trip to **Jordan: A Petra Exclusive!** Six people in six wheelchairs, six pushers, and three on their own legs. She wondered idly what they should call the walkers collectively – sans-seats like the sans-culottes of the French Revolution? She sniggered. Still, better stick to the 'Ables', then at least everyone knew what she meant.

What would this trip be like? Their last trip to Hong Kong had been a breeze. Most of the people knew each other as the majority were from the same family, and they'd had a good laugh. The one before that, on the other hand, was like something out of Hell. On the first day, five of the six wheelchair sitters complained about their rooms. Then the Ables insisted on having a meal up the mountain – completely ignoring the fact that more than half the party could not climb. The cost of carrying the sitters up the mountain in sedan chairs had really eaten into the profits. The only good thing was that everyone was massively overcharged for those 'extras'.

This trip was unusual in that there was only her and the local guide, who was also the bus driver. Usually she had a helper who could run around doing the duff jobs, and a driver and a guide, but there had been staff cutbacks and she was alone. On the bright side, the company was flying her to Amman a day early so she could check the details, while the local guide was meeting the group inside the airfield to arrange their visas, so, with luck, any complaints would be made to him, not her.

She fluttered through the guest list and as she did so, her phone rang. The legend said: Prize Winner.

Abbey sighed. As though the paying guests weren't difficult enough, this one was a prize winner who had put her profession down as author/writer. They wouldn't have let a writer win, except no one else had entered the competition. Abbey hoped to goodness she was not a journalist. Journalists were always trouble.

CHAPTER 5

THE REWARD IS THE NATURE
OF THE WORK: YOU REAP
WHAT YOU SOW

Abbey stood with her sign that declared **Wheelchair Warriors Holidays**, watching the people come out of customs at Amman's airport in ones and twos. Everybody looked tired but only a few people came towards her board. The local guide should have brought the group together but instead sent them a WhatsApp, telling them to wait in the baggage area, which most of them didn't, or couldn't, read.

Everybody looked tired, but only a few people came towards her board. Many of the guests were old and not in the best of health, and the five-hour flight, plus all the waiting around at the airport, had left them exhausted. Abbey could see they were ready for bed but she had to check she had all the right people. On one previous occasion in Sri Lanka, still talked about at WWH, the guide had thought all the people sitting in wheelchairs were his guests and had guided them onto the bus, oblivious of the fact that some were not on holiday at all. The bus had arrived at its destination in Kandy before he discovered half the people were destined for Gaul and several of his guests had been left at the airport. He was no longer with the company.

She brought out her list.

Five couples were now sitting beside her and two of the walkers who were talking to each other. She was still missing one wheelchair pairing and one single walker. She looked over the group and was certain she'd spotted the *prize winner who might be a journalist.*

'Are you Sandra Blee?' she asked the heavily pierced young woman in black.

'Nah. Jade,' said the girl. 'I'm here with Mrs Tank.'

Abbey looked at her list and ticked them off. The others, now realising officialdom was starting, began to call out their names.

'Mr Cox.'

'Roxanna Victory.'

'Mr Jarvis...'

Everyone had either brought or been allotted pushers apart from the woman with Mediterranean looks called Roxanna. Roxanna was annoyed about it.

'Who's going to push me? I hope he's not one of those idiots who thinks a wheelchair is a sports car.'

Abbey looked at her list and discovered it was the prize-winning writer, Sandy Blee.

'Actually,' Abbey said, 'she's an extremely careful young lady, very experienced and capable, with an excellent pushing history.'

Roxanna raised her eyebrows and sneered. Abbey noticed she had buck teeth. 'And where is she?'

Abbey looked at her phone. She hoped there was some sort of message, but there was none. However, she did have Sandy's phone number. 'I'll give her a call,' she said, smiling sweetly and walking away in case she was going to have to shout.

Sandy answered immediately. 'Hello?'

'Is that Sandra Blee?'

'Yes, of course. It's my phone.'

Abbey gritted her teeth. Not just *not here*, but also an idiot. 'Where are you, dear? We need you to meet your client to push her to the bus, and then into the hotel.'

She wanted to scream, *Didn't you read the instructions I sent? Those details were clear and large.* But Sandy's position between an employee and a guest and the possibility she was writing for a travel magazine made Abbey more careful.

'Oh, sorry!' said Sandy. 'I had no idea.' She gave a little giggle. 'I suppose I should have read all the bumf, but what with one thing and another, arguing with my brother and making arrangements for the dog, well, you know. Shall I come and join you now?'

'Yes, please. We have a big board just outside arrivals.'

'Oh yes,' said Sandy cheerfully. 'I saw it, but I imagined it was for the guests... I thought there'd be a smaller one for the workers. I'm at the café, won't be long.'

Abbey bit her lip and muttered to herself, but she didn't want bad publicity. Who does?

She returned to Roxanna Victory and said sweetly, 'She's just coming. The dear one thought you'd like a coffee...'

'No. I don't drink coffee.'

Abbey hoped Sandra Blee had not brought her charge a coffee, but if she had, she might just throw it over her. She had a bad feeling about Roxanna – bit of an oversight putting someone who might be a professional complainer with the journalist.

Once Sandra Blee and her coffee had finally turned up,

they set off for the specially adapted bus. Luckily, this one had arrived. On a previous occasion, the company had sent a normal one and a claim that all the adapted buses were in the garage. Abbey and her helper had had to carry six elderly and overweight individuals up the bus steps and down again at the hotel. It was not an experience she (or her back) wanted to repeat.

Once they were underway, she stood up to give the clients all the holiday details. Everything was in their packs, both emailed beforehand and given to them in printed form at Heathrow airport, but Abbey knew Sandra Blee was not the only person who did not read the small, or even large, print.

As she went through the statutory welcome, she looked at her guests. As well as Sandy and Roxanna, Jade and Mrs Tank, there was a Mr Jarvis with his disabled daughter – was she really ill or just fat? – but perhaps life in a wheelchair did that to you. They were not talking to each other but although they were silent, they didn't appear antagonistic. One couple, a Mr and Mrs Cox, however, were quite different. Abbey never liked married couples on trips; they always brought their arguments from home with them. These two were currently disdainfully silent, but she had heard them sniping at each other at the airport and it didn't fill her with confidence.

There were two single women in their forties who wanted to be known as Jolly and Spice – they were giggling and whispering to each other, clearly dissecting their fellow travellers – and a Mrs Williams, who had been given a pusher at Heathrow airport. Her helper was called Harry, a large, strong-looking man of forty-something. Abbey was torn between hoping to get to know him better and praying he wouldn't make trouble with the younger guests.

There were also the three walkers, who were meant to be useful if anything happened to the pushers, but very seldom were. On a previous trip – possibly the same one as the sedan chairs – two pushers had hurt their backs and were unable to work, but the four young male walkers, instead of filling in, disappeared into town to get drunk every night. Holiday from Hell. Which was fine if you were the one getting compensation, but not so good if you were the company giving it. Since then, the company had created a rule that none of the pushers could be related. A fatuous rule, Abbey thought. Yes, two of the drunken louts had been brothers, but boys were quite able to get drunk with friends and didn't need relatives to do it. In her opinion it just showed how out of touch WWH were.

Having said her piece, Abbey sat down and started making notes. It was useful to put short descriptions beside each name so she could remember them. Clients always seem to appreciate you knowing their names. However, she'd only just started making notes when she felt a presence at her elbow; it was Sandra Blee. It would be.

'Can I help?' she said, smiling angelically.

'Yeah,' said Sandy, kneeling down beside her, although Abbey had just very clearly told the clients to remain in their seats unless it was an emergency. No doubt Ms Blee had been drinking her coffee or examining the view when she was speaking.

'I wondered…'

'Hmm?'

'Could I have a list of all the clients? Then I can remember their names. After all, I am working, aren't I? I should know who to help.' She smiled.

Abbey thought, *Is this an emergency or could it have waited until the hotel?*

'I'm sorry,' she said, 'client confidentiality doesn't allow it. You'll have to ask them yourself.'

Sandy returned to her seat and Abbey thought, *So there, Miss Journalist. Do your own dirty work.*

CHAPTER 6
THE CAMEL DOES NOT SEE
ITS OWN HUMP

In the hotel in Amman, Sandy was given a room with a shared balcony next to Roxanna. *Wonderful hotel this*, she thought, sighing. It was the first time she'd been outside of Surrey and everything was so different, cleaner and, honestly, so much better and more exciting. Even the air had a distinct tang.

Roxanna seemed OK. Definitely an improvement on her brother. She hadn't had much time with her yet, but Roxanna was relatively young (compared to most of the guests), maybe early fifties or something, and so thin it was painful. Sandy had never suffered from being too thin – even on the carotene-only diet – but Roxanna's skinniness would mean easy pushing and the hotel was brilliant for wheelchairs – all flat floors, wide doors, big lifts – and she had a huge bathroom with a walk-in shower. It was true, thought Sandy, scratching her head with her pen absent-mindedly, that Roxanna did have rather noticeably protruding teeth. They looked like the sort of thing people wore in school plays or as a disguise. But surely Roxanna couldn't be in disguise, could she? Maybe Sandy could write a crime novel about this trip and make her the villain. Or would that be unkind?

Sandy walked out onto the balcony. Interesting view of Amman's streets, she thought; it looked like a very modern city. She took a few pictures and sat down in the sun to update her blog. OK, she only had two readers, but after this trip she might get more, maybe even up to ten or twelve if she was lucky. A trip in Jordan must make more interesting reading than the listing of life in Guildford.

She had other plans too. She was going to write a brilliant short story about this trip. This time she would win the competition – whichever one it was – and get a proper, hopefully monetary, prize. Could she write about her fellow travellers, or would that be too invasive?

Miss Abbey seemed a bit of a schoolmarm! Big woman, school gym-teacher type. Bossy or what? Still, perhaps it was difficult trying to run a group of people who didn't know each other, and with all the added complications of wheelchair travel. Sandy longed to discover how Roxanna and the others ended up in wheelchairs. Would they think her nosey? Perhaps she could explain she was writing a blog. Or would that make it worse? People don't always like journalists, on the other hand most people do like authors. Perhaps she should stick to the truth and say she was trying to become an author. Or did that sound too limp? Best to say nothing at all and just listen.

Bang!

The adjoining gate between the two balconies was flung open, hitting the wall and bouncing back as though in complaint. Roxanna wheeled through, smiling in a diffident manner.

'Sorry to barge in, but although I can open the gate, I can't knock on it first without falling on the floor. I didn't think you'd want me flying headlong at your feet and finding your first duty was to lift me back into the chair. I don't know who designs this accessible stuff but it certainly isn't anyone in a wheelchair.' Her laugh wasn't entirely happy.

Sandy laughed too, but slightly anxiously. She wasn't sure that disability was a source of humour, but perhaps Roxanna was going to show her otherwise.

'I thought we'd better get to know each other, Sandra,' said Roxanna. 'I mean, we're going to be together for the next two weeks.'

'Yes,' said Sandy, twisting a lock of hair in her index finger. 'Actually, I like to be called Sandy, if that's OK. What do you like? Roxanna or something else?'

Roxanna gave a weird smile that Sandy didn't understand and then said, 'You can call me Roxy.'

'Thanks, Roxy, that's a fun name.'

'Yes, it means reborn.'

'Oh. Great. And, er, if we're getting to know each other can I ask a couple of questions?'

'Sure,' said Roxy. 'What would you like to know?'

Sandy gave an embarrassed shrug. 'Oh well, you know, all the usual things. Parents. Siblings. That sort of thing. Like, are your parents still alive?'

'No,' said Roxy. 'I have a sister but she's a bitch and we don't speak. She lives in Hong Kong. My parents moved there to be with her, and died there. I didn't speak to them either.'

'Oh,' said Sandy, wishing she hadn't asked. 'I'm er...'

'Don't say you're sorry. It was the making of me. They were shits. When I was in an accident, not my fault at all, they did a runner. Left me to make my own life, which I did. Believe me, Sandy, friends are much better than relatives.

What was that joke we used to have in our old maths text-book? "Friends you make yourself, relations you are blessed with."'

'Oh.' Sandy smiled and hoped Roxy wouldn't notice she hadn't a clue what she was talking about. 'I have a brother,' said Sandy, trying to continue the mood of shared confidences. 'He's not very nice either. We live together, but only because we can't afford the rent individually.'

'Where do you live?'

'Surrey. I work in Guildford. Receptionist. But really I want to be a writer.' Sandy blushed; she was being brave admitting that, but thought Roxy seemed friendly and wouldn't judge her.

'That's good,' said Roxy. 'We should all have ambition. Especially when you're young. How old are you, Sandy?'

'Twenty-six.'

'Really. I put you much younger, twenty-two or so.'

Sandy grimaced. 'Yes. My brother says that's because I haven't really lived. Before I was a receptionist, I looked after my mother until it was too much for me and she went into a home, but by then she was about to die. I was lucky to get the job. I haven't got any A levels. I had to leave school to look after Mum.'

Roxy looked at her with a twisted smile. 'So you also know what it's like to be without parents. Father?'

'Died when we were young kids. Mum brought us up, but she got cancer. I thought I owed her one.'

'And your brother?'

'Well, he lived with us, but you know...' She shrugged 'He's a boy. They're different.'

Roxy nodded. 'Yes.'

There was a knock at the door and Miss Abbey's voice could be heard. 'Sandra, are you coming to drinks?'

Sandy opened the door. 'Oh, sorry, was it on the itinerary? I haven't...'

Miss Abbey gave a weary smile. 'Yes, I realised. Oh, and, Miss Victory, are you coming to join us at the Get To Know You drinks?'

'Yes, if dear Sandy doesn't mind pushing me.'

Sandy noticed a change in her tone and wondered if Roxy didn't like Miss Abbey; there was an odd feeling of friction in the air.

'Yes, yes, of course,' she said, getting behind Roxy's chair and pushing it. It wouldn't budge.

'The brakes!' said Miss Abbey, smiling helpfully.

'Oh, yes, of course. Sorry, sorry, so sorry, Roxy.'

'Don't worry, dear, you'll soon learn,' said Roxy. 'It takes time to become an *experienced pusher*.' Again there was that edge in her voice, but it seemed directed towards Miss Abbey, not Sandy.

They followed Miss Abbey down to the main hall where there was a gathering of the group. They were the only ones not there.

CHAPTER 7

FOR LACK OF A HORSE, THEY PUT SADDLES ON DOGS

Abbey had spotted Sandra Blee was missing immediately she entered the hall. She only hoped she was in her room and not off trying to ride a camel or something ridiculous. Competition winners were always trouble.

The other guests were making some kind of desultory conversation. Unlike normal Get to Know You drinks where guests could mingle easily, wheelchair guests had difficulties. Either they stayed in their chairs and were in danger of getting entangled with other chairs as they moved around, or they decamped into a comfy chair and discovered they were stuck with the person next to them for the whole party. She had tried to get the able-bodied guests to walk about between wheelchairs and make conversation, but most of them were young men and not in the least interested in talking to oldies in chairs. At least the young woman was doing her bit to be friendly. What was her name? Abbey took a quick side eye at her list. Oh yes, Elsa. Remember Elsa the lion, thought Abbey, although frankly she'd hardly ever seen anyone who looked less like a lion. More like the lion's prey: tall, skinny thing without a bit of excess flesh. I suppose, she thought grudgingly, some men might find those slender curves sexy, but blondes were so passé.

She passed a quick eye over the party and then the clock. She'd better go and get that Sandra Blee before the party ended. No chance of forgetting her name.

As Miss Abbey made her way upstairs, Jade watched her. It didn't take rocket science to know she was going to look for that curly-haired plank, Sandra Blee. What kind of name was that anyway? You certainly knew what sort of movies those parents watched. Pity she wasn't John Travolta, he at least was sexy.

'Jade!'

'What?'

'Are you getting me a drink or not?'

Jade shrugged and moved towards the bar. Flipping artful dodger. Only brought her as her servant. She wouldn't even drink it. She just liked holding it as a sort of weapon. Weird, weird woman.

Three blokes were standing at the bar talking to each other. The Ables! Ha! Jade jostled the nearest one so he spilt his beer on the next one.

'Hey!'

'Sor-ry. I'm just getting a glass of champagne for my gran, right.'

'You did that on purpose.'

'Nah, just your muscles were in the way, Arnie.'

'Ha ha. I'm Tony, the handsome one.'

'Jade.'

'These two are Cyril, the dreamer, and Faisal, the bar maestro.'

She looked them over. Faisal looked OK. Not too sure about Cyril. In his chinos and cashmere he looked like the sort of Tory twat who would make jokes about her tattoos or ask if she was a pincushion. Like she hadn't had it already from her gran a million times.

'You mates already?'

'No, we met tonight. We all wanted to go to Petra and this was the cheapest trick; half price provided you say you'll help if any of the pushers get sick. We both signed up for that, but we're hoping your gran will be the one we have to push; she's tiny. Love her blonde curls by the way!'

He winked and Jade sneered.

'Yeah? She's not really me gran. Me gran was supposed to be coming, but she's in hospital and this is her replacement. I call her gran to make her happy.'

'Oh, I'm sorry,' said Tony, and the others murmured agreement. 'That's terrible, so sorry. I love my gran, she's the best.'

'Yeah. Right. See you around.'

Jade took two glasses of champagne back to her charge.

'Thank you,' said Mrs Tank. 'I saw you chatting up those boys. What is it with your family, can't keep your pants on for ten minutes?'

Jade sneered. 'Yeah. Did you see me having a quick shag then?'

'Oh! Language, Jade.'

'Yes, Gran!'

A wave of annoyance passed across Mrs Tank's face. 'I told you not to call me that. You can call me Mrs Tank.'

Jade stuck out her tongue and wriggled it derisively. 'OK, Mrs Tank, your ladyship!'

'What are those boys' names?'

'Tony, he's the chatty one. The looker who does bar is

Faisal and the other one who looks like he might be a Tory is Cyril. Anything else you want to know?'

'Yes, the other guests. Who are the people in the wheelchairs?'

'Well, the one that's just arrived with Miss Abbey is Roxy, her pusher is called Sandra Dee – can you believe it?'

Jade began singing 'Look at Me, I'm Sandra Dee…'

'That's enough, Jade. Besides, she's not. I've seen the list. She's Sandra Blee, so don't try it on, OK.'

'Yes, Gran!'

'Go on, then. Who are the couple?'

'That's Mr and Mrs Cox. They've been sniping at each other ever since they arrived. I think he likes telling her what to do, and she doesn't like doing it. I heard her calling him a fat toad, not that she can talk! I've seen thinner sumo wrestlers.'

At that moment an altercation between Mrs Cox and Roxy began on the other side of the room. It wasn't obvious what started it, but they could hear Mrs Cox calling Roxy a skinny witch and Roxy yelling back it was lucky that Mrs Cox was not in a wheelchair or her husband wouldn't be able to fit her between the tables.

Mrs Tank snorted and edged her wheelchair so they were behind her. 'And… the young girl with the man?'

'That's Mr Jarvis and his daughter, Mavis.'

'What about a wife?'

'Ooh, getting interested, are we?'

'Maybe. It's nice to have a man who cares about pushing his daughter, sounds kindly.'

'Might be, or she might be an heiress and he'd like the money.'

'Cynical, aren't you?'

'Then the two giggly women are Jolly and Spice.' Jade gagged.

'Oh yes, the jokey ones who call themselves "girls". Fifty if they're a day.'

'Yeah! But not old compared to you, are they?'

'Mind your tongue. And finally, there's one more chair and pusher and the walking girl, what's her name?'

'She's Elsa, and the other chair is Mrs Williams and her pusher's called Harry. He looks nice but I haven't talked to him.'

'Elsa the lion? Did Elsa come with the boys? Your chat-ups?'

'No, separate.'

'OK. Push me over to the father and daughter. I'll see if I like him.'

'Right ho, great white chief!'

CHAPTER 8

IF YOU WANT TO CONFUSE SOMEONE, OFFER THEM MORE CHOICES

Abbey looked at her watch. It would soon be time for dinner. The Get to Know You hadn't gone very well. The only people who got to know someone else were Mrs Tank, who was pushed over to the father and daughter and then talked at them, and the two boys, who seemed to have formed a gang with the barman. She sighed. Let's hope they don't go off and get drunk every night. Before you know it, they'll be in with a bad lot and she'll have to get the police involved. It happened a few years ago in Russia – when they still took trips to Russia – the boys had been chatted up by a load of prossies and gone off somewhere. They were given something to drink. Passed out. Robbed. Left at the side of the road with only their underwear on. Boys could be a right pain on trips.

The dinner bell rang and Abbey jumped forward to help anyone who needed it.

'As it's a Get to Know You night,' she purred, 'I've done a seating plan so everyone should be next to someone new.'

Slowly they started wheeling into dinner. She hoped the kitchen staff had understood the problems of getting chairs under the tables; not all the guests could do transfers – they were often just too old for those sorts of games. She hurried in behind the last one, but it seemed everyone was so hungry they had found their place and were settled. She gave a sigh of relief. Now, where was that Sandra Blee?

However, Sandra was sitting demurely beside Roxanna, with Tony from the walking group on the other side. Abbey had put herself next to Tony so she could keep an eye on Sandra, and encourage him, as he appeared to be the chattiest of the boys, to make friends with the less mobile guests.

She looked down the table. Already it was clear that Mrs Tank and Roxanna ate almost nothing, while both the Coxes were working steadily through huge piles of food. With this age group of uncertain health, how much food they ate often depended on what prescription drugs they were taking. Abbey paled slightly when she thought of the amount of undeclared drugs her group had, no doubt unwittingly, brought into the country. It clearly stated on the 'Rules of Travel' that all drugs must be accompanied by the prescription, but very few read it, let alone complied.

On her other side was Harry, and next to him, Mrs Williams. She knew nothing about either of them, so that seemed like a good idea too.

As Tony was already attempting to chat up Sandy and making her blush, Abbey turned to Harry. 'So, Harry, what made you decide to join us here in Jordan?'

Harry smiled at her and said, 'Sorry? Come again. Not much English.'

Right! No one had thought to tell her that. 'What language should we talk to you in?'

'Sorry? What?'

Mrs Williams lent across Harry to Abbey. 'He's from Bulgaria but he knows some Spanish. Any good for you?'

'No,' said Abbey. 'French might work. Do you speak Spanish or Bulgarian?'

Mrs Williams shook her head. 'No. So far we've been using sign language, but it would be useful if someone was able to communicate with him.'

Abbey stood up and asked for silence. 'Does anyone here speak Bulgarian?' she asked. *The boys, perhaps, or Elsa, may have spent gap years in Bulgaria*, she thought hopefully.

A few heads were shaken. Nobody said yes.

'Or anybody speak Spanish?'

Again there was silence, then little Sandra Blee put her hand up. 'I've done a year on Duolingo. And I've got a translation app.'

'OK,' said Abbey, laughing from the sheer ridiculousness of the situation. 'I guess that will have to do.'

Sandy lent forward so Harry could see her and said, '*Yo hablo un poco español, es verdad por tu*?'

Harry put his thumb up. Sandy sat back down and Mrs Williams said to Abbey, 'I think he's the strong, silent type.'

Tony turned to Sandy and lifted his glass, clinking it against hers. 'Well done, that was brilliant. Your accent was super. Gave me chills. They're multiplying!' He grinned at her and, winking, added, in case she'd missed the Sandra Dee reference, 'It's from *Grease*!'

'Oh.' She smiled politely. 'Is it? Thanks. I'm not sure how much sense my Spanish made but, well, I tried.'

Perhaps, thought Abbey, *we might get a little romance for our journalist, then she'll love the trip and write nice things. Unless, of course, he breaks her heart, and then it'll be our fault. It really was very difficult managing people.*

CHAPTER 9
BLIND IN YOUR HEART

Abbey came down early for breakfast. She liked to be ahead of the clients and, although the two-hour time difference made it only five o'clock in the morning in the UK, she was sure there would be some early birds. Sandy was ahead of her. Her breakfast was spread out in front of her, making her table look like a war zone as she tried a little bit of everything on offer.

'Morning, Sandy,' said Abbey.

Sandy looked up, her eyes shining with excitement. For a moment, Abbey wondered if she really was some hard-bitten journalist or exactly what she seemed: a young girl travelling for the first time. But old ideas are hard to shake and Abbey assumed it was a clever ploy: Sandy was just pretending to enjoy every little thing to disguise the fact she was an investigative journo. Just to be sure, Abbey took out the WWH indemnity form.

'Sandy, would you mind signing this? It's just to say you won't sue us if something goes wrong. Purely theoretical, of course.'

Sandy took it and started reading. Abbey frowned. If

ever she needed proof that Sandy was a journalist, this was it: none of their previous prize winners had bothered to read the form before signing it.

When she saw Sandy's signature, she was even more certain (Abbey had done an online course in graphology). It was not the loopy schoolgirl curls she expected but the knife-ended uppers and small, insignificant middles of a sarcastic thinker: in other words, a journalist. She took the form and stalked off to another seat where she could watch the arrivals.

Sandy was about halfway through her tasting trip when Cyril, Tony, Jade, and Elsa crept into the hotel having clearly been up all night. Tony, Jade, and Elsa grabbed a coffee and went back to their rooms but Cyril brought his over to Sandy's table and sat opposite her.

'Hello, you enjoying your breakfast?'

'You bet,' she said. 'Most of these things I've never even heard of, in spite of the fact I spent hours on Google looking up what to expect.' She grinned at him and he grinned back, shaking his head. 'I must have watched *Lawrence of Arabia*, *Indiana Jones and the Last Crusade* and *Jinns* three times each!'

'Funny girl,' he said, but not unkindly. He knocked back his coffee and got up. 'I think we must have visited every single night spot in Amman last night,' he said. 'You should have joined us.'

It was Sandy's turn to shake her head. She didn't say anything but it was clear to her that the others had a lot more money than her and she knew better than to get into their type of deep water. She'd spent a lot of years, when she was looking after her mother, learning from books and films about girls who fell into rich men's traps, and she was warned.

Giving a quick wave at Miss Abbey, he left to go and get ready for the day's activities.

Abbey stared at him, trying not to feel annoyed. If she could, she would have restricted all travel to the over-fifties. Young boys, and any girls with them, always caused trouble. The only good thing was that the journalist had somehow got left behind when they went on their visit to the watering holes of Amman.

By the time the rest of the party was at breakfast, Adam, the local guide, had arrived. He was walking around the group, politely saying 'hello' to the guests he had left behind in the baggage department.

Abbey was a little annoyed he hadn't turned up at the Get To Know You party, but when he offered her a bunch of dried desert flowers, she forgave him.

'I'm so sorry, Miss Abbey, for my absence last night. As you know, because of the war in Israel and Palestine, we have no tourists, but last night I was asked to do a quick moonlight trip through Wadi Rum for one foreign guest, and when there are so few, you must take what you can.'

His smile was lovely. It was annoying but it was true; she knew there were almost no tourists here. Even though Jordan was not itself involved in the Israeli–Palestinian War, many airlines refused to fly here. WWH had been forced to move the guests who were originally booked with BA to Royal Jordan Airways when BA cancelled all Jordan flights less than a week before they left.

He turned back to Abbey, saying, 'When I met them all yesterday I hadn't... er...'

Abbey bit her cheek to prevent a sneer. She knew what was coming. It wouldn't be the first time the local guide was shocked at the number of people in wheelchairs, had not noticed they were called Wheelchair Warriors Holidays, or had thought that was some kind of allusion or joke.

'I hadn't noticed,' he continued, 'that you had so many young men, eh.'

Oh! That was a first. Given this was a Muslim country, she'd expected a complaint about the number of women, not the boys who could be useful. Or was this going to be something like the Russian experience again... she did hope not. She frowned. There weren't so many young men; only Tony and Cyril, and she supposed Harry could be considered young. Could she trust that Sandra Blee, though? A journalist snooping around was probably worse than a horde of young men.

Adam recovered himself and addressed the group. 'Lovely to see you all again. We are going to have a brilliant day, eh... The museum is our first stop and I know you're going to find it so interesting, and then we visit a few of Amman's many Roman remains.'

Yes, thought Abbey, who had already checked it out, *and the museum is one of the few places, other than the hotel and airport, with easy disability access*. She hadn't had time to check the amphitheatre or the citadel, but given what he had just said, she hoped they would also live up to expectation.

They did, but not the way Abbey had been expecting.

CHAPTER 10
NEVER MISS AN
OPPORTUNITY TO PUT A
SMILE ON SOMEONE'S FACE

I n Amman, the museum trip had gone without a hitch, although it had been slightly disappointing to discover it did not have a coffee shop. Fortuitously, Adam had managed to find a nearby restaurant where they could sit outside on a big patio, and so avoid the inevitable steps and narrow passages inside that made life difficult for someone in a wheelchair. The guests were so pleased with the visit and the lack of hassle that they enthusiastically bought the ubiquitous keffiyeh, as the Jordanian scarf was called, which the street sellers presented to them in abundance as soon as they sat down. Laughing with pleasure at the men's sales techniques, most of the guests donned their keffiyehs immediately.

The amphitheatre trip, however, was not to be so enjoyable.

Six people in wheelchairs sat at the top of the steps, staring down into the amphitheatre and across at the Roman site, an impossible rampless descent of several metres.

'How is Sandy going to push me up and down those

steps?' asked Roxy in an aggrieved voice. 'She'd have to be a gladiator.'

Abbey had no answer but Mrs Cox, delighted to be able to contradict Roxy, declared, 'I've found somewhere down the side I think will be possible for me. Come on, Charlie, let's see how we manage.'

She dived off to the right, pulling her husband's chair, and soon went out of sight. A few moments later, the wheelchair returned into view, without its pusher and heading fast down the steps towards the columns at the bottom of the ramp. Mr Cox was holding on to the sides of the chair as it careered bumpily down, yelling for help, his long keffiyeh streaming out behind him in protest. Mrs Cox was nowhere to be seen.

Abbey sighed. 'Come on, Adam,' she said, jumping off the top step and heading, even faster than the wheelchair, down the steps towards Mr Cox, who had arrived at the bottom and smashed into a Roman column, the chair jumping back but fortunately remaining upright.

'It's normal,' said Adam as they galloped down. 'He doesn't seem hurt. A bit dazed, eh.'

Abbey bit her cheek. He might not be physically hurt but his pride would be wounded. Had Mrs Cox just taken him to the top and pushed? Oh dear, she did hate working with married couples.

'Why,' said Mr Cox as they arrived at the bottom of the steps, 'were there no cushions on the pillars? I could have been seriously hurt. Does no one care about the disabled?' He stared at Abbey, his eyes shining and his double chins trembling in fury.

She sighed quietly. Would it simply annoy him more if she pointed out the post had been there nearly 3000 years, so by now the cushions would have deteriorated?

'Where's Mrs Cox?' asked Adam.

They all looked up the slope to where Mrs Cox should have been standing, but there was no one in sight.

Mr Cox gave a deep breath and yelled at the top of his voice, 'Ophelia! Where are you?'

Blimey, thought Abbey, *how did I miss that name*? She couldn't think of anyone less Ophelia-like than the substantial Mrs Cox.

The words echoed around the amphitheatre. Ophelia! Ophelia! Ophelia!

But instead of the appearance of Ophelia, they got Jade, who galloped down the steps the way the wheelchair had come.

'Can I help?' she asked.

'What have you done with Mrs Tank?' asked Abbey snappily.

Jade shrugged at this irrelevance. 'Oh, she's asleep in the shade. She's fine. Adam, can I help you? You'll need another pair of hands getting over the edges and up the steps...' She smiled.

Adam looked at her. 'Thank you. You're a very kind and thoughtful lady.'

'I'll go and find Mrs Cox,' said Abbey in an exasperated voice. 'Adam and Jade, can you take Mr Cox round the amphitheatre now we're here? Afterwards, we'll get some help to carry him back up.'

'No problem,' said Jade while Adam pointed out a disabled ramp at the side of the columns.

Even Mr Cox laughed. 'Well!' he said. 'Imagine that! As long as you fly down the first lot of steps, they make accommodation for you.'

Abbey climbed back up the steps wondering if Mrs Cox had re-joined the party. As she got to the place where Mr

Cox had started his descent, she stopped. One of the young men was there with Mrs Cox, who was lying on her back, her head propped up against a pillar.

The rest of the party were crowded behind him, giving advice, while he attempted to bathe a cut on her temple with some baby wipes. It was hard to imagine why a young man would have baby wipes in his pocket, but she was glad he did. With an effort, Abbey remembered his name was Cyril. *Nice aquiline nose*, she thought.

'Well done, Cyril,' she said.

He smiled. 'It's OK, not deep. She must have fallen over and hit her head on the pillar when the wheelchair sped away.'

Mrs Cox opened her eyes. 'I was hit, I tell you. I leant down to put the brakes on and one of those hanging-around fellas hit me. One of those would-be guides. "*Please, my lady, very good English-speaking guide.*"' She imitated an Arabic accent. 'Then whump! Pha! Foreigners!'

Cyril raised his eyebrows at Abbey but didn't speak.

'I've hurt my ankle too,' said Mrs Cox. 'He may have kicked me as well.'

Cyril looked down at her leg. 'It does look a bit swollen,' he said.

'Are you a doctor?' asked Abbey hopefully. Perhaps doctors carried baby wipes wherever they went.

He shook his head. 'Sorry, no, my sister is though. Perhaps I've gleaned some knowledge from her.'

The rest of the party were now loud with their opinions.

'Nasty-looking cut.'

'Easy to get gangrene out here.'

'I heard there's a Roman virus that's still embedded in the stones.'

'Dust in a wound is the worst thing. You can never get it clean.'

'Clearly,' said Roxy smugly, 'Mrs Cox will have to be in a wheelchair too. So! Thus Ables find themselves so easily dis'ed!'

Mrs Cox looked up, a delighted smile spreading across her face. 'Why, so I will! My leg is far too sore. I can't possibly walk and this nice young man, what's your name, dear, can push me.'

He smiled. 'I'm Cyril, Mrs Cox, and certainly, I would be delighted to be your pusher. However, Miss Abbey may not have a spare chair.'

'She'll find one.' Mrs Cox smirked, and Abbey noticed a touch of threat in her voice. Oh dear, it was indeed going to be one of those trips. She smiled politely.

'I'm sure we have a spare,' she said, 'but who will push Mr Cox?'

'I will,' said a gentle voice behind Cyril.

Abbey thanked Heaven for the young people – they were being so much nicer than the old ones. 'Thank you, Elsa.'

It took three people to carry Mr Cox back up to the bus, an uncomfortable and embarrassing journey in which he screamed furiously at his helpers and the company for not having proper disabled access in the places they were going. However, when he discovered that Elsa had offered to push him, he stopped complaining and smiled.

'Why, that's fantastic. I think we're going to have a lot of fun.'

'We will indeed, Charlie. May I call you Charlie? You went down those steps so elegantly, I was impressed. You must have excellent balance; many others would have fallen.' Elsa smiled and winked at Cyril over Mr Cox's head.

Abbey saw the wink and thought, *Ah ha, so was that why she offered to push? Well, as long as Mr Cox is happy and Mrs Cox is happy, we may get through this unscathed. And if Cyril and Elsa want to make a go of it, all the better. The Jordanians may say 'a happy wife is a happy life', but here in WWH, a happy punter is a happy guide.*

CHAPTER 11

WINDS BLOW COUNTER TO
THE WAY THE SHIP DESIRES

After the disaster at the amphitheatre, it was a relief to get to the citadel and discover there was only a small lip for the wheelchairs to get over, and then wide paths and relatively easy pushing with excellent views of Amman.

The Coxes, Elsa and Cyril were now happily sitting in the sun discussing the difficulties of wheelchair access, so Abbey went to find out how the other guests were doing.

As she turned a corner, she saw Adam deep in conversation with Harry. Well, that was a surprise. Who would think that a guide in Jordan would speak Bulgarian? Still, perhaps they had a lot of Bulgarian guests. Or perhaps they were conversing in Russian. Bulgarians often spoke Russian and before the Russian–Ukrainian War, Aqaba had a lot of Russian tourists, so maybe he did speak Russian. She must ask him later. As Mrs Williams had fallen asleep in her chair and seemed quite content, Abbey moved on to see if anyone else needed her help.

Sitting on the side of some tall columns, she found Jolly and Spice discussing something that appeared to be worrying them. They stopped talking when they saw her and signalled.

'She's right, you know,' said Jolly.

Her tone made Abbey feel nervous and she answered a bit more sharply than she would normally do with a guest. 'Who's right about what?'

Jolly winced. 'Mrs Cox. Someone pushed her over. We were following her to see if there was disabled access and we saw a whole kerfuffle and pushing event.'

'A whole kerfuffle,' echoed Spice.

Abbey felt sick. 'Who?'

'We couldn't see who. We could only see a head. You know how everybody wears those red and white Jordanian scarves. Whoever it was was wearing one. It could be a tourist or a local.'

Abbey sighed. She'd have to report this to head office and there was bound to be a fuss. They might even insist on making a police report. She decided to ask Adam for his advice. He must have had similar problems in the past. Certainly, Abbey quailed at the idea of involving the police. She turned to the girls.

'Have you told anyone else about this?'

'No. We were waiting to talk to you,' said Jolly.

'OK. If you don't mind, it would be better to say nothing for the moment. If it turns out to be a police matter, they may well stop us going to Petra and none of us wants that, do we?'

She gave a bright smile, but realised even that slight threat might come back to haunt her. Petra was everyone's goal and she didn't really believe anyone had pushed Mrs Cox. It was more likely that she fell over; the terrain was rugged and, Abbey had noticed, Mrs Cox was wearing sling-backed high-heeled shoes.

The threat worked well. Spice said, 'You know, Jolly, we couldn't actually see very clearly. It might be there was just someone passing her. Then the wheelchair rolled away and all our attention was on that and not Mrs Cox.'

'Yes,' said Jolly, squishing her nose, 'you're right. There were lots of people passing.'

Leaving the two women, Abbey went back to find Adam. Mrs Williams had woken up and Harry had wheeled her over to see the view and was making her laugh with sign language. Adam was walking towards Jade and Mrs Tank when Abbey caught up with him.

'Adam, can I have a quick word?'

He stopped politely and she saw he was smoking a cigarette. For a moment she was tempted, but she had given up six years ago. Silly to start again now just because of a little crisis.

'Hello, Miss Abbey, I've just been talking to Harry. Interesting man.'

'Oh good,' she said absently, 'so do you speak Russian or Bulgarian?'

Adam frowned. 'No.'

'No? So what language were you speaking in?'

He gave her a puzzled look. 'Arabic.'

'Arabic? I thought he was Bulgarian.'

Adam took a long drag on his cigarette. 'I don't know. His Arabic name is Messiah, but it may be that Harry is a Bulgarian name. I didn't ask him.'

Abbey looked back at where Mrs Williams and Harry were pointing out various birds. She examined him thoughtfully. It wouldn't be the first time a guest had lied about their origins. 'Is Messiah local then?'

'No, he's from Morocco, although I believe he lives somewhere else now. We were speaking together in MSA,

Modern Standard Arabic; it's understood by most Arabic speakers.'

Abbey didn't ask any more questions but she was bemused by that. She needed time to think through why Harry/Messiah might not admit to the languages he spoke. Still, since he clearly didn't speak English, perhaps it wasn't relevant. She certainly didn't want to stir up a nest of unnecessary bees.

CHAPTER 12
RESPOND TO RUDENESS
WITH A SMILE

'Don't get me wrong,' said Mrs Cox, and Abbey felt her jaw muscles clench while she tried desperately to keep her sunny smile. 'I really like the people on this trip. And, now I'm in one too, I feel so, so sorry for the people permanently in chairs. It must be so awful being...' her voice dropped to a whisper, '...disabled. But I'm afraid Roxanna is really too rude and unpleasant and I must ask that she isn't placed anywhere near me at any time. Just today she said she was glad I was in a wheelchair as now I'd stop being so snide about people who were disabled. As though I ever was. I am never rude!'

Abbey sighed internally. Adam had advised her not to worry about Mrs Cox's apparent incident and even Mr Cox, who was now delighted with his new pusher, said his wife was always making things up, so that, at least, was past. Only now, Mrs Cox was back to complaining about other things. Apparently, Roxanna and Sandy had pushed in front of her at the buffet.

'... although I don't blame Sandra, who is a lovely, gentle girl and not at all worldly, but sadly, that Roxanna is all too worldly. Moreover,' she said, 'when I said I was glad of my chair because I felt very tired these days, something I put down to the altitude, Roxy gave a very callous laugh and said it was more likely my spherical abundance than the spatial altitude, which wasn't making anyone else tired. No doubt she thinks that kind of language is funny! And,' she continued, just as Abbey thought she had finished, 'as for those "girls" Sugar and Spice...'

'Jolly,' said Abbey.

Mrs Cox sneered. 'Jolly indeed. They are clearly Lebanese!'

Abbey stared at her. 'Lebanese?' This trip was getting madder and madder. First of all, the Bulgarian turns out to be Arabic speaking, and now these two English girls are Lebanese. Was anybody on the trip who they claimed to be?

Mrs Cox laughed and wiggled her hips in her chair. 'No, lebanese! You know...' She touched her nose.

Abbey suddenly understood what she meant and tried to repress the laugh that bubbled up in her throat. 'Oh,' she said, 'lesbian.'

Mrs Cox looked as though Abbey had just sworn. 'Sssh,' she said, 'no need to be rude.' She signalled to Cyril to push her over to join her husband. Abbey rushed out to collapse in giggles.

Jade was outside having a cigarette. 'Oh, sorry,' said Abbey, dropping down and laughing hysterically. 'It's just...' She waved her hands. What could she say?

'Yeah,' said Jade, 'I heard. Fucking Boomers. My gran's the same.'

Abbey sobered up suddenly. 'Your gran? I thought...'

Jade shrugged. 'Yeah, she's not really. I call her that. Makes her feel like one of the family.'

'Oh,' said Abbey. 'OK.'

Jade stubbed out her cigarette and sloped off. Abbey watched her curiously. There was another mystery there, but she wasn't quite sure what it was. Jade and her grand-mother, Lady Bumstead, had originally booked together on the trip. But then they were informed Lady Bumstead was in hospital and her place was being taken by a Mrs Tank. They had paid a hefty excess for a change of passenger so it would seem odd if they were smuggling in the original guest. Abbey had seen people pretending to be the guest and hoping to get a free holiday, but this would be the other way around. A guest pretending not to be who she actually was and paying double. That was a first, and it was hard to imagine why anyone would do it.

This trip was turning out to be concerning for someone with a hungry journalist on board. For some reason, Abbey thought about that Agatha Christie film where everybody on the train knew each other but pretended they didn't. And then there was a murder. There'd better not be a murder on this trip; that really would give the journalist something to write about.

CHAPTER 13

OH MOUNTAIN, DON'T LET
THE WIND SHAKE YOU

Mrs Tank was sitting alone, watching a couple of women in the bar, with a strange look on her face. Abbey glanced at them briefly before strolling over to get to know her guest a little better. The women probably were an interesting study; one was a tall red-head, and the other a short dark woman who was literally bouncing in her chair with excitement. Perhaps if she too had nothing to do, she might sit and watch the other punters. But she *did* have far too much to do.

She approached Mrs Tank, smiling politely. Could she find out the real relationship between her and her pusher? They had paid a lot extra for a name change. Abbey didn't want to stir things up, but she didn't like being surrounded by mysteries at work.

One thing Abbey never did was ask the clients how they were enjoying the trip; that was almost certainly a prelude to a complaint and she'd had quite enough with Mrs Cox. She started instead with a neutral question.

'Hello, Mrs Tank, where do you hail from?'

'Hail from?' said Mrs Tank, grudgingly removing her eyes from studying the couple at the bar and raising an eyebrow at Abbey. 'That's an expression from the past. I wonder if Jade even knows what it means. But, since you ask so nicely, I'm a Londoner through and through, how about you?'

Abbey's smile became more strained – she hated it when guests threw back the questions. 'I live in London too, which part are you in?'

'Chelsea,' said Mrs Tank. 'I believe I heard that you come from Battersea. How charming. It's always nice when you meet people from other walks of life. So refreshing, don't you think?'

Abbey bit her cheek and ploughed on. 'How are you liking Jordan, Mrs Tank?' Yes, that was a better opener. She should have started there. But that, like asking how you were, could so easily lead into a complaint.

Mrs Tank gave a comedic look of surprise. 'Well, the bus trip was a revelation – so educational to travel with a group and not in a chauffeur-driven limousine – and the hotel has quickly realised that I need to be given the best, so they have stumped up nicely, thank you. It was a shame you gave me such a small room, but luckily I was able to negotiate with the manager, and Jade and I now have a suite. She's up there moving my things at the moment. I do so hate to be cramped at night, don't you? So bad for one's health.'

Abbey wondered if Mrs Tank would be paying the inevitable excess herself or if she would have to argue on the company's behalf. The good thing was that with the dearth of tourists, thanks to the war over the border, they were getting the best rooms at a much cheaper price than usual. She saw Jade returning and excused herself to go and talk to some of the other guests. Let's hope they were happy with their rooms and not trying to change them. Would Mrs Tank do this at every hotel, at every place on the trip?

She stopped by Mr Jarvis and his daughter, Mavis. Could Mr Jarvis also not be who he said? Who then would he be? And Mavis? Perhaps she didn't need the wheelchair at all; perhaps she was a Moroccan belly dancer. Abbey felt the giggles rising again and had to hastily tell herself that there was a journalist around somewhere longing to pounce on her every mistake. Amazing how quickly that can destroy joy.

'Now, Miss Abbey,' said Mr Jarvis, staring above her head, 'I wonder if you realise that when it says on the information leaflet that it will take forty-six minutes to get to Jerash from our hotel, it is actually not taking into account the quality of the road, the other traffic, and the difficulty of getting buses down roads normally intended for mules.'

Abbey blinked. 'I believe the road is very good and well-travelled.'

'Exactly,' he said, now examining the floor at her feet. 'Well-travelled. There you have it... camels, mules, carts, local buses, rock falls... I would definitely look again at that estimate. I, personally, would allow at least two hours because you never know what obstructions might be found on these types of roads, bathed in sand, wind-blown and so forth. And then there's Israel!' He suddenly looked right into her eyes. 'We mustn't forget Israel.'

'No,' said Abbey weakly. 'No, of course not. And we are all aware of the problems there and the war taking place, but we're some distance from the border. The Foreign Office—'

'Indeed! The Foreign Office. You do realise that it's only

eighty-seven minutes to the King Hussein Bridge Crossing. Eighty-seven minutes! Hardly distant, is it? And there are parts of the road between Amman and Petra that run along the Israeli border. And I suppose you do realise that when Iran sent missiles back to Israel, lights were seen over Amman and fallout was found on the streets. Hardly safe, is it?'

'Ah. No,' said Abbey and saw with relief that Adam was beckoning her over. 'I'm so sorry, Mr Jarvis, I must go and talk to Adam.'

Mr Jarvis nodded his head. 'You tell him what I said – the King Hussein Bridge Crossing is eighty-seven minutes from Jerash and fifty-three minutes from Amman!'

Abbey had hoped that Adam was saving her, but it seemed there was another problem. For a moment, she wondered if her nightmare was coming true and there was a murdered guest, but it seemed it was something simpler.

'Miss Roxy has had a problem,' he said. 'A wheel has come off her chair and rolled away. No one in the hotel has a spare tyre.' He gave a wry smile, adding, 'Or not of that size. Miss Sandra has asked everyone in the hotel but so far no one has any ideas, eh.'

'Um,' said Abbey, wishing it had been anyone except the journalist involved in the affair. However, this should be easy to resolve. 'OK, I'll ring over to the agency and see if they have a spare wheel in the workshop. How are Roxanna and Sandy managing at the moment?'

'Miss Roxanna can walk a bit, so Miss Sandra found some crutches and took her down to the shops in the hotel buggy. They're going shopping. I think the women are enjoying themselves. Miss Sandra said it really didn't matter what happened, it was much more fun than working at Percy's Bifold Doors, whatever that means, eh.'

Abbey frowned. Could the journalist have gone undercover at Percy's Bifold Doors? Had they had some dreadful exposure recently? She must look them up. An investigative journalist would be even worse than the ordinary kind.

CHAPTER 14
MOVEMENT IS A BLESSING

Both Mrs Tank and Miss Abbey would have been surprised if they had heard what the women at the bar were discussing.

Cat said to Miranda, 'Did you see that woman leaving the bar, pushed by the young man?'

Miranda swivelled around on her chair. 'What, that little old lady with incredibly perfect skin and unlikely blonde hair, talking to the sturdy woman in blue? The one with a WWH badge on her lapel, who's bending down to hear her better?'

Cat then also had to turn, but she did it more discreetly than Miranda. 'No, not that woman, although strangely there is something about her that also looks familiar, not the face but the way she's moving her arms. Is it just that there are definite types, so you think you recognise someone when you don't? With this kind of job, you find a fossil in every stone.'

Miranda made a face; she was not into philosophising as much as Cat. 'Are you talking about them, or another woman?'

'No, another woman, also sitting in a wheelchair, only she was being pushed by a young man with a big nose.'

'Ooh, pity I missed that. I like noses, makes it so easy to identify them. What were his ears like?'

'I didn't notice. But anyway, what I was going to say was that I'm sure I've seen her somewhere before, although I can't remember where. But then, thinking I'd also seen the other woman makes me sound like an idiot.'

Miranda laughed and put her hand on Cat's arm. 'Shame I didn't see her; I'm much better at remembering faces than you.'

'True.'

'OK, well let me know if you see her again. Was the young man handsome?'

Cat wiggled her nose thoughtfully. 'No, not really. But nice-looking, you know what I mean? Attractive.'

'While we're on the subject,' said Miranda, her eyes still scanning the room. 'These people you think you recognise... are you thinking any of them might be our subject?'

Cat blew out thoughtfully. 'Possibly.'

'Would it look too obvious if we got up the list of WWH guests and tried to identify each one of the people here?'

'Not if you can deign to look at my phone,' said Cat. 'Then we could just be sharing some joke or something... ironic, isn't it, that a list on paper is now more threatening or suspicious than a digital device that can hold a thousand times more information?'

Miranda leant over and looked.

'Well, let's start with the woman wearing the badge. She must be Miss Abbey, team leader and chief guide at WWH. It says here she's been working at WWH for ten years and quickly rose to group leader thanks to her charm and expertise.'

Cat snorted. 'And the fact they are a small company with only ten employees, most of whom only stay a couple of years.'

'Yes, that too.'

'And the one she is talking to must be either Mrs Tank, Mrs Williams, Mrs Cox, Roxanna Victory, or Spice Spain. They're all marked down as elderly women and, as you said, she has improbably lovely blonde hair, so it must be dyed.'

'What about the men? Remember our man said she might have had gender surgery. Who have you got on your list there?'

'These are the pushers: chap called Harry from Bulgaria. Oddly, the workers don't get surnames, only the guests. Then there's a Cyril, a Tony, a Jade, a Jolly and a Sandra Blee; she does get a surname. Oh, and so do Mr Jarvis and Mr Cox. Charlie Cox is the only man who is elderly and in a wheelchair; he was pushed by his wife, but she's marked as having had an accident and now in a wheelchair too. She's pushed by Cyril and Mr Cox is pushed by Elsa. Mr Jarvis is pushing his daughter's wheelchair.'

'I don't think this list is very helpful,' said Miranda. 'Let's find another way of getting to know the guests. I'll sleep on it. OK?'

'Fine. But before you go to sleep, let's just weigh up what we know about our absconder.'

'OK, the first thing we know is that she was, when we knew her, a woman. In those days she was calling herself Bella Chantry. She escaped from prison six months ago – which seems to indicate she has been getting some deep disguise work done (possibly even surgery) – and has reappeared on this trip to Jordan. She may now be a man or a woman as he/she is a master of disguise.

'Secondly, he/she has killed twice and won't hesitate to kill again if it suits her/his purpose.'

'When we knew her,' pointed out Cat, 'she was a woman in a wheelchair but could walk a little.'

'Indeed. So, an excellent disguise here where so many guests are in wheelchairs.'

'True. Which presumably was the reason he/she joined this group. However, that does allow us to eliminate the guests who are not in wheelchairs.'

'But does it?' said Miranda, moving the bowl of nibbles and surprising the barman, who glanced at her hoping she wanted another drink. 'Remember how manipulative she was... she might implicate one of the Ables. Make him or her do something that looks completely innocent, which then leads to something far more serious. The same way she convinced Stevie into taking her for a flight in the Tiger Moth, only to jump out and disappear so we thought she was dead.'

Cat nodded. 'You're right. So, we should also look for a possible accomplice. Perhaps two people working together.'

'So,' Miranda moved the crisps to join the peanuts, 'she must be one of the seven people in the wheelchairs: Mr Cox, Mrs Cox, Mrs Tank, Roxanna Victory, Mavis Jarvis, Mrs Williams, and Spice Spain. Since Bella could walk a bit, could Mrs Cox's accident have merely been a ruse to get her into a wheelchair too? Yes, it sounds like convoluted thinking but we know Bella Chantry did indeed have a highly complicated mind.'

'OK, and her accomplice could be any one of the Ables.'

'Yup.'

'So, the final thing is, why is she here? We know about the other wheelchairs being a good disguise, and that going into a war zone is a good way to protect an ordinary criminal, but remember the third thing Mr UIO said: she wants to hook up with someone here for some unknown reason. All we have to do now is discover who she is and who that person is, and everything will fall into place.'

'Ha, easy!' said Miranda. 'Now I have that all implanted in my brain, it's time to go to sleep and let my instinct take over.'

CHAPTER 15

TRUST IN GOD BUT TIE YOUR CAMEL

The next morning, when the buses arrived to take the WWH group to Jerash, Mr Jarvis was already out the front with Mavis long before the others had finished breakfast. As soon as the driver opened the doors, Mavis got out of her chair and walked onto the bus, throwing her father the independent sort of look he would have hated had he noticed. He was busy checking each person against his watch as they arrived and looking a little more despondent as each minute ticked by.

'Five minutes to load,' he said, 'and still three more chairs to come.' He looked at Abbey. 'No sign of Mrs Tank this morning?'

Abbey sighed quietly. 'She's just having breakfast,' she said. 'Jade has gone up to fetch her things.'

He glanced at his watch again. 'I didn't envisage the extra time it would take for guest gallivanting,' he said dismally. 'How good is wheelchair access at Jerash?'

Before Abbey could answer, one of the waiters came out of the hotel. 'Excuse me, sir, I think your daughter left this behind.'

Abbey saw the waiter was holding out a handbag. Mr Jarvis tutted and muttered thank you in a rather ungenerous fashion, snatched the bag and turned towards where his daughter was sitting on the bus. Abbey had already looked to see where Mavis was and, to her surprise, saw a look of triumph passing over her face before she limped off the bus to get her bag.

'Families,' muttered Abbey, 'almost as bad as married couples.'

The bag collected, Abbey answered Mr Jarvis's question. 'Very good. Much of the Roman town is flat and there are no steep inclines, at least none like the amphitheatre.'

Mr Jarvis stared at his watch, his gloom obvious. 'That's lucky for Mr Cox then. How's his chair? I'm surprised it didn't break when he hit that column. He was lucky not to have an injury. Ha. And that would cost you a lot. Insurance is so high these days. And what about Miss Roxy? Has she got a new wheel yet? Your wheelchairs don't seem in very good shape.'

'We gave her a new chair,' said Abbey sharply, and moved off to talk to Jolly and Spice who were weaving towards the bus remarking on everything they saw and comparing it with home. Sharing happy giggles. They said good morning and passed by, still weaving. Abbey wondered why Jolly found it so difficult to push a simple chair: surely the Jordanian chairs were not that different from UK ones and presumably she pushed Spice around at home. Still, at least she and Spice were enjoying themselves. They appeared to be guessing why the other guests had chosen to come to Jordan and finding it hilarious.

Abbey saw Mrs and Mr Cox and their new pushers coming out of the hotel. They were apparently having a serious discussion with Adam.

Despite a nervous feeling in her stomach, Abbey stopped. Cyril looked at her, frowning.

'We've just been examining the chairs,' he said. 'After Roxy's wheel came off, I thought I'd better check the others. Have a look at Charlie's brake cable.'

Feeling sick, Abbey bent down. She could see the cable had worn to almost a thread. It was ready to break at any moment.

'This isn't wear,' said Cyril, his voice quiet so only Abbey and Adam could hear. 'It's been cut.'

Abbey frowned. She could see there was a clean edge where the cable had been sliced, but who would do it, and why? And could this be directed at Mr Cox or someone else? The chairs were given out randomly, so a cut cable was not necessarily aimed at the Cox family. It was more likely this was a disenfranchised former employee wanting to cause a stink, hoping to get at either the boss of the travel company or the wheelchair company.

'Have you had any sackings recently?' she asked, turning to Adam. 'Anyone who might want to make your company look unreliable?'

Adam paused before replying. He glanced at his phone. Eventually, he spoke. 'Miss Abbey, tourism is down hugely ever since the October 7th Hamas attacks on Israel and their response. We have had to let people go, Miss Abbey, we just don't have enough work. The first people to stop coming were the Americans, and most of our clients were American or Russian, and since the Ukrainian war, those are down too.'

She nodded.

'But, Miss Abbey,' he said, 'none of our employees would want to hurt the company. It could be something against your company, or something personal against Mr Cox, eh?'

Abbey frowned. 'How would such a person get access? Once the chairs are allocated, they keep them in their rooms or use them constantly. I'm afraid this must be a disgruntled employee.'

She walked away. She didn't want any further discussion on this subject and she was glad that it was Adam's problem and not hers.

However, she did have a quick glance at her list of who had the company chairs.

Mrs Tank was using her own. She had also arranged her own flight to Jordan and had travelled out to Amman in Lady Bumstead's private jet, so bringing her own wheelchair had been no problem.

Mr Cox had one company chair. Mavis had another. Mrs Williams, a third, Roxy, a fourth and a fifth as she had a new chair. And Spice, of the Jolly and Spice pair, the other. And now, of course, Mrs Cox also had a wheelchair.

Abbey went back to the briefing notes she had been given for each guest. The Cox pair, it seemed, had filled in the form themselves (people often ignored the questions and the office filled in the omissions). The writing looked like a man's, so she assumed it was Mr Cox. It said he had a business in industrial use of plants, had been injured in a workplace accident and had been unable to walk ever since. (The office had added a note that he acquired considerable compensation in the accident, using it to start his own business). *Oh dear*, thought Abbey, *one of those*. Mrs Cox, the form declared, was a housewife who did voluntary work and had recently been on jury service. They had no children and no pets. Their next-door neighbour was marked on the form as their next of kin to inform in case of an accident.

Mr Jarvis had also done his own form, in spidery handwriting that tested Abbey's patience. Why couldn't people use the typewriting feature? He was a university lecturer and his daughter received benefits owing to her various unspecified illnesses. In consequence, they were carrying a variety of prescription drugs. He had attached a doctor's permission form. They were travelling on a bonding exercise. Abbey snorted.

Mrs Williams, the form said, could walk but only slowly owing to her age – she was eighty-two – and hence required a chair. At home, she used a stick indoors and a wheelchair outside.

Spice was the most unusual; her problem was partial sight and thus not directly related to wheelchair need. However, she had discovered on previous holidays it was safer for her to be in a chair with Jolly pushing, rather than explain her visual difficulties. People, she had written on her form, do not understand blindness but they can't really avoid a wheelchair.

Abbey gave a cynical smile. That could have been expressed better. She imagined Mrs Cox pushing Mr Cox off the top of a hill, watching him career into several walkers on the way down. Still, it made it even more important that she had ignored their belief that Mrs Cox was hit; one of the two witnesses could not actually see. Honestly, how people loved to scandalise!

Roxy had not filled in her form but the office had added a brief note that she had been injured in a car accident and she could walk a little with a stick or help but that she tired easily. When tired, the office had added, she tends to get emotional.

Abbey bit her cheek. Did Roxy shout at the office staff? Give them a 'piece of her mind'? Seemed likely. Roxy was doing her best to ruffle a few feathers here too.

CHAPTER 16

YOUR MANNERS INTEREST ME MORE THAN YOUR BEAUTY

Once everybody had finally arrived, the bus set off for Jerash. Contrary to Mr Jarvis's fear, the road from Amman to Jerash was extremely good – better in fact than most of the roads in the UK. There had been no camels, donkeys, chickens or even potholes on the road, most of which was the Jerash Highway.

Access to the site was perfectly suitable for wheelchair users, but once again, there were problems that only someone in a wheelchair would have considered: large cobblestones. These were beautifully preserved but made pushing the wheels along the colonnades a huge effort.

Jade sat back on her heels and puffed. 'OK, Gran! Which bits do you actually want to see?'

Mrs Tank snorted. 'Didn't they have wheelchairs in Roman days? No wounded warriors like us?'

'Funny,' said Jade. 'They knocked 'em off in the gladiator's ring. Shall I take you there and leave you to wait for the lions? Nice flat area that.'

Adam hovered over politely. 'Miss Jade, if you push Mrs

Tank up the side to the amphitheatre, there is a lovely view of the whole site, and no cobbles.'

'Thanks, Adam. Can you show me the route?'

He smiled and led the way.

Cyril turned to Mrs Cox. 'Would you like to see the view too, Mrs Cox?'

She snorted. 'Views. I've seen a few, too bloody many to mention. Take me to the visitor centre, I'll check out Roman coffee.'

'Hey!' said Roxy. 'Sandy can push you down there, then lovely Cyril can take me up to the view. Sounds like it's quite a push, and Sandy's still learning, aren't you, duck? I wish I'd brought my own chair; it has a bike attachment at the front, which is much better for cobbles. You'd have thought WWH would know that, wouldn't you?'

She glared at Miss Abbey, who, luckily for her, was too far away to hear her complaint.

Sandy nodded and took over pushing Mrs Cox. She felt rather down. Clearly she wasn't impressing Roxy with her skills and yet she had tried so hard. She was particularly careful with Mrs Cox's wheelchair as they went down the ramp to the visitor centre.

'Coffee, Mrs Cox?'

'Lovely,' said Mrs Cox, snuggling herself more comfortably in her chair. 'And a couple of the little buns I see over there. Must keep up one's blood sugar levels, mustn't one, dear?'

Sandy wondered if she would be reimbursed for the buns, and then felt ungenerous. Poor old woman, there probably weren't many things in life she really enjoyed.

Jade had been hoping for a nice quiet time with Adam, Mrs Tank, and the view, but instead she heard the clunking of the other chairs following behind them. Gnawing her lower lip, she sent disdainful looks their way, which no one noticed.

First up was Mr Cox, whose pusher, Elsa, was proving to be a real superwoman despite looking like a sexy skeleton. Mr Cox was busy telling Elsa about nerium oleander, a plant that he said was found at this time of year in Jordan, particularly in sandy, scrubby areas.

'This plant,' he was saying as she pushed him over the stones, 'loves the heat... But you be careful, my dear, poisonous to the touch, it is. I wouldn't want you brushing against the leaves and keeling over... I might have to give you mouth-to-mouth resuscitation...'

Jade heard him giggle boyishly and sneered. *Git.*

'Is that it, Charlie?' asked Elsa, pointing to an attractive pinkish red flower. 'With the fringed corolla you described.'

'Yes, how... oh no! Someone has stubbed out a cigarette on its leaves. Ugh, how disgusting. Was that you, Adam? You're a big smoker. Still, I suppose I shouldn't have expected anything else. Arabs, of course, don't care a hoot about the environment... not really civilised, are you? Not that I blame you... takes years to reach our level...'

Jade felt Adam beside her tighten his fists but he was far too polite to say anything. 'Why you racist bastard,' said Jade. 'Pity you didn't smack into the column and kill yourself. You git! You've had nothing but nice treatment here even though you behave like a boar straight out of the forest.'

Mr Cox turned towards her and began laughing loudly. 'Well! Look at you, the human pincushion. How would you know anything about anything? Still in the Victorian age, aren't you? Goth, eh? You know what happened to them? They were all destroyed by the Romans and raped and mutilated, every one of them. Died screaming, they did. In agony!'

'Please, please, Mr Cox,' said Abbey, running up the hill from the Roman forum. 'Of course I know you're upset and don't mean a word of what you say. I'm sure Jade will forgive you.'

'I won't!' said Jade. 'He's an ugly, fat git and racist to boot. He should have been left in his suburb in England to prey on his neighbours.'

'I meant every word of it,' yelled Mr Cox. 'Disgusting little shit shouldn't have been allowed out until she learnt some manners – look at her covered in tattoos and pins, it's a disgrace.'

'Did you know,' said Cyril quietly, as though talking to Roxy, 'that the elevation here is just under two thousand feet, which can make people feel dizzy and emotional if they aren't used to it?'

'Truth,' said Adam, turning towards him. 'It can make you breathless. You feel it, Miss Abbey?'

Abbey, panting from running up the hill, said she did and suggested they all move into the amphitheatre to test out the acoustics, which were most unusual.

'It all depends where you put your chair as to how your voice sounds...' she was saying as they went out of earshot.

The other chairs trundled away but Jade stayed watching the view. 'You're an idiot!' said Mrs Tank. 'You leave that boy alone! I can't always be saving you. Now push me into the theatre so I can be amazed by the fools in there.'

Jade said nothing and turned the chair sharply, letting it jolt on the stones.

The only people in the visitor centre, apart from Mrs Cox, who had fallen asleep in her chair, and Sandy, were a couple of women sitting drinking coffee. Sandy watched them, wondering what nationality they were. One of the women was extremely tall and red-headed. Dutch, thought Sandy. They were always tall but were they red-headed? That was more Scottish, wasn't it? Oh dear, was she falling into stereotyping? She mustn't do that in her novels or her blog. She bit her lip and looked at the other woman, who was much smaller and rounder and kept jumping up to fetch things. One of those people who cannot keep still. *How would I describe that in a novel?*

Sandy rubbed her nose, pulled out her notebook and started jotting down ideas. Might as well fill the time with something. Would she get to see Jerash at all? That was the trouble with winning a working prize – you were the slave, not the master. Perhaps she could write some kind of Roman-themed story.

Sandy was concentrating so hard on her writing, she didn't notice Cyril entering the room until he appeared at her side. He said 'Sandy' in a quiet voice to avoid waking Mrs Cox, who was snoring lightly. She looked up and smiled. He was nice-looking in a big-nosed sort of way. Oh dear, there she was judging again.

'I've left Roxy in the amphitheatre,' he said. 'She wanted to take a short walk and then sit for a while. I can look after Mrs Cox if you'd like to see something of Jerash. You can walk around and be back before anyone misses you, you know how slowly we move with the chairs.'

'Oh wow, thank you, Cyril,' she said. 'That's so kind.'

And she was out of there.

Jade might say that Cyril was a *fucking Tory* but frankly,

he was kinder than anyone else on the trip, and he had the most entrancing blue eyes, unusual with such dark hair.

Over on the other table, Cat was talking to Miranda in a low voice. 'I've got all the WWH details and I think we can identify that young guy as Cyril, and the old woman asleep in the chair as Mrs Cox. She's the one I'm sure I've seen somewhere before.'

Miranda, who was much better at recognising faces than Cat, was just turning to look when most of the wheelchair group arrived. Jade and Mr Cox were once again yelling at each other, this time about history.

'Your horrible Goths were totally annihilated by the Romans.'

'Not so!' said Adam quietly. 'The Visigoths sacked Rome in the early fifth century. Alaric I was the leader and when they marched north in 410, he died. He was succeeded by his half-brother Athaulf, who marched them to what is now France to establish a Visigoth Kingdom.'

The warring parties turned to stare at him.

'Jeez!' said Jade. 'You know your stuff.'

Adam shrugged. 'I'm a guide. Here in a Roman ruin, people ask many questions. I research the answers and tell the next group. The last group was from France and was interested in Roman conquests and what happened next.'

Mrs Cox woke up with a start. 'There you all are. Oh, how lovely, I've got my original pusher back. Where is that awful Roxy woman?'

'In the amphitheatre,' said Cyril. 'She wanted to think. Sandy went to get her.'

CHAPTER 17

CHOOSE THE FRIEND BEFORE CHOOSING THE ROAD

After walking the whole way around the Roman ruins, Sandy headed for the amphitheatre. She wasn't sure if Roxy would still be there – she could walk a little and seemed able to manoeuvre her wheelchair herself. The way back to the visitor centre was downhill, so not too difficult in the chair, even given that these ones that Roxy had declared were 'from the ark', were harder to push than her mother's chair had been. However, when Sandy arrived at the amphitheatre, Roxy was still sitting in the centre of the area. Her eyes were closed and for a moment Sandy wondered if she was asleep. Then she spoke.

'Nasty incident between Jade and Mr Cox,' she said. 'He looked like he might bash her if he could reach her.'

'Oh dear,' said Sandy, 'what happened?'

'The old fool started abusing the locals,' said Roxy. 'Bet he's the type to beat his wife. He was certainly quick to start shouting. One of those men who think they are superior to women and other races.'

Sandy sighed, thinking about her brother and

wondering what would happen there when she got home. Still, it was early days yet, anything might happen to make a good story on the trip. Moreover, she had noticed two extra people had signed up for her blog; that meant four in total.

Would Mr Cox bouncing down the Amman amphitheatre steps with his pink keffiyeh streaming out behind him make a good story? Perhaps he could smash his head on the pillar and she could turn it into a crime novel. Who did it? Almost certainly Mrs Cox but was that too obvious? Perhaps she could implicate someone else...

Roxy's voice, still talking about men who consider themselves superior, broke into Sandy's thoughts. 'Suppose in the future the world gets rid of all men. Men cause wars. Are unnecessarily violent. Can't have babies and don't further humanity. The population is too big. Get rid of men and we have room for the future. Men can't exist without women but women can easily exist without men; all we need is science.

Then, looking back at this time, the women of the future will be shocked at the behaviour of women of our time, women who allowed themselves to be dominated, who fell in love. Love, indeed! A construct to allow themselves to be dominated...'

Sandy laughed. 'You are joking, right?'

Roxy looked at her, raising the side of one lip.

'We should start down the slope to join the others in the visitor centre,' said Sandy. She could feel her heartbeat speeding up anxiously. It was hard to miss that Roxy had some odd ways of thinking. And yet she was very kind to her, so she must be a nice woman to put up with all her fumbling around the chair. Her jokes were sometimes a bit harsh, though.

'Do you like men, Roxy?' Sandy asked.

It was rather a daring question and bordering on rude, but on the other hand, if she was going to write better, she had to know what made the world tick. She spent so much time watching television, she knew very little of the world outside its fantasy land.

'Not much,' said Roxy. 'It was a man who put me in a wheelchair. He was driving – drunk – and left the scene of the accident. I was lucky that I was found by a little boy who got his mother, who called an ambulance. Otherwise, I'd be dead.'

'Oh gosh, I'm so sorry,' Sandy said, feeling awful. 'But there are bad women as well as men.'

Roxy snorted. 'Yes, I've met some of them too. And stupid ones. And bitches.'

Oh dear, thought Sandy. She shouldn't have asked the question. What an idiot she was. She always made things worse.

CHAPTER 18

THE MONKEY IS A GAZELLE
IN THE EYES OF HIS MOTHER

After the trip to Jerash, Roxy said she was tired and went to lie down. Sandy didn't feel a bit tired. She needed to find something exciting to write in her blog. She walked out of the hotel into its large, well-cultivated grounds.

Mavis was sitting in the garden on a bench to the left of the hotel, behind a hedge and slightly hidden from the main doors.

'Hello,' said Sandy. 'You all right?'

Mavis nodded. 'Yes, I'm fine, I just needed to get away for a bit.'

'Ah. Am I disturbing you?'

'No, I'd like a chat, Sandy. I just need a break from my dad.'

Sandy looked around. There was no sign of Mavis's wheelchair.

'Don't you need the wheelchair?'

'No. I have weak joints and a bad heart, so it helps with all this walking. But sometimes I like to walk a bit, to stretch myself. But my dad doesn't like people to know. He says people don't understand and will think we're only after benefits.'

Sandy had never heard Mavis talk so much. Previously she had wondered if she had a speech impediment. Clearly that was wrong.

'Oh. I'd love to chat, I didn't realise you could er... wanted to ...talk much.'

Oh dear, was she being rude? She had spent so much time alone, she wasn't always sure what was OK to say and what wasn't. But she knew from her reading that sometimes people were dying to tell you their problems and you should let them.

'My father and I,' said Mavis, her voice bitter, 'have nothing in common, so we have nothing to talk about. And anyway, he doesn't listen to me. I can talk all right, if only someone would listen.'

'Ah,' said Sandy. 'I'll listen.'

Mavis lapsed back into silence and stared at something in the far distance.

'You know,' said Mavis, suddenly, 'we don't even like the same things.'

Sandy cocked her head on one side. 'What do you like?'

'Cats, but Dad won't let me have one.'

'You must be having a good time here then,' said Sandy. 'There are cats everywhere.'

'Yes, but not mine, and they don't want to cuddle.'

'Oh. Is your mother still alive?'

Mavis looked around her. Then back at Sandy. 'I don't know.'

Ah ha, thought Sandy, this sounded promising. Perhaps there was a mystery here she could unravel to the benefit of everyone concerned, including herself. For a moment, she saw herself on a podium being awarded a prize for bravery in investigation.

Then Mavis continued. 'She was when I left home, but I suppose she could be dead now. She likes climbing on high shelves to get things down and she won't use the ladder.'

Ah, no mystery then, merely an overactive imagination and not just hers.

'She didn't fancy a trip to Petra?'

'No, she thought she should stay with the kids, my little brothers. She's worried they might develop UFA like my dad.'

'UFO?'

'No. UFA, unfounded anxiety. Or sometimes UAS – unfounded anxiety syndrome!' Mavis giggled. 'She makes up lots of acronyms like that. You'd be a YSB.'

'YSB?'

'Young single blonde. Not as funny as UFA but not as catching either.'

Sandy laughed. 'You are funny, Mavis.'

The girl beamed. 'I know! Mum says you have to laugh because the world is full of HHBs and if you didn't laugh, you'd give up.'

'Horrible hairy bugs?'

'Horrible human beings.'

'Oh, Mavis,' said Sandy. 'Why did she say that? Did something happen?'

Mavis shrugged. 'A man in the street spat on me. He said I was taking the air and water from healthy humans and I should be put down like a dog.'

Sandy gasped. 'Wow! What a... a... HHB.'

'Yes. But Mum said it's his problem and he must really be very shy and scared, so he takes it out on the vulnerable like me. She says we must be kind to people like that.'

Sandy was going to say Mum sounded like a Kind and Sensible HB but they heard Mr Jarvis calling from the other side of the garden. Mavis got up. Shrugged at Sandy. She took something out of her bag and, putting the bag on the bench, turned to Sandy.

'Sandy, can I give you something?'

'Sure,' said Sandy, hoping this wasn't something Mr Jarvis wouldn't want his daughter to give away.

Mavis put a pair of pliers into Sandy's hands. 'I found these in the Amman amphitheatre and I didn't know what to do with them. Dad doesn't approve of me picking things up. He says anything on the floor could be contagious and I must be careful.' She sighed. 'I'm tired of being careful.'

'Sure,' said Sandy, taking the pliers and wondering what to do with them. She could put them in her luggage and maybe ask Miss Abbey about them when she looked less harassed than she normally did.

'Oh, and, Sandy, do you mind not telling my dad we've been chatting?'

Sandy nibbled her lower lip, wondering if it was OK to keep secrets from Mavis's father.

She must have looked surprised because Mavis brushed her hand across her face impatiently. 'Thanks. Dad doesn't like me talking to people.'

'Oh,' said Sandy. 'But yes, of course, I won't say anything. Do you know why he doesn't like it?'

Here was a mystery indeed and perhaps she could put it in a story.

'He says I'll pick up odd accents and he likes the way I speak now.'

'OK,' said Sandy, baffled. Odd accents? What did that mean? Was it just an excuse? Was Mr Jarvis a tyrant? Perhaps he thought Mavis might be led astray by someone on the trip, but who? Mr Cox? Mrs Cox? Cyril? Elsa? Miss Abbey? Mrs Williams or Harry? Impossible to say which ones might lead his little duckling astray. Was Mavis making a joke at her expense? Did she have an odd accent?

Mavis walked away and Sandy saw there was a bag on the bench where she had been sitting. She jumped up and hurried after the girl.

'Mavis, you left your bag behind.'

Mavis looked around her vaguely. 'Oh, yes, so I did.'

She took the bag and for a moment a strange expression swept across Mavis's face; it looked almost triumphal. Did Mavis control her father as much as he controlled her? Families were odd. What would it be like to be part of one?

CHAPTER 19

FOREWARNED IS
FOREARMED

After breakfast next morning, the kerfuffle of moving a tribe of sixteen people to another location began. Mr Jarvis was, of course, the first out, with his watch in one hand and his stopwatch visible on his phone. He greeted Miss Abbey sadly.

'After the slow start yesterday,' he said, 'I thought I'd time each arrival so we'll know how much time to leave for boarding in future. Forewarned is forearmed, Miss Abbey. Forewarned is forearmed.'

'Thank you,' she said politely, wondering how upset he would be when they inevitably left late.

However, something else was worrying Abbey: Israel. It wasn't only Mr Jarvis with his pessimism and his distance from the border in minutes that had alerted her to the possibility of trouble. Israel itself had been far more aggressive towards Gaza and Lebanon since they arrived here, and there was no doubt Abbey and her partially disabled crew were a very vulnerable target should either side decide they wanted hostages. Abbey shuddered at the word hostages. The Israeli hostages, taken over a year ago, were now mostly believed dead, although a few were still in captivity and a minimal number had been released. Would anyone care about her motley crew of hostages? Could Mrs Tank pull rank and get herself released before anyone else? The idea made Abbey smile, even though she was worried.

Abbey quickly reviewed her list. As far as she knew there were no US Americans here, but then it was hard to tell with all the duplicity she had already encountered. Abbey had been very young when the New York Twin Towers were bombed but she remembered her parents saying it had a lot to do with the hatred towards the USA, owing to their foreign policy, and that Americans made good targets. And she was aware everyone in this region blamed the USA for Israel's actions. None of the guests had USA passports, but could any of them have sneaked a second passport? You never knew with groups – there was usually at least one member who was too clever for his own good. And then, of course, there was Sandy Blee, the journalist. Could she actually be an activist? An activist and a journalist? Where was she now?

Then, as though she wasn't worrying enough on her own, Adam joined her, his face also full of anxiety.

'Oh,' she said, 'I see you've heard the news.'

He jumped nervously and looked at her. 'Which bit?'

'That the Americans are sending troops to help protect Israel.'

'Oh, yes,' he said. 'Tricky.'

'This could well lead to an escalation,' she added.

'Yes, yes, terrible.'

She wondered for a moment if he was thinking about something different. He didn't seem to be concentrating on what she was saying. But what could be worse than an escalation of the Palestine–Israel War into Jordan? Nothing she could imagine.

Her glance fell on the guests, now finally assembled in their wheelchairs and ready to go to Petra. Having been able-bodied all her life and a regular swimmer and runner, she had never really thought of what might happen to disabled people in a war zone. Now it was brought upon her very fast. They would need transport. It wasn't just that they couldn't walk through the desert; they couldn't walk at all.

'Is the airport closed?'

'No.' He sounded surprised. 'No, everything's fine.'

'Oh. Good.'

The driver brought down the ramp and the wheelchairs started boarding. However, if only Abbey had known it, the war in Israel was the least of their problems right now.

CHAPTER 20

HALF A PERSON'S BEAUTY COMES FROM THEIR TONGUE

The staff at their hotel in Petra were so glad to see them arrive that Abbey immediately wondered if many more guests had cancelled their holidays to Jordan.

'We have upgraded all your guests,' said the manager, smiling happily. 'Such lovely rooms and a beautiful villa for Mrs Tank.'

Wow, thought Abbey, *word gets about. Did the last hotel send this hotel a message about Mrs Tank?*

As befitted their cheap vacation prices, the wheelchair pushers were originally going to share bedrooms, but thanks to the lack of tourists, the myriad of empty rooms and the subsequent upgrading policy, they were now going to receive 'a beautiful chamber of their own, some with pool access'.

Abbey started distributing keys. Most of the rooms were easy to find, but Mrs Tank and Roxanna both had named villas, so Adam said he would show them where to go. Abbey nodded. 'Good idea. OK. Jade, Sandy, we'll take Roxanna and Mrs Tank. Can you go and find your own rooms? Here are the keys; one's on the pool side, the other's got a balcony. You choose between you, off you go.'

And she swept away with her more important clients.

'Git!' said Jade. 'You can see where we come in the pecking order. Well, let's have a look at them, these beautiful upgrades.'

She shot off and Sandy, walking behind her, was wondering if she needed poolside access given Petra was currently quite cold and windy, when she heard Jade singing 'Look at Me, I'm Sandra Dee...'

Sandy sighed. This wasn't the first time Jade had sung that song, especially the ruder parts. At first, Sandy had been slightly amused, although she had also heard it from girls at school, but after the fourth and fifth time, she'd had enough. It was true, she hadn't had much education, but before coming out to Jordan, she had read and watched everything she could find about the country and had enjoyed her research. She doubted Jade had read anything, preferring to mock and tease those who did.

She thinks I'm an idiot, Sandy thought. *She thinks I'm too wet to fight back. Just because she's the granddaughter of the infamous and rich Lady Bumstead, a woman who was recently the defendant in a celebrity murder trial.*

Jade, no doubt, had a private school education. She thinks she's better than me. Well, thought Sandy, *I bet she doesn't know this.*

'But you, of course,' she said, catching up with Jade, 'are rather less of a Sandra Dee and rather more of a Jane Digby character, aren't you? *Jade* Digby, perhaps. I wonder if there's a song about her.'

Jade sneered and lit a cigarette, in spite of the large no smoking signs. 'No fucking idea!'

'No,' said Sandy, her voice sugary. 'I didn't think you

would. She was a wild child who ended up married to a Bedouin sheikh and lived until her seventies in a Bedu tent, much to the disgust of her family. Rather cute, isn't it? A sweet story of lust turned into love.'

'I'll have this room then,' said Jade, throwing the other key at Sandy and slamming the door.

Sandy felt depressed. She might have got one over on Jade but really, did that matter? Wasn't it all awfully petty? She bit her lip and reminded herself how wonderful it was to be here and not at work. What was that tiresome phrase they used at Percy's Bifold Doors? Push forward? Onwards and upwards? Yup. Onwards and upwards. She climbed the stairs.

Sandy's room was lovely with a huge balcony that was positioned towards the west so she would be able to see the sunset. It was directly above Jade's room and in front of them both ballooned a huge but completely unused pool. Would Jade go swimming, or was it just the idea of the pool she liked?

By the time Sandy got downstairs, everyone was already gathered in the drawing room. Guiltily, she hurried to Roxy's side.

'There's a candlelight show tonight at the Treasury in Petra, if anyone fancies it,' Abbey was saying as Sandy arrived. 'For those who are interested, it starts with a candlelit walk down to the Nabatean ruins, followed by entertainment from local artists, before another candlelit walk back up the slope.'

'Local artists!' said Mrs Tank. 'Ha ha! I know what that means... they were too cheap to get anyone any good and these old boys with their flat voices and horrible instruments were only too keen to play.'

Everyone else was shaking their heads and looking towards the nearest dining room, which offered Mediterranean delights.

'I'll go,' said Sandy. 'I love the idea of a candlelit walk. So romantic.'

Roxy groaned. 'Not for me.'

'Jade'll go with her,' said Mrs Tank. 'It'll keep her out of trouble.'

Jade sneered but agreed. 'OK. Whatever.'

Abbey looked at the other young ones. 'Tony? Elsa? Cyril?'

They shook their heads. 'We heard that it isn't worth going to,' said Elsa. 'Sorry, Sandy.' She turned to Tony. 'We could check out the Wadi Musa nightlife.'

Tony made a pouting face and spread his hands and the three of them exchanged glances. 'If there is any,' he muttered.

Sandy shrugged. She wasn't surprised. Of course they thought she was unsophisticated, but who cares, she was enjoying herself. Probably they would go off spending their money on boozing. She smiled internally. Let them! She was here to learn. To improve her life. To see the world, she told herself, although oddly she didn't feel as happy as she wanted to.

At eight o'clock, Sandy and Jade set off for the walk. One of the cats decided to follow them and Sandy stopped to pet it. Jade carried on, sighing, and was soon out of sight. Sandy and the cat walked on alone until the cat stopped to eat something a tourist had dropped.

Sandy looked for the things she had seen on TikTok: this was the Siq Trail and there were tombs and shrines of past people. Here, cut into the rock, were the conduits that led from the five springs in the distant hills that carried water to the Treasury and beyond; water that had made life here in Petra possible in the past. Here was the tunnel that had been built to prevent tourists drowning in sudden flash floods, as had happened in 2018 when eleven people were killed.

Further down, she passed some djinn blocks that took her mind back to *Jinns* and her preparatory film watching. And finally, she reached the narrow split in the rock that gave out to the Treasury.

She stopped for a moment, waiting to savour the excitement to come. She knew what to expect, but she still held her breath. Eventually she could wait no longer and she walked through the narrow split, and as she did so, her body gave a huge sigh of contentment. Positioned in front of the elegant temple of the Treasury, giving a warm glow of light, were hundreds and thousands of lit candles bathing the building in purplish light, making it eerily stunning: nothing at Percy's Bifold Doors was like this.

Jade, seeing her arrive, came over. 'Load of rammies, isn't it? Disney without the steroids. And, look at that, here comes the local laity. Oh my God! One chap's brought a flute. And what's that thing with three strings? Christ! What a shithole. I'll listen for one song and if it's as bad as I expect, I'm off. See you tomorrow.'

Jade sat down on a small folding stool by the exit and got out her phone. Sandy walked past her, past many rows of stools and deckchairs, and positioned herself at the front on a hand-woven rug and under the full splendour of the Nabatean architecture. She lay back on the rug and gave herself up to the music that was about to start. She looked up; the sky was full of stars, and she sighed happily. Life, she told herself, was just beginning, and everything was about to change. Which was true, but not in the way she thought.

Miss Abbey and the others were still finishing their dinner when Jade came back. 'It's pants,' she said. 'A complete waste of time. I left Miss Goody Two-Shoes down there breathing in the atmosphere, but I came back. I've seen better rubbish in Peckham.'

'What were you doing in Peckham?' asked Mrs Tank. 'Chasing some butch boy, were you?'

Jade sat down and poured herself a glass of wine. 'Nice dinner, Gran? Lots of delicious home cooking, was it?'

'Yes, thank you. Do you want anything or will you exist on alcohol and crisps?'

Jade jeered.

Before long, the tiring bus journey and the thought of tomorrow's excitement caused most of the guests to start yawning. Once dinner was over, they all said they were ready for bed.

'I won't need you, Jade,' said Mrs Tank. 'So you can check out the local talent, see if it's better than in Peckham.'

This amused her so much she was still laughing when she arrived at the lift.

Jade wandered over to the bar. She was bored. Sandy seemed to get high on this cultural rubbish – even her gran said it was amazing to think this stuff had lasted so long and it was a pity she couldn't live as long. Just think how many marriages she'd get in if she lived 2000 years – yeah right! Who gave a stuff?

Jade twiddled her nose ring and asked for a glass of Jordanian wine. She'd tried arak in Amman but it made her feel queasy. How long was her gran going to stay here? Yes, they were on a trip but the great Mrs T might do anything at any time; she was that unpredictable and had the brass and the guts to do whatever she felt like, so who knew? She took a crisp from the bar and stared at the television. Earlier, they'd been showing football, now it was kick-boxing. Who liked it? The tourists or the locals? The staff, perhaps. She looked around for someone to give her a cigarette.

Adam was talking to the bartender but seeing her look around, he came over.

'Would you like something, Miss Jade? Are you enjoying the boxing?'

He smelt of smoke. She wondered if he rolled his own. 'Got a fag?'

'Please?'

'A cigarette? I'm gasping.'

'Oh, yes, of course. In Jordan, it is allowed to smoke in bars, but not many places, eh.'

'Yeah!' she said, indicating the ashtray in front of her. 'I figured.'

He got a packet out of his pocket and offered her one. She took two. 'I'll light you one,' she said. 'I hate to smoke alone.'

His handsome face puckered slightly. 'I'm on duty,' he said. 'Miss Abbey—'

'She's gone to bed.' She looked at him. 'You want a drink?'

He looked around. 'Yes, OK, but don't tell Miss Abbey. I don't think she'd approve.'

Jade raised an eyebrow and shrugged. 'You think? Aren't you supposed to drink in public?'

'I'm a guide,' he said simply. 'I'm always on duty.'

She turned to the bartender. 'Give me a bottle of Jordanian Sauvignon Blanc and two glasses,' she said. To

Adam, she added, tilting her head, 'Let's sit over there, away from the TV.'

She got up and went to a small table in a private nook screened from the bar and the door. He followed her, looking slightly dubious. She sat down and grinned. 'Ah, you're OK, I've got my eye on the door. If anyone comes in, I'll pretend both glasses are mine.'

The bartender brought the drinks and smiled at Adam as he opened the bottle. 'Enjoy,' he said and returned to the bar.

Jade raised her eyebrows.

'It's OK,' said Adam, 'he's a friend of mine.'

'At school together, were you?'

'No. I'm from Egypt. I studied archaeology...' He sighed softly. 'I had a dream to be an archaeologist, but it's expensive. My father, he wanted to help me; he took two jobs, and he worked hard to put me through university in Luxor. I did six years, but when it came to getting a job...' He shrugged. 'I come from a middle family. I have no connections, so I couldn't get anything. No work.'

He glanced at Jade – she was listening, watching his face intently. He took another drag of his cigarette. 'Tourism here was good then. Egyptian workers were cheaper than locals. I got a job washing dishes in a Bedouin camp in Wadi Rum. I didn't forget my dream, but I must eat!'

Jade nodded. She finished her glass and poured herself some more wine. He had drunk very little of his but she topped it up anyway.

'So, I enjoy the tourists, they teach me a lot, and they like me. Then an English archaeologist arrived at our camp in Wadi Rum. He was on his way to Petra and stopped with us first – maybe he too had seen the *Lawrence of Arabia* film. Many people talked about Peter O'Toole.'

He smiled and spread his hands. Jade smiled back. He was a good-looking man; she could see why the tourists liked him. Sexy. Appealing.

'This man, John,' said Adam, 'was driving himself in a hire car but he nearly had an accident. He said the driving in Jordan is mad.' Adam laughed. 'I told him it was mostly young Saudi boys with lots of money who come over the border and drive like idiots, but he didn't care who it was, he was just scared. We talked archaeology; sites and digs. And John asked me to be his driver, to take him to Petra.'

Adam tilted his head. 'You don't know this, maybe, but Egyptians aren't allowed to be drivers here, no Egyptian taxi drivers – the Jordanians say they will take our jobs, that we are cheap labour – but they don't mind us washing dishes! No Jordanians want to do those jobs.'

'So how could you be his driver?'

'Because he has a 70 car.'

'A 70 car? What does that mean?'

'It's a hire car. He hired it so I can drive it as another tourist, but I can't work for him. You understand?'

Jade nodded but hoped desperately he wasn't gay. What a waste if he was. 'I understand,' she said, stubbing out her cigarette. He did the same, on top of hers.

'John is keen *not* to drive, you understand. So, we make an arrangement. I will come and learn about the Petra dig, and I will drive him. No money. I will become a tourist too.' He laughed and raised his eyebrows. 'A student tourist, eh.'

'But what about your job at the Bedouin camp in Wadi Rum?'

Adam half shrugged. 'Yes, it was difficult. They had no one like me. No one to replace me but I have a dream. I want to learn more about archaeology, so I leave and they say don't come back. Ever! We move to Petra.'

'So? What happened to the Englishman, John, you said?'

'We worked for several months, then he must to go back to England. He has family, young children. But before he goes, he pays for me to train as a guide to thank me. So now I am guide in Jordan, including Petra and Jerash. And I care more than many guides. The subject interests me and I still have my dream to be an archaeologist, but it is waiting.' He stared sadly at the wine bottle. 'A dream in waiting is like a corked bottle without a corkscrew.'

She laughed. 'Nice! Yours? Old Arabic saying?'

'Mine.'

Jade leant back and stretched out her long legs, letting her naked knee brush his thigh.

'So, if you lot don't drink except on sufferance, what do you do to have a good time?'

He smiled at her, but he left his leg where it was. 'Mostly we work. I read a lot of archaeology. I'm still hoping one day I get a job working on a dig.'

'Is that so?' she said. 'I think I brought some archaeological books with me. Want to come up and see if there's something I can lend you?'

He looked nervous. 'We are not allowed in the guests' rooms,' he said. 'Perhaps...'

She grinned. 'Know what? I think I fancy a late-night swim, but as I always swim naked, I'll definitely need a bodyguard with all these randy young men around... number twelve, ground floor, poolside. I'll give you ten minutes!'

She walked to the bar, signed for her wine and left Adam to make his own decision.

CHAPTER 21

WE TRY TO HIDE OUR
FEELINGS BUT WE FORGET,
OUR EYES SPEAK

Next morning, Sandy got up early to see the sunrise. She opened the curtains and then remembered she was looking west. Getting dressed, she stared out at the pre-dawn stillness. Suddenly, below her, a shadow slipped through the discreet pool lighting. Its direction was away from the room underneath hers, hurrying towards the main hotel. He was barely visible in the green glow of the pool lights, but even so, she could see from the shape it was Adam.

The crime writer in her wondered if he'd just killed Jade and was now making a getaway, but the realist said it was likely to have a more basic explanation. Did Jade know it was illegal in Jordan to have sex with someone you weren't married to?

Would the girl care? She was a tourist. If caught, she would probably be shipped back to her own country, given a slap on the wrist and a short ban on entering Jordan again, but what about Adam? That must be so dangerous for him, crazy fool. What if Miss Abbey had been the one looking out to see the sunrise?

Sandy waited until she was sure Adam had got away from the hotel, and then hurried down to watch the dawn's transformation.

'Good morning, lady,' said the doorman as she wished him *sabah alkhayr*, hoping he understood her Duolingo Arabic. 'Your colleague awaits you outside.'

Sandy was surprised. She had mentioned, before leaving for candlelit Petra, that she would be up to see the sunrise, but nobody else had said they were getting up too. She wondered who this colleague was. Through the glass door that led outside, she saw Cyril. Sandy very much doubted he came out to be her companion; more likely he was just coming back from a night out on the town.

As she left the hotel, the cold wind blew through her jacket and she shivered, wondering if she had worn enough layers. Still, a brisk walk would warm her and the sun would soon be up.

Cyril was sitting on one of the stone bollards. He jumped up and walked over to her.

'Hi.'

She smiled. 'Hi. You just coming back from a night out? Like Amman?'

He laughed, his blue eyes twinkling. 'What nightlife? This place is more dead than a country village! No, I thought I'd come and see the sunrise. They told me at the desk you were coming down too.'

Sandy shivered again.

'Hey, you're cold. Want this?' He proffered a dark blue puffer. 'I brought it in case it was colder than I remembered. But now I'm too hot.'

'Thank you.'

She put it on and felt extremely grateful, even if it hadn't been intended for her. It fitted her perfectly and she frowned; although he wasn't a big man, it would be a very tight fit on him. Had he actually been waiting for someone else?

'I know a very good place to see the sunrise, unless you have ideas of your own?' Cyril said.

'No, I was just going to hang around by the museum, but if you know somewhere better...'

He nodded, looked at his watch, and whistled at a nearby man holding camels. The man came over, smiling, and said something to Sandy. She smiled blankly, totally focused on the large animal approaching her.

'Can you ride?' Cyril asked.

'Er, yes, I guess. If I can get up there.'

Cyril smiled and said something to the camel man. The Bedouin tapped the camel on the shoulder, and with a lurch that made Sandy's heart jump, the large animal knelt down beside her.

'Slide your leg over and hang on as it gets up. You need to hold tight and throw your body forward, but once you're up, it's a breeze.'

'Ah, right!'

She took a deep breath. This was all about learning to live, but *wow*. How many people at home had ridden a camel? She wondered what her brother would say about this.

The Bedouin tapped the camel again and it rose, front legs first, so Sandy felt herself slipping backwards and grabbed the saddle. Then the back legs came up and she felt better, if a little unstable. She looked over at Cyril, who was already sitting on another camel. He was laughing, but not unkindly. 'You'll get used to it. I've done it hundreds of times, but the first time is always the worst.'

'Right.'

'*Shakran lak*,' she said to the Bedouin and he politely replied, 'welcome!' although Sandy doubted she had pronounced it right. Especially when she stole another look at Cyril's face.

'It was meant to be "thank you". Not quite right?'

He shook his head. 'But good you tried. Not many tourists try to learn Arabic.'

'Thanks. I learnt a few other words like "good morning" and "where is breakfast?"'

Cyril roared with laughter. 'Sorry, but why did you choose the last one? That's hilarious.'

She shrugged, smiling. 'I don't know. I thought it would be useful. I wasn't sure what to expect but I knew I would need breakfast.'

'Wonderful.'

As the camel started moving, Sandy needed all her concentration to stay on while the animal rolled and dipped like a rough day on the Guildford bus. Gradually, she got used to the animal's swaying gait and was able to look around her, now only holding on with one hand. Once her mind was back in thinking mode, she licked her lips; there had been something she'd missed in Cyril's speech. He said something unexpected, but what?

The camels now turned up a stony track and, holding tightly to the saddle, she looked down at their broad feet and was impressed. This was not easy walking, and it was quite different from the *Lawrence of Arabia* film, where the camels galloped everywhere across the sand and Lawrence looked as though he was racing a horse with complete mastery. Here, the paths were mostly loose stones, and no one was racing.

At the top of the ridge and the bottom of a large rock, the camels stopped suddenly, as though they knew the place.

Cyril said, 'We'll get off here.' And he slipped down from his mount without waiting for the Bedouin man following behind them on foot.

She stared at the distant ground. Was she supposed to jump? She'd break something. Should she hold and slip? Throw herself wildly into the abyss? How?

As she was pondering on her descent, the camel man arrived and gently tapped the animal on its foreleg. It sank down with its front legs first. Sandy gasped and she grabbed the pommel as her body swept forward and she nearly landed on the camel's neck. Would she break it? Poor camel. The back legs descended too and she held her breath. Was she slipping back this time? Her body gave a clumsy jolt to the left and she bit her tongue, trying desperately not to yell out. The Bedouin man reached up and a strong hand held her steady, helping her onto stable earth. He looked at Cyril, who smiled supportively.

Cyril said something to the Bedouin and she realised what it was she'd missed.

'You speak Arabic,' she said.

He half-smiled at her and nodded.

'OK, now concentrate. We're going to have to do some climbing up this rock, so follow me and put your feet where I put mine. These are what the Bedouin laughably call Nabatean steps, after the builders of Petra, which means they aren't really steps at all but little indentations.'

She followed him slowly, but to her relief, he didn't hurry ahead, like her brother would have done, waiting at the top, laughing at her incompetence. Instead, he moved slowly and kept watching her, making sure she could see the indentations and where to put her hands. After a rather arduous climb, they finally came out on top of the rock, and

Sandy was amazed to see the whole valley spread out beneath her in the pink tinged morning glow.

Cyril laughed with real spontaneity. 'My sister and I used to come up here as kids. Amazing, really, that our parents let us, but I guess they trusted her. Having an elder sister has benefits.'

Sandy stared at the rising sun, slowly taking in what he said. 'You've been here before. So, you speak Arabic because...?'

He kept looking at the view but said, 'I was born here, my parents both worked for UNICEF.'

'Wow. So you went to school here?'

This time he turned to her. 'I went to the French lycée in Amman. It was the cheapest of the foreign schools. We went back to England when I was thirteen and my sister was fifteen but we come back regularly. In some ways it feels like home.'

Sandy could hardly think of a life more different from her own. Not only was he born here and had living parents, but he went to a paid school, not the local rubbish tip she attended. He might even have gone to university. She stared at the beauty of the growing light, her mind whirling. It was so kind of him to show her this. She hoped she wasn't being too boring a companion, but really, she couldn't think of anything to say; he was so out of her league it was laughable. Even the rich bitch Jade was more understandable than this incredible boy.

She gave up thinking and watched the changing environment, feeling a huge sense of elation. She gave a sigh of contentment. 'Wow.'

He smiled at her. 'I feel as though I'm seeing this for the first time through your eyes.'

'Double wow,' she said, laughing. 'If only we could all do that. What stories I would write!'

He laughed with her.

Life could only go downhill from here, but what an experience.

CHAPTER 22

WITHOUT PAIN WE
WOULDN'T KNOW JOY

The first morning in Petra was one of those breakfasts Abbey dreaded. The only people up in time for the morning briefing were Mr Jarvis and Mavis, Elsa and Mr Cox, and Mrs Williams.

Elsa had opened her bedroom door to find Mr Cox trying to get rid of a bag of rubbish. She disposed of it for him in her own bin and pushed him along to the lift. Mrs Cox, he'd said, was having breakfast in bed.

Mrs Williams was also waiting for the lift but had misplaced Harry.

Elsa dutifully pushed both chairs into the breakfast room and then, since Harry was absent, happily fetched everything for both Mr Cox and Mrs Williams.

'Much easier,' said Mrs Williams, 'than sign language. I wish you could stay with me. Perhaps I could do a swap with Mr Cox.'

Elsa smiled, glancing across at Mr Cox, who shook his head.

'No chance,' he said, taking her hand. 'I'm not losing this lovely girl for anything.'

Mr Jarvis tutted and looked at his watch. 'In two minutes the others will be late for the briefing. Is it worth going if we're late?'

Abbey ignored him. She knew Sandy had gone to watch the sunrise but had assumed that would just be a quick walk up to the museum and a stroll back once the sun was up. Instead, she appeared to have disappeared. Roxy had not come down yet, even though she could move her chair herself and did not need Sandy. Mrs Tank and Jade did sometimes eat breakfast in their rooms, but even so, she was expecting them down by now. And where were the boys, Cyril and Tony? Or Harry the Bulgarian and Mrs Cox?

Surely they couldn't all have overslept. Had those boys been out on the razzle again? She did hope not.

Then, as though all these non-arrivals weren't enough, when she was getting her food at the buffet, a small bouncy Englishwoman cannoned into her, spilling her yogurt all over the floor and narrowly missing pouring her coffee on Abbey's WWH jacket.

'Oh, I'm so sorry,' said Miranda. 'I was looking at someone who had just come into the dining room and not where I was going. I do hope I haven't hurt you.'

Abbey shook her head, but Miranda's apology was so genuine that she couldn't help but be appeased.

'It's OK, it is just turning out to be one of those days, and I wish I could have stayed in bed.'

'Oh! Poor you. Can I help? Shall I carry some of your things to your table? It's the big one, isn't it?'

And before Abbey knew what was happening, Miranda had taken her plates and was heading for the guests.

'Hello, everybody,' said Miranda, smiling at the few people installed at the table and others who were just arriving. 'I just cannoned into your leader and I'm trying to make amends. How are you all today?'

Elsa looked at Miranda and laughed. 'Good. Very good. How could we not be happy here in Petra with a beautiful morning and a day of treats ahead?'

Some of the others then also murmured good morning, clearly puzzled about who Miranda might be and why she was chatting away to them. However, before they knew it, they were telling her their names and various other things. The only person who seemed to find Miranda annoying was Mr Jarvis, who looked at his watch and pointed out that the crowds really started at 10 a.m.

'I read it,' he said emphatically, 'in the guidebook.'

Miranda beamed at him. 'Oh yes,' she said, 'but that was before the Gazan War. Now there are only 800 tourists as opposed to the 3000 they normally expect.'

Mr Jarvis sighed and wrinkled his nose, muttering, 'You never can be too sure.'

By the time Abbey returned to the table, Miranda had offered to push Mrs Cox if Cyril did not return in time, and was suggesting various extra delights for breakfast, which she would be happy to get for them.

Abbey sighed. 'Anyone have any idea where Cyril is?'

'Yes,' said Elsa. 'He said last night he was going to watch the sunrise this morning. I expect he's on his way back from Camel Rock.'

They all turned to her. 'Camel Rock?'

'What's Camel Rock?'

'Where?'

Elsa blushed. 'Oh! I er... read it on Quora. It said it was a great place to see the sunrise in Petra. I think I told him about it last night.'

She smiled and Miranda was not the only one to think she was lying. However, while the others clearly thought that what she and Cyril got up to was their business, Miranda was silently intrigued. What was the real relationship between Elsa and Cyril? She must investigate.

By ten o'clock, everyone had arrived at breakfast except Jade, Sandy, and Cyril.

'I'd better have Miranda push me,' said Roxy, 'if Sandy can't be bothered to get back in time for her duties. Mrs Cox can limp. She's only sprained her ankle.'

'Then I'll have Tony,' said Mrs Tank imperiously, although Tony was yawning and looking far from ready for a day pushing wheelchairs.

'It's all right, Gran, I'm here,' said a weary voice and Jade appeared with a cup of coffee.

'So sorry I'm late,' said Sandy, rushing in, her curly hair dancing all over her face. 'I just didn't realise the time. So, so sorry, Miss Abbey, Roxy, everyone. Can I help anyone now?'

'So,' said Abbey, 'the only person missing is Cyril. Elsa, do you know where he is?'

Sandy shot a look at Elsa and felt a bit sick. Why would she know? What had she missed? Sandy sucked her lower lip. The beautiful morning seemed to have grown cold. She shook herself. I must be realistic, she told herself. I'm just a nobody. She realised Miss Abbey was talking to her.

'Sorry, what did you say?'

'I asked if it was a lovely sunrise.'

'Yes, yes it was.'

'And did you go to Camel Rock?'

Sandy nodded. 'Is that what it's called? It was so beautiful. And the sunrise with that view... just wow!'

Before anybody could say anything further, Cyril arrived with a cup of coffee for himself and one for Sandy. 'I thought you might like this,' he said, smiling at her. 'Milk, no sugar, I hope that's OK.'

Sandy nodded and blushed.

'Ah,' said Abbey, 'were you watching the sunrise together then?'

Sandy fidgeted and stared at the floor. She didn't know what to say and Miss Abbey's voice sounded annoyed. They hadn't done anything wrong, had they?

Cyril answered. 'Yes. I showed Sandy how to ride a camel and we rode up there. It was fabulous.'

Over the other side of the table, Elsa laughed. Miranda watched all these things and wondered what was happening here. There was clearly either a budding romance or a mystery. She must find out which.

CHAPTER 23

THERE'S MORE THAN MEETS THE EYE WHEN YOU ARE LOOKING INTO DEEP WATER

After breakfast, the guests all assembled in the drawing room, where Miss Abbey was ready to give them the plan of the day.

'For those of our guests who prefer it or cannot walk,' she said, 'I have organised transport to take you down to the Treasury. As Mrs Cox has now joined this number, I will walk and Adam will ride down with you in the bus – he will be able to tell you various things about the Treasury on the way there.

'The group will then re-form at the Treasury. The wheelchairs will come out of the van so the various pushers can take their guests to see the sites and we will then join up again at the Nabatean restaurant at the bottom of the steps to the monastery.

Is everybody happy and clear about what's going to happen? If not, this is the moment for questions.'

'I thought we were planning to be at the Treasury at 10 a.m.,' said Mr Jarvis. 'Does this mean we'll be late? How long does it take to get there, a, by electric vehicle and b, on foot?

I would also like to know if there will be any delay for various people,' he glanced at Sandy, 'wishing to take animal transport?'

Sandy shook her curls and stared at the floor in embarrassment. She hated being singled out. 'No. No,' she stuttered. 'Happy to comply with whatever.'

Miss Abbey's plans worked without problem. The electric vehicle disgorged the wheelchairs outside the Treasury, the walkers arrived at the same time, and clients and pushers were reunited and the wheelchairs and their occupants were pushed on to the end of the Roman colonnade. The only anomaly was that Mavis decided she wanted to walk, pushing her own chair.

Speaking so quietly that it was hard to hear her, she said, 'It's flat here.' She shot a forceful glance at her father. 'It will be good for me. Stretch me!'

Her father looked like he was going to object, but since she was determined and the others were encouraging her, he got out his watch. 'Half an hour at most, Mavis. Have you got your handbag?'

She had not.

Adam hastily called the bus, which returned immediately and Mavis was reunited with her handbag.

'Very well,' said Mr Jarvis, his foot tapping, 'the half an hour starts now.'

The girl nodded. Sandy thought that after half an hour, Mavis would probably be exhausted anyway and glad to comply. She was pleased the girl was learning to stand up to her father. Perhaps it would improve their relationship.

'What's wrong with Mavis?' she asked Roxy, leaning

forward to hear better as she pushed the chair across the rocky sands. 'Any idea?'

'Her father said she had multiple problems including a weak heart. Seems they travel with a cocktail of drugs supplied by the doctor.'

Sandy wondered what it would be like to have a father. Clearly he loved Mavis, even if he was over-protective.

By the time they arrived at the end of the colonnades, most people were ready for lunch.

'These large columns were built,' Adam said, stopping and pointing at them, 'by the Romans after they conquered the Nabateans. The last monarch, Rabble II, wanted them to move in after his death and the Romans agreed to hold off until then.'

There were lots of nodding heads and 'oh really's, but most of the group were streaming steadily towards the Nabatean lunch place.

'When was that?' asked Jade, pushing Mrs Tank up beside Adam. 'When did the Romans take over the kingdom?'

Adam smiled at her. '106 AD.'

Jade was about to continue the conversation when Mrs Cox broke in. 'After lunch, what about the monastery? Everyone says that's worth a visit.'

Miss Abbey shook her head, clearly annoyed. 'It's an impossible place for wheelchairs,' she said testily. 'Eight hundred steps. Just not possible.'

'It is 800 steps on the short route,' said Adam. 'But I have an idea. I can drive the bus and take Mr Cox and Elsa, Roxy and Sandy, Mrs Tank and Jade, Jolly and Spice, and Mrs Williams and Harry in the van, while anyone who wants to walk can go up the steps.'

'What about me?' said Mrs Cox angrily, although her

husband looked quite pleased at the idea he would be alone with Elsa.

'Actually,' said Mrs Williams, 'I'm tired and I think I've had enough of old buildings. I'm happy to give up my place to Mrs Cox and Cyril.'

Sandy was looking at Adam and saw a flash of annoyance pass over his face, before being replaced by acquiescence. Miss Abbey, however, was only too glad to have agreement.

'Right, that's it then. Once we've had lunch, you lot go in the van, and anyone who wants to, can walk. Anyone else can stay with me and we'll explore the area around here. I believe there's a sacrificial stone somewhere.'

Adam shrugged.

Lunch over, Adam reappeared from the back of the restaurant with the electric transport, which was not allowed to travel through the centre of the Petra site. Slowly the guests began loading into the van. Mr Jarvis gave a glance at his watch and a big sigh and wheeled Mavis away. Mavis was asleep.

By the time all the wheelchairs were loaded into the van, all the other groups had moved off to climb or wander as required.

'OK,' Adam said, 'we have guests, pushers, and wheelchairs. Everyone ready?'

There was a murmur of accord and they set off.

Sandy and Cyril sat on the bench at the back, which had no access for the physically impaired. She glanced at Adam and saw he was concentrating on driving in the rather difficult terrain. She scrolled down her phone, got up an article she had downloaded, and showed it to Cyril. She had high-lighted a phrase.

There is no motorised access to the monastery; the only way there is on foot or by donkey.

She raised her eyebrows.

He nodded and bent his head down to her ear. 'Yes, I know,' he whispered. 'Adam is up to something, but don't worry, we are just pawns in a bigger game. Trust me.'

He put his hand on her arm and squeezed it gently, making an OK sign with the other hand. Sandy repressed her sigh. In some ways she wished he wouldn't be so kind. He was clearly out of her league and yet he was so nice. She wondered what he meant by pawns in a bigger game. Did his knowledge of Arabic mean he knew something?

As they drove up the mountainside, the road became rougher and narrower. On one side the mountain soared steeply up, while on the other side of the track, it spilled off into nothing. Periodically, stones dislodged by the van cascaded down the slope, bouncing on outcrops and only just missing any goats attempting to graze on the precipitous ledges.

Sandy glanced out the window and decided to look inside instead.

Eventually, Adam stopped on a wide platform at the mouth of a large cave. 'We will go in here for a rest,' he said. 'This is a wonderful cave and needs to be seen.'

He went round and opened the side door, switching on the electricity to the ramp so the wheelchairs and their occupants could be lowered down and pushed out. One by one the guests went into the cave.

As each one entered they gave a gasp at the spectacular sight: water over thousands of years had run through the limestone, sandstone and silica, and created striations of red, yellow, brown, and white. Into these layers, the Nabateans of former years had sculpted niches, both large and small, and even seats. The effect was like some crazily coloured art deco architecture springing out of the stones.

'We believe,' said Adam, 'that the Nabateans lived here and certainly the Bedul continued to do so until the government threw them out, taking over their ancestral land and making them live in new villages.'

Cyril looked at Sandy and raised his eyebrows. She gave a half smile in return. She wasn't quite sure what his look meant but clearly he knew something.

'Now,' Adam said, 'if you would like to wheel further back into the cave you will see evidence of an early well.'

The group did as they were bid and rolled deeper into the cave. Here, it was possible to see, through the semi-darkness, what looked like a reservoir dug down into the rocks. 'We think that when the five springs were still giving water, the Nabateans were able to channel water in here. If you look along the side you will see there is an indentation cut into the rocks. This is similar to the channels they had already built to harness the water down to the Treasury.'

The guests peered into the darkness, leaning forward in their chairs, but it was hard to see clearly.

'Go and have a look, Sandy,' said Roxy, 'and then let's get on to the monastery. I'm bored of all this decorative rock; give me modern carvings any day. And coffee.'

Sandy looked down the hole but instead of seeing an indentation for water, she saw what looked like blankets, water bottles, crisps, and Thermos flasks. She looked back at Cyril, wanting to get his opinion but saw he was talking to Elsa in what appeared to be a very flirtatious way. He had his hand on her arm and she was looking up into his face with a huge grin. Moreover, she was wearing a dark blue puffer. Was it the same blue puffer Sandy had worn on the camel this morning? The one she had borrowed from Cyril and returned when they got back to the hotel. It could be. She had thought it would be too tight on him but on Elsa it fitted nicely or perhaps was a little too big.

Her heart hit the floor and she walked back to Roxy in a daze. What a fool she was! A silly little fool. She thought they had had a rapport, but in fact that was how he treated everyone. Elsa was probably his girlfriend or he wanted her to be. Clearly she was much more his type. Bet she went to public school.

'Well!' said Roxy. 'You learning, are you? I told you men are all shits! Don't bother with them.'

Sandy sat down on a rock beside her. She didn't speak, lost in thought.

Adam stood up in front of the group. 'Are you all comfortable?'

There were murmurs of yes, although Mrs Tank and Roxy both muttered something that sounded like 'as long as it's not for much longer'.

'Good. Jade, can you come up here, please?'

Jade, who had just sat down on a rock next to Mrs Tank, got up and threaded her way through the wheelchairs to the front.

'You'll have noticed the beautiful striations on the rock,' Adam said. 'This is years of water streaming through the limestone and wearing away at the sandstone. Very few people come up to this cave, because if you don't know the back route, it's very hard to get to.' He smiled. 'Consequently, no one will come up here so we are perfectly safe.'

Sandy frowned, pulled out of her reverie by a changing note in his voice. What did he mean, safe? From what? From whom?

The next moment she found out.

He put his hand in his pocket and pulled out a gun, which he placed against Jade's temple.

'I'm so sorry to do this, but I'm afraid you're all my hostages until I get notice from below. I will explain the situation, but first, Mrs Cox, if you don't mind, can you get out of your wheelchair and go and sit at the back, on that flat stone?'

Mrs Cox appeared to waver for a moment and Sandy feared she would refuse to go and Jade would suffer. Indeed, they would all suffer. Mr Cox leant over and patted her hand encouragingly.

Slowly Mrs Cox got up and moved to the back, weaving slightly as though she was trying to think of a way to cause a diversion. She sat down heavily on the flat rock and leant back against the wall with a huge sigh.

'Now, Sandy, can you get Mrs Cox's chair and put it there, with its back to me? Cyril, if you don't mind sitting in Mrs Cox's chair. Thank you. And Sandy, if you move to the indentation in the wall at the side... yes, that's right... there's some rope in there. Could you please tie Cyril to the chair? And tie his hands. And don't think you can cheat me, I can see what you're doing from here.'

Sandy shivered. His voice was so gentle. He was so polite, and yet he was holding a gun to Jade's head and giving cruel instructions. Why was he picking on Cyril? Must be because he was the only active young man in the group. None of the others would be able to contest him, but Cyril might have done so. The young bull might challenge the stallion! She had to stop herself from giggling. Perhaps she could tie Cyril lightly, so he could escape.

However, that idea had apparently occurred to Adam too. 'Were you perhaps a Girl Guide, Sandy?'

No chance, thought Sandy, any spare money went to her brother, not her. She shook her head.

'No,' he said, 'I thought not. So, wind the rope around tightly. Not so tight as to stop the circulation. We don't want anyone hurt.' Adam stopped talking and looked at his terrified hostages. 'It's OK. This is not a Hamas-type situation. I will explain in a moment, but we, the Bedul of Petra, have a problem that the government refuses to address. We are highlighting this in a variety of different ways today. Please don't be scared.'

Sandy looked at Cyril. But he just sat quietly, letting her wind the rope around his body. He wasn't even flexing his muscles, to make the bonds easier to escape from, the way they did in James Bond movies. He seemed relaxed. She made an apologetic face. Even if he was a flirt and not serious, he was another human being and she didn't want to hurt him. He gave her a deep smile, which made her chest flutter despite everything.

'Now, Sandy,' said Adam when she had finished, 'go and get some water bottles from the back.'

'Water bottles?'

'Yes, they're in the cave to the left of Mrs Tank. Please distribute them. I don't want anyone to die of dehydration.'

She shuddered. All rather creepy. He didn't want them to die of dehydration but he didn't mind shooting them. She gave everyone a bottle. She was about to return to Roxy, in case she needed her, when he said, 'I think the temperature is dropping. Can you get the blankets and gloves from the back as well, please, and distribute them? Jade, you'd better help her, but don't try anything. If I shoot the gun in here we'll get ricochets and more people will be hurt.'

Jade and Sandy pulled the blankets, gloves, and crisps from the holes at the back and distributed them. Some people clearly were cold as they pulled on the gloves and huddled into the blankets. As they were all still wearing their pink keffiyehs, they looked like a group of elderly Bedouin. Sandy caught Cyril's eye and he winked. She wondered if the idea had occurred to him too, or if he was just trying to bolster her spirits.

Having given out all the goodies, Jade returned meekly to Adam's side.

'Now, Sandy,' he said, 'sit on Cyril, facing me.'

'What!' said Sandy, shocked. 'I'll hurt him.'

Adam made a noise. 'Sit on him and look at me. That way neither of you is going anywhere.'

Oh, thought Sandy, was he worried she too might try and jump him? The only young person he hadn't targeted was Elsa. Why not? A glance at Elsa showed she was holding Mr Cox's hand and hunched over, staring at the floor. She appeared terrified. It was unlikely she would move at all.

Adam's voice cut into her thoughts again.

'Go on! Sit on him!'

'Oh dear,' said Sandy to Cyril, 'I hope I'm not too heavy. Sorry, Cyril.'

Cyril's lips twitched, but his eyes smiled encouragement and she sat down. In any other circumstance she would have loved to sit on Cyril, even if he was a flirtatious bastard, but right now, with the ropes around him and her weight pressing on him, she felt certain he must be in a bit of pain. She felt terrible.

'OK,' said Adam, 'now I can explain.

'I think some of you know I am from Egypt, but my mother was Bedul, the tribe of Bedouin who come from Petra. When I returned here to work on the dig, I met many of her relations. I discovered that the Bedul have a problem with the government. And of course I want to help my relations.'

He moved a little and, apparently forgetting he was supposed to be holding Jade hostage, lifted the gun and waved it demonstratively. The hostages all gasped and shrank into their chairs, their eyes following the moving weapon.

Apparently realising what he was doing, he frowned apologetically, and returned the gun to Jade's temple.

'In the past, no motorised transport was allowed into Petra, but in 2021, electric cars were permitted entry. The government said this was to improve animal welfare but instead it was to stop the Bedu making money from the camels, donkeys, donkey carts and horses, and to give that money to the government. Now we have no way of making money from the tourists.'

'You have shops,' said Jade suddenly, and everyone jumped at her loud, clear voice. 'We're constantly pestered by people trying to sell us junk – most of which probably comes from China.'

Jade, Sandy thought, surprised, did not seem to be at all intimidated by the gun at her head. Did she have some kind of death wish?

'OK, yes,' said Adam, 'we're allowed to sell *local goods* but that brings in very little income from the tourists in comparison to the rides on camels and donkeys. We are starving without sufficient income and the government doesn't even want us to live on our traditional lands. They want us to live and sell in that new village on the hill. We are dying: not only our bodies but our souls.'

There was silence from the people in the cave. *We*, thought Sandy, *are simply pawns in a game between the government and Bedouin. Would anyone be happy to die for this? Let's hope we don't have to.*

'Many guides are from Egypt,' Adam continued, 'and they don't understand the problems. They side with the government; they have no sympathy for the Bedu cause. They say the tourists prefer the comfort of the shuttle but they don't understand they are undermining our traditional ways and polluting the environment.'

Jade snorted. 'Don't give us that! You're from Egypt too.'

'Yes, but I am half Bedu. As I said before, my mother was from the Bedul Tribe. They are descendants of the Nabateans and so the rightful owners of Petra.'

Jade shrugged. 'Whatever. But I'll help you. It's better for the environment to have animals, not those polluting cars. What do you want me to do?'

Adam's face suffused with joy but all the others looked shocked. *Hmm*, thought Sandy, *she had agreed to help him awfully quickly. What was going on here*? She hadn't forgotten seeing Adam leaving Jade's room this morning. Did she know all about this? Was the gun even loaded? She glanced down at Cyril. He smiled back, totally relaxed. He understood Arabic. What had he heard? She looked back at Jade and Adam.

'OK, Jade. I'll give you a map. You must go down to the tents and talk to the Bedul sheikh. You will see him. Big man. You must tell him we are ready to negotiate – he will understand.'

Jade took the map and studied it. 'So this is where we came in, where the van is... so, if I go out the left side and... this is the track?' She looked out of a small slit to the left. 'Yes, OK. I'll go down.'

Wow! thought Sandy. *Clearly Jade is a Girl Guide or perhaps she does orienteering. Or perhaps it's a bluff. Maybe she's pissed off with Adam and all of us and is just getting herself out of trouble and leaving us here to die.*

After Jade had left, Adam turned to Sandy.

'So, Miss Sandy,' he said. 'You're an important journalist. You will write big articles in the English *Times,* the American *New York Times*, and the *Washington Post*, eh? We will get international support. The government will be unable to put in their shuttles and we'll return to the traditional ways and have our animals again.'

Sandy stared at him, fingering her lips. 'What! Did you think I was a journalist?'

Adam stared back. 'You are, yes? Miss Abbey said you're a very tiresome investigative journalist.'

Oh dear, thought Sandy, *was this all my fault*? She didn't know what to say.

Roxy laughed. 'She's a receptionist. She wants to write novels.'

And suddenly all the kidnappees started laughing too. Great spurts of emotional relief. It was all so ridiculous. Adam stared at them. He looked totally confused. Sandy wondered if he had promised the Bedul sheikh huge publicity all over the world.

Once Jade was out of sight, Adam moved to the edge of the cave. He was holding a satellite phone and Sandy wondered if he was expecting a call. The whole thing seemed like a monstrous dream and she had to remind herself that only a week ago the most exciting thing in her life was informing Mr Percy at the bifold doors company that a potential client had arrived.

Adam's satellite phone pinged, making the hostages jump.

Without thinking, Adam replied, turning his back on the group and wandering over to the rocks outside, his gun now back in his pocket. Sandy wondered whether to be heroic and jump him, but, even as she thought it, she felt Cyril nudge her with his leg. She looked at him and he shook his head. He was smiling. *He does know something*, she thought.

Adam turned to the group.

'Now, as you say, the fun begins. Truth. The government is sending up a negotiator. She will arrive with Jade in maybe an hour. It is easier to go down than up!'

CHAPTER 24
WHOEVER GETS BURNED BY SOUP BLOWS ON YOGURT

Miss Abbey was sitting with the Jarvis family and Tony. Mrs Williams had said she was tired and Harry had taken her back to the hotel. What, Abbey wondered, had happened to Adam and the rest of the crew? Tony had already walked up to the monastery and back, and said there was no sign of them there; he seemed a bit annoyed. He was fiddling with his phone and looking bored. Abbey suspected he had agreed to meet Elsa there. That girl had something about her; Cyril, Tony and even Mr Cox seemed besotted with her. OK, she was pretty, but rather too helpful and flirty, and her clothes showed far too much of her body. Sexy in a rather obvious way.

There was a bang outside and Abbey was dragged out of her thoughts. What was happening? There was a big kerfuffle around the shuttle boarding area. The whole place seemed to be full of camels and donkeys and people shouting at one another. She bit her cheek and wished she hadn't when she tasted blood.

'Tony,' she said, 'go and find out what's happening.'

He got up and saluted ironically, moving off towards a couple of women entering the tent with a local guide. One of the women was a tall redhead, the other was the short, dark-haired woman who had been so friendly that morning. Miranda, thought Abbey. That was her name. Why was she suddenly everywhere?

The guide was pointing at Abbey. The red-haired woman nodded and walked towards her, stretching out her hand. 'Miss Abbey? Cat Harrington, SeeMs Detective Agency and currently your chief negotiator.'

'What?' Abbey stared at the woman, who was now sitting beside her, while the short one had moved off to talk to Tony. 'What do you mean, *my* chief negotiator?'

Cat rubbed her neck. She paused as though not sure how to break bad news and then said, 'Miss Abbey, I'm sorry to have to tell you that some of your group have been taken hostage.'

Abbey clasped her hand over her mouth, her job and her whole life teetering on top of a cliff in the back of her mind. This was worse than her worst nightmare.

'Oh my God! Hostage? Hostages? My group taken... oh no, no, no. Is this Hamas or Hezbollah?' And then she thought of the terrible publicity that was bound to accompany this. 'Is Sandy with them?'

Cat seemed a bit shaken by her last comment. 'Sandy? Would that be...' She glanced at her list. '...Sandra Blee. Is she your daughter?'

'No. No. No. No. She's a journalist. If there's a hostage taking and she's there... oh God, the publicity... I can't bear...' Abbey breathed deeply and asked, 'Who has taken the hostages? Is it Hamas? All the remaining group? And why? They're all old. Who wants old hostages? Worse, elderly, disabled hostages. What if they die? Oh my God. Oh my God!'

Cat put her hand on Abbey's arm. 'No, no, nothing like that. This is a local issue. Nothing to do with the war in Israel.'

Abbey stared at her. What was she saying? How could anything here not be to do with the war in Israel? What? But her body, understanding quicker than her mind, gave a shudder of relief. 'Not Hamas? Not Hezbollah? Thank heavens. For a moment I...' She took another deep breath and licked her lips. 'OK, what's this about?'

'Well, you may have noticed that the Bedouin are demonstrating here, outside the café and where the electric shuttle starts its journey.'

'Yes, sort of...'

'This is because the local Bedouin tribe, known as the Bdul or Bedul, are against the use of the shuttle instead of camels and donkeys in this area. Your hostage situation appears to be an extension of that. We'll know more shortly; one of your number is on her way to the sheikh. We just got a message from your guide.'

'Adam? Has he been taken hostage?'

Cat shook her head, grimacing. 'No.'

Abbey had a sick feeling in her stomach. She *was* about to lose her job. 'Adam? He's involved?'

Cat nodded. 'He's half Bedouin and I guess he agrees with their cause.'

'And this cause is?'

'Returning the area to as near natural as possible while still having tourists. So, that means animals for transport and no mechanical activity, plus allowing the Bedouin to live in their ancestral caves.'

Abbey sighed. It didn't sound as though there would be

a job to have. 'And people in wheelchairs. How would they get to the sites without cars and vans?'

Cat looked at the commotion outside and back at Abbey. 'There used to be donkey carts to carry people who couldn't walk... that's a possibility. But we're getting off the point. I need to know all about the hostages, their state of health and exactly who they are.'

Abbey felt like screaming. Half of them were clearly not who they said they were, and who knew about the rest? This was a complete nightmare.

'Well,' she said, 'there is a Mrs Williams, an eighty-two-year-old lady who seems to have led a blameless life, and her pusher, a youngish man called Harry. They went back to the hotel because Mrs Williams was tired.'

Cat glanced at a list on her phone. 'She's eighty-two, you say? And Harry?'

'We've had problems there because he says he's Bulgarian and can't speak English. He and Mrs Williams communicate with sign language. However, he does speak Arabic, although he didn't admit this to any of us. I know because he was speaking to Adam, the guide.'

Cat made some notes on her iPhone and nodded thoughtfully. 'OK. Tell me everything you know about this Adam... and then we'll move on to the rest of the hostages.'

CHAPTER 25

THE WORLD IS LIKE A BELLY
DANCER WHO BRIEFLY
DANCES FOR ALL

M iranda sat down outside the restaurant and offered Tony a can of beer.

'I think I met you this morning, briefly, at breakfast. Can we have a chat?'

Tony smiled. 'Thanks, I'll grab the beer. What do you want to know?'

'Can you give me a quick run-down of your companions? I guess you know by now your guide, Adam, has taken several of them hostage...'

Tony grinned, as though finding it funny, but he answered seriously. 'Hostages? Adam? But he seemed so friendly. I think he mentioned he loved archaeology. Is this something to do with the war in Gaza? Is he a terrorist?'

Miranda broke in quickly. 'No, no, he's a Bedouin, or rather his mother was and so he's espousing their cause about the shuttle... they think allowing motorised vehicles into Petra is destroying the environment and taking their livelihoods.'

'Oh, OK, yes, I see their point,' said Tony. 'Frankly, I was surprised to see any cars and whatnot in Petra. I'd always understood that we'd travel by donkeys and camels. I was expecting the wheelchairs to be put in donkey carts. Much cleaner that way... I'm going to get an electric car as soon as I can afford it. Chinese one, they're better.'

Miranda nodded. That the young tourists supported the environmental view didn't surprise her. However, she'd already talked to some of the guides and they took a contrary view, thinking it would reduce the number of elderly tourists. Because Jordan was expensive it was inevitable that most tourists were older and wealthier and preferred travelling in mechanised transport.

'So which of your companions, do you think, would agree with you?'

'Elsa for sure. She's a great believer in using animals rather than cars, healthier she says. I think she's considering doing something for the environment in the future. Not sure about the old crowd but most of the young ones would probably agree with her. Not the dreadful Coxes, though. Right pair of Moaning Minnies they are and Mr C is a bit racist. I wouldn't put any faith in him.'

'What about Mrs Cox?'

'She's odd, self-important, I'd say. One evening she spent several hours telling me and that funny old woman, Mrs Tank, about how she'd been on the jury of some murder trial a few years ago. According to Mrs Cox, and frankly, I don't believe a word the old girl says, she was the only one who thought the defendant was guilty but she brought all the others round to her point of view. She says they made her foreman. To be honest, I expect that was to get rid of her.'

'What happened in the end? Was the defendant found guilty?'

'Yes and no. She thought she'd convinced them all it was

murder, but they insisted on the manslaughter charge. She was really narked.' He laughed. 'Silly old fool.'

'Any idea why they went for the lower charge? Did the man have a lot of extenuating circumstances?'

'Woman. It was a woman. Mrs Cox got all flirty suddenly and said she couldn't say who it was because the criminal was a big *celebrity* and she tapped her nose and was highly annoying. But yes, apparently the woman had been taking prescription drugs and the rest of the jury thought that might well have influenced her judgement.'

'Did Mrs Tank say anything about the case?'

'Well, you know, I wasn't quite sure how much she heard. She seems awfully deaf and sometimes I think she's actually asleep. They're a bit of a weird crowd. I'd no idea it would be like this. My brother did this trip a few years ago and he said they had a great time climbing up mountains and getting drunk. It certainly isn't like that with this group.'

CHAPTER 26

LIKE A CAT WITH SEVEN SOULS

When Cat returned to the sheikh's tent with the information about Adam and the hostages, the government negotiator was waiting for her. He rose politely and offered her a cup of tea, which she accepted.

'Thank you for your quick response,' he said in fluent and unaccented English. Somewhere, Cat remembered, she had read that most Jordanians learnt English at school as a second language to Arabic, something to do with the Anglo–Jordanian pact that existed. But it was also possible he had been to university in the UK.

'I think you'll find the government is very happy to compromise and deal fairly with the Bedouin position, which, of course, they understand. However, I must stress that before any serious negotiations can take place, we do need to release the hostages, who must by now be suffering seriously. These people are old and were not well in the first place. I believe the majority of them are in wheelchairs. They need to be released immediately.'

Cat could not agree more. Everything Miss Abbey had

told her about Adam and the hostages he had taken seemed crazy, and rather amateur. She wondered why he had agreed to such a foolish idea that could only get him into trouble and would probably mean he'd be used as a scapegoat and be returned to Egypt in disgrace. She could only assume a young man's enthusiasm for his family cause had somehow clouded his better judgement.

'I'm happy to go up to the cave now and talk to Adam,' she said. 'Is there anyone available who can show me the way?'

The negotiator clapped his hands and a young boy came in with a girl wearing black leather and covered in tattoos and piercings.

'Jade?' said Cat.

The negotiator looked at Cat. 'You know Miss Bumstead?'

'I know who she is,' said Cat. 'I don't think we've been formally introduced.'

Jade walked over and squinted up at Cat. 'I think I *do* know you. You're that bitch detective who got my grand-mother arrested. Well, I hope you can do a better job with Adam.'

The negotiator gave a structured smile and informed Jade she could now lead Mrs Harrington up to the cave where Adam was holding the hostages.

Jade looked at Cat, one lip raised in disdain. 'You think you can climb up to the cave? It's quite hard going, stony track and all. How fit are you?'

Cat gave her a side-eye. 'See my feet? Climbing shoes. Normally I would prefer Louboutins but today I'm prepared. Are you ready?'

'Whatever.'

The first part of the path was relatively easy but soon there was a steep incline. Occasionally there were steps cut into the rock as though some of the Bedouin had indeed lived up here.

'Do you know if any Bedouin still live here?' Cat asked.

Jade made a noise in the back of her throat. 'If you ask the guides, they'll tell you no. They say this was a tomb area and no one actually lived here, but Adam and the Bedu say different. He says Bedul have always lived here, are descendants of the original Nabateans and still do. So who knows.'

Cat nodded and looked up to the rocks beyond. By now they could see the cave they were heading for, but it still towered a long way above them.

'How old are you?' asked Jade as Cat stopped for a breather and Jade finally caught up with her. 'You seem fitter than me.'

Cat's snort turned to a laugh. 'Look around you, Jade, what do you see?'

Jade scratched her eyebrow, dislodging one of the pins. 'Mountains? Stones?'

Cat shook her head. 'Look down. Look up the track. What animals are following us and what are ahead of us?'

Jade looked. 'Cats?'

'Yup. And you know what cats are good at?'

Jade laughed. What was this? She was halfway up a mountain with some giant red-headed British detective-cum-negotiator, and the woman wanted to discuss cats. She must be a loop. 'I don't know. Getting their own way?'

Cat grinned. 'Well, that too, let's hope so. Cats are good at survival. Look at them all. There are more cats in this place than I've ever seen, and not only here, throughout Jordan. Cats everywhere. No dogs. The only dogs are working or wild. Cats are survivors. Shall we go on?'

Jade followed behind her, shaking her head but smiling. Yes, the woman was a loop, but she was a characterful one. When the sheikh had told her this English woman was going to be the negotiator she nearly threw up her breakfast. But it seemed that Cat, as well as cats, were good at getting their own way. What did Cat really want? She couldn't possibly have a beef about the shuttle, so why was she here? OK, negotiators are neutral but they're not usually far away from home and detectives. What was this woman about?

When they got a bit further, Cat stopped again, puffing a bit. 'How are you managing?'

Jade shrugged. 'I guess I'm OK if you are.'

Cat sat back on a rock. 'What made you choose to come out to Jordan, Jade?'

Jade looked at her thoughtfully before replying. This woman was a negotiator and a detective, so she was pretty sure she didn't do casual questions. 'It's a job. My gran was going to come and, as she likes to have me around, I was going to push her chair. But then she had medical problems and went into hospital, so her friend, Mrs Tank, came in her place.'

'Lucky she was free, wasn't it?' said Cat, smiling brightly. 'Mrs Tank! What a coincidence that she should have the same name as Lady Bumstead's second husband. Not a relation, is she?'

Jade spat at a passing cat. 'You were at the trial, weren't you? You thought she was guilty of murder. This isn't a coincidence, is it? What you doing here, Cat?'

Cat shook her head. 'Actually, it is. I was amazed to see you here. Still, it's a small world and there seems to be a path of tourism that many people take. Shall we make the final push?'

When they entered the cave, Cat looked around. A sea of worried faces looked back at her. All of them, except one woman at the back, were wrapped in blankets, wearing gloves, the keffiyeh scarf, and holding plastic bottles. It was an incredible sight and Cat wished she could get out her phone and take a picture. But it would be unprofessional. If only Miranda was here, she would have done it without thinking, but Cat had none of her heedless lack of propriety.

She turned to Adam. Jade was talking to him in a rather urgent manner. Possibly she was giving him the run-down about the SeeMs Detective Agency and who they were. Chances were Jade was not an unbiased party but closely involved herself. Cat noticed the gun balanced precariously in Adam's pocket and thought, *I bet it's not loaded*. That would be a wise move. Killing a tourist would not help the Bedouin cause.

'Hello,' she said loudly to the group. 'I'm Cat Harrington. I'm here to negotiate on behalf of you and Miss Abbey. Don't worry, this will soon be over and we'll get you down to the hotel for hot baths and supper. I'm sorry you've been inconvenienced.'

'Well,' said a voice at the back, 'it's Superwoman. Or should I say Catwoman?'

Cat looked at her. Late middle-age and thin, red hair, glasses and buck teeth with an aggressive attitude. She had never seen the woman before, however, recognition is a strange thing. We think we identify someone by their looks, but actually that is not the case – it's other factors: voice, speech patterns, mannerisms, attitude. The whole package. She recognised this woman but now was not the time for reunions.

'Adam,' said Cat, 'come outside and talk to me.'

Turning to her, he looked lost and vulnerable, like a

little boy who knows he's done something stupid and wishes he hadn't. Cat's heart went out to him. She had three children, and he looked just like them when they were young and had done something foolish. How did he get involved in this?

Adam looked uncertainly at the group in front of him, vacillating.

Cat smiled at him. 'It's OK, they understand negotiations are ongoing.'

He nodded unhappily and they walked outside.

'Let's be brief,' said Cat, 'it's getting dark. We need to get the hostages down now. I have spoken to the Bedul sheikh and the government negotiator and they both agree that the first and most important thing is to bring the hostages down. Then we can discuss what everybody wants. Are you prepared to do that?'

Adam nodded again and automatically put his hands on his head. Cat wondered if he realised what he was doing. Jade, who had followed them out, spoke sharply. 'We want safety for Adam,' she said. 'We don't want him to become the scapegoat in this. He was only doing what his family asked.'

A true granddaughter of Lady Bumstead, thought Cat. Jade believed she could mould the world into the shape she desired.

Adam clearly did not have such confidence. He looked at Jade silently, his hope resting on her skinny, tattooed shoulders.

'OK,' said Cat. 'Adam, are you willing to drive the hostages back to the hotel without any detours? That will go in your favour. Then we can start the negotiations.'

Adam nodded. Cat thought his punishment was going to be much greater than his reward. After all, what did he really want? A job in archaeology? He'd blown that. Yet again an example of ordinary people getting swept into political situations that damned them. Even though this was only a local dispute, Adam had been foolish and although she would negotiate on his behalf, she was quite certain he would be sent back to Egypt.

'So, Jade, Adam has given me his demands on this paper. Are you coming with me, or do you want to go in the van?'

'I'll go with him,' Jade said. 'Come on, Adam, let's get the guests into the van before the darkness completely closes in.'

Cat took the map and started the climb down. As she reached the halfway point, she saw Miranda climbing up, sweat pouring down her face.

'Hello, I thought I'd come and see how you were. If I'd known what a climb it was, I'd have stayed at the bottom. How did they get the wheelchairs up here?'

'There's a track at the back. He drove up.'

Miranda laughed. 'Ironic. He's campaigning for the shuttle to be replaced by a donkey-only state and yet he makes a kidnapping that could only happen with the use of the shuttle.'

Cat tilted her head. 'Strengthens his cause, I'd say. If there are no shuttles, there'll be no kidnappings in the future, at least not of disabled tourists, and so the government doesn't need to worry about it happening again.'

'Well, if you say it, it should help him. You are his negotiator!'

Cat shook her head. 'We're neutral.'

'Of course.'

When they arrived at the base of the hill, they could still see the camels and mules milling around, some being ridden, some tied to posts. There were several tourists on donkeys starting up the steps to the monastery.

'I see they haven't stopped tourists coming into the site then,' said Cat.

'No.'

'Well, that's a good thing. Means they don't expect any violence. If they did, they'd be sure to shut the site.'

A man rode past them on a donkey and as he did so, he wound his long scarf tighter around his face.

Cat gasped. 'At the risk of making you think I see a ghost in every bush, I recognised that man but I can't think who it is. I could only see his eyes.'

Miranda looked after the retreating donkey. 'Famous pop star come to help in the negotiations? Former American president? I'd say it was Bella reborn but no way could she change her size that much.'

'No. Something else... someone. I can't quite... maybe it will come back.'

Miranda watched the donkey. 'He seems to be going up towards the cave. Could he be...?'

He veered off the path Cat had used and disappeared behind an outcrop of the mountain.

'No, I think he's going elsewhere. You know the Bedouin are saying that some family members still live up in the caves part-time, and only return to the created village occasionally. Perhaps he's on his way to one of those.'

They carried on down the hill and then across the sandy paths to the sheikh's negotiating tent on the edge of the former shuttle base. Cat gave his advisor Adam's written demands and came away.

'I don't think they're really taking Adam's part seriously,' she said, 'but it will have terrible consequences for him. I wonder how he got involved in such a self-destructive enterprise.'

Miranda sucked her lip. 'Family. It's everything with the Bedouin. I was told one family has 900 members, all living in Wadi Rum. If his mother was Bedu, then he must feel he has to do his part. But yes, you're right. They'll probably make him the scapegoat... What do you think? A few years in prison or worse?'

'Poor Adam.'

CHAPTER 27

SPEAKING IS NOT LIKE SEEING

It was with great relief that Abbey heard the hostages had been released and taken back to the hotel.

Mrs Williams, who had gone back to the hotel and, consequently, knew nothing about what was going on, rang her in great distress.

'Miss Abbey! What's happening? Adam drove the van into the hotel car park with the others and then he was arrested and taken away in a Public Security Directorate van. They didn't even let him unload. Where are you?'

'I'm coming,' said Abbey, getting up as she spoke. 'Can you ask the hotel staff to help unload our guests? I'm sure they are all exhausted.'

She closed her phone and looked at Cat and Miranda, now back in the café.

'Thank heavens,' she said. 'I was terrified they'd have to spend all night up there... I don't know how many of them would have survived.'

'Adam's in more trouble than he should be, really,' Cat said, hoping Miss Abbey might intervene on her employee's behalf. 'I'm not sure how well he'll be treated.'

Abbey shrugged. 'You aren't expecting any sympathy from me, are you? My tourists could have died from the shock, hypothermia, or anything. He was foolish at best and a criminal in my eyes. Sure, go and negotiate for him, but don't expect me to care.'

She started walking to the hotel with Tony. Mr Jarvis had already taken Mavis back and although Harry had briefly returned, he had disappeared again long ago. Abbey wasn't sure if he knew about the hostage situation.

'I'll go and see what I can do for Adam,' said Cat to Miranda. 'You'd better go back to the hotel and chat to the tourists, find out if any of them feel sympathy for him. It might help his cause if anyone supports him.'

Miranda nodded and hailed one of the donkey boys. 'How much for a ride to the Hotel Rummy?'

The boy grinned. 'Let's go, we talk price as we ride. I love walking beside pretty women.'

She laughed. 'OK, but if you try and cheat me, I'm jumping off.'

Cat watched them go and walked towards the tent. Ahead of her, she could see the PSD van arriving at the tent and Adam being bundled out. His head was bowed and he was wearing handcuffs. She hoped he was OK. He didn't seem the right person to be involved in this. Too humble. She walked over to join the negotiations.

CHAPTER 28

IF GOD PROPOSES THE DESTRUCTION OF AN ANT, HE ALLOWS WINGS TO GROW UPON HER

When Miranda reached the hotel, she discovered a new problem had arisen. Somehow, in all the chaos of moving the chairs, getting people into the vans, and helping everyone, Mrs Cox had been left behind.

Miranda wondered how Mr Cox could not notice, but seeing how deeply involved he was in chatting to Elsa, she saw why he wouldn't bother about his elderly wife. However, when Miss Abbey came up to tell him the news, he did suddenly look very concerned.

'Silly old fool. What was she doing? And now what? How will she get down? It's getting dark. They won't be able to send a van up there in the twilight... it'll be too dangerous. She'll be furious when you get there. She might even start walking down and get lost.'

He breathed deeply as all the likely scenarios passed through his mind.

'I'll go,' said Jade. 'I can ride a donkey up there. I know the short path. If Cat and I can walk it, so can a donkey. I've got a head torch.'

'And how'll she get down?'

'On a donkey too,' said Jade. 'One of the donkey boys can come up with me.'

'What about Mrs Tank? Won't she need you?' said Abbey, who was now looking queasy and clearly feeling she was losing control.

Jade glanced over at the old woman, who appeared to be asleep. 'Ah, she won't care. Or if she does, you can get Cyril to push her. With Mrs Cox AWOL, he won't be needed. OK, is that agreed?'

Abbey shook her head. As usual there was no stopping Jade.

'I'll go with you,' said Miranda. Funny, she thought, that Cyril hadn't noticed Mrs Cox was missing if he was normally her pusher. She might pump Jade for information on the way up to the cave.

Jade looked at her and shrugged. 'OK. Can you ride a donkey?'

'Just did. In fact, we might use the same guy to take us up.'

'Whatever.'

As they rode up to the cave through the darkness, the donkeys' way now lit only by the moon, Miranda thought again about how difficult living must have been in the past. The Bedouin must have depended so much on their animals to protect them, to take them places, and even to feed and clothe them. No wonder they were so close to their livestock. No wonder they didn't want to move to mechanised transport. What would happen to the animals? She switched her mind back to her job.

'Was it chaos as you left the cave?'

'Of course. What do you think? That we all filed out one by one like the animals off the ark?'

Miranda grimaced. Talking to Jade was not easy.

'Did you notice what Cyril was doing? How come he missed Mrs Cox not being there?'

Jade slew around on her donkey and stared at her through the dark. 'What, Wonder Boy? You detectives blame Wonder Boy? Wonder Boy, the Tory. Yes, I do believe you're right. He's the type of dark horse who suddenly springs on one as the bad guy. What would Poirot have made of him?

'Adam, on the other hand, was working hard to get everyone down safely, and then they came and put him in chains, like one of the gladiators on the way to his death. Poor Adam, he was only trying to help save the environment and his family.'

Miranda sighed. 'So what was Cyril doing that kept him from thinking about Mrs Cox?'

'Oh, canoodling with Sandra Dee, of course. He only ever has eyes for her, silly little virgin.'

'Ah, so there's a love affair there, is there?'

'Whatever,' said Jade. 'Love? Who knows... lust, I reckon!' She started singing 'Look at Me I'm Sandra Dee...'

Miranda stared at the donkey's ears. Jade was not an easy companion.

When they arrived at the mouth of the cave, Miranda dismounted slowly. She was beginning to feel the effects of all this walking and donkey riding and thinking it would be nice to travel in a warm, comfortable shuttle. Jade had already jumped off and gone ahead into the cave. Miranda gave the boy her reins and followed her.

As she walked in, Miranda stood on a plastic bottle. 'Oh!' she said, as their torches highlighted several more discarded items. 'Blimey. Did you have a party in here? Crisp packets.

Blankets. Gloves. All strewn around the floor. At least you were well fed and watered.'

'Ha ha,' said Jade. 'Bet you've never been a hostage. It's not a party, OK!'

'Sorry.'

Both girls swished their torches around but Mrs Cox had disappeared. There was no sign of her anywhere. Miranda trod on another bottle and another crisp packet.

'Adam was worried the hostages might get sick without water,' said Jade, clearly feeling he needed more defence, even if it was only Miranda she was talking to. 'So he'd packed the cave with goodies before getting everyone up here. He even thought we might have to stay the night so he brought up blankets and cooking equipment. He's a really good guy and now they're treating him like a criminal. It's wrong.'

Miranda frowned. 'You seem to know a lot about it. Did he tell you what he was planning?'

Jade snorted. 'He held a gun to my head, you know.'

Miranda exhaled. 'And, as Cat has already discovered, an unloaded gun. Did you know all about it beforehand?'

Jade swung round at Miranda, the glare from her head torch blinding the detective who staggered back, nearly tripping over another plastic bottle. 'I'm a tourist here, OK. I don't want to be thrown out until I'm ready to go. You tell your negotiating friend I'm ready to tell her things when she ensures my and Adam's safety. You got that?'

Miranda bit her lip. 'Yes, I got that. Now concentrate on looking for Mrs Cox, OK. If we find her, you're on much safer ground.'

They moved through a sea of plastic bottles and other detritus. However, Miranda couldn't see any of the cooking equipment Jade talked about.

'Where's the cooking equipment?'

'Down the hole at the back. We didn't have to stay the night, did we?'

'Show me.'

Jade walked over to a flat rock in front of a large hole and pointed. 'If you look down there you'll see blankets and provisions. He told me he put them there the night we were all at the Get To Know You Party. Fucking awful that was.' Jade gagged at the memory. 'Not surprised he made some excuse to get out of that shitshow.'

Miranda shone her torch into the hole and saw all sorts of blankets and... She gasped.

'Jade, come here.'

Jade came up behind her. 'Oh shit!'

She swung her torch across the blankets and clothing. 'It's her all right. That's Mrs Cox. She must have fallen in. She was sitting here. On this flat rock. Mrs Cox! Mrs Cox!' she yelled. 'Can you hear me?'

They stared down at the woman, who was lying in an almost foetal position except her head was up and back. Her eyes were closed and it was possible to believe she might just be asleep or unconscious.

'She's alive, don't you think?' said Jade. 'I can see her chest moving.'

Miranda heard the fearful hope in her voice. This did not look good for Adam. If Mrs Cox had died because of his actions this was negligence at best and murder at worst. Do the Bedouin still have blood feuds? She wondered and almost giggled. However she suppressed it, sure Jade would not understand.

'Mrs Cox! Mrs Cox!' Jade shouted again. 'Can you hear me?' She swivelled around and said to Miranda, 'I bet she's deaf, they all are.'

Even though it was looking more and more as though she was dead, Jade continued calling. Miranda watched her sadly. She'd seen too many dead bodies to expect this one to return to life.

'Stay here,' she said. 'I'll get the lad to come and help us.'

As Miranda walked towards the opening of the cave, she saw the rope that had been used to tie Cyril. She picked it up and walked out to the donkeys.

'We need some help. There's an old woman who's fallen down a hole in there. Can you climb down and check how she is?'

The boy hobbled the donkeys and walked inside the cave to the lip of the hole. He looked over into the dark depths and returned to Miranda, who tied the rope around his waist. He paused a moment on the edge to check Miranda had secured it and was ready to pay it out. Satisfied, he slipped lithely in and was soon being lowered gently down by Miranda and Jade.

'Lucky he's so light,' Miranda said, bracing her muscles against the weight. The rope went slack as the boy arrived at the bottom.

'Oh!' the boy called. 'Not good. Dead.'

'Oh my God,' said Jade. 'No! This isn't true. I saw her move. She's alive. She is!'

Miranda put her hand on Jade's arm. 'Don't panic. Let's get the boy up then you can go down and we'll make sure. OK? I would go down myself but you're a lot lighter than me.'

Jade nodded and silently she and the boy changed places. Jade was only down there for a few moments when she shouted up to them. 'She's unconscious. She's got a big bump on her head. I think she's breathing. Bring me up. We'll need a doctor and a stretcher.'

The boy shrugged. It was clear he thought the woman was dead.

They pulled Jade up. She was shaking so much she could hardly put her feet over the edge. Miranda put her arms around her and gave her a big hug. Instead of resisting, as Miranda expected, she clung to the detective, her body riven with vibrations.

'Oh my God, Miranda. What will happen? Everyone will say it's Adam's fault. If she is dead, they'll say she died because of him. Did she have a heart attack or something? They'll say he brought it on with his actions. Oh my God. Oh my God, who will save him now?'

Miranda looked at her phone. No signal.

'Don't panic, Jade. Anything might have happened. Keep calm. Can you ride? We'll have to go down and tell the others. Miss Abbey isn't going to be happy.'

'No.'

They rode down in silence. Even the donkey boy was bereft of speech. Something that had started out for one purpose had had the most dreadful result.

Miss Abbey was waiting for them at the donkey stand near the hotel.

'Did you find her?'

'Yes,' said Miranda. 'Jade, can you pay for the donkeys while I talk to Miss Abbey?'

'Yes.'

Miranda took Miss Abbey gently by the arm and led her back towards the hotel. 'Is Cat here?'

'No, she's still up at the negotiations. They've not sent any information. I think she's trying to help Adam. This is a bad situation.'

Miranda sighed. 'I'm afraid it's about to get worse.'

They were now in the light of the hotel but hadn't yet gone into the hall where they could see the others waiting.

'Tell me.' Miss Abbey's voice sounded strained.

'We found Mrs Cox. It looks like she fell off the edge of the stone she was sitting on and into the hole behind. She's dead. She may have broken her neck or had a heart attack, and although Jade wants to believe she's alive, she is definitely dead.'

'Dead? Oh my God!' said Miss Abbey. 'Oh my God.' She stared at Miranda, her mouth opening and shutting. 'I... er... but how...?'

'Looks like she fell off the ledge,' said Miranda again, not surprised Miss Abbey couldn't take in what she was saying. Of course, she thought to herself, she might have been pushed, but no one was ready for that idea yet.

'She fell...' Miss Abbey took some breaths before continuing. 'So it's entirely Adam's fault.' Her voice was now hard and decisive. Miranda could almost hear her brain computing how to save her job, and her future, by putting Adam in the firing line.

'Sooo,' said Miranda, 'shall I...? If you like, I'll tell Mr Cox. Would that make things easier?'

For a moment Miss Abbey vacillated but then she shook her head, threw back her shoulders and said, 'No. I'll take him into the drawing room and you can talk to the others in the hall. He must be allowed to hear the information first, and from me.'

They entered the hotel and Miss Abbey went quietly to Mr Cox's side. She told Elsa to go and sit with the others as Miranda had something to tell them all, and then she wheeled Mr Cox away into the drawing room.

Miranda walked behind them to close the door and as

she did so, she saw Mr Cox collapse. She heard him say, 'The bastard! I'll get him for this. He won't get away with it. My darling Ophelia.'

And she swung the door closed.

In the hall, Miranda said, 'I'm afraid we did find Mrs Cox. She appears to have fallen down the crevasse at the back of the cave, and she's probably dead. We'll need to get a doctor up there as soon as it's light...'

Elsa stood up. 'I'm a doctor,' she said. 'I didn't mention it before for various reasons but if you wish, we can go up there now. I'm happy to ride up on the donkey in the dark if someone shows me the way. If she is alive, we'll need to get up there as soon as possible.'

'Oh, well, OK.'

Cyril stood up too. 'I'll go with her. We'll take Ahmar, the donkey boy, with us. He knows the way well by now. Between us, we should be able to get her down tonight.'

'OK,' said Miranda. 'I'll tell Miss Abbey.'

Cyril smiled at her, slightly cynically. 'You'd better wait until we've gone. I don't think Miss Abbey wants to lose two more tourists.'

Sandy watched them go. Miranda looked at Sandy. Although the girl looked sad there was also resignation on her face, as though it was inevitable. Knowing what Jade had said, Miranda felt a great deal of sympathy for Sandy. She too had flirted and lost. Love was not always straight-forward.

CHAPTER 29

NOT ALL PATIENTS TAKE THE SAME MEDICINE

I t took three hours to get Mrs Cox out of the cave and back down the mountain. Her body arrived, strapped unceremoniously across a donkey, and was taken by the staff to the hotel's cold room.

'We'll need an autopsy,' said Elsa.

Abbey, who by then was feeling like her life was about to end, but was glad to have all her tourists returned, even if not all alive, stared at her.

'What do you mean, an autopsy?'

Elsa bared her teeth and sucked her lip. 'Look, Miss Abbey, I haven't been qualified very long, couple of years. My last training placement was with a forensic pathologist and I learnt a lot about dead bodies there. I agree I'm not a complete expert, but I'm pretty sure Mrs Cox was already dead when she fell off the wall and hit her head on the bottom. There's no blood on her head and yet there was a deep cut, which looks as though it was caused by hitting the wall on the way down. Rigor mortis has already happened and I wonder if it was rigor that caused her to fall.'

'Also,' added Cyril, 'she fell onto the extra blankets, as

Ahmar and Jade saw before, and I think Miranda may have seen too. Falling on those would have saved her if she hadn't, as Elsa says, been dead already. It wasn't such a long fall.'

Abbey stared at them, trying to process what they were saying. Eventually she said, 'Is Miranda still here?'

Sandy came up quietly. 'Yes,' she said, trying not to look at Cyril and Elsa, although she'd obviously been waiting for them to return. 'She's in the café. We were talking. Her colleague is back too.'

As they were talking, Cat and Miranda joined them.

'OK,' said Cat, 'most of the others have gone to bed, including Mr Cox. They were all exhausted and, of course, none of them are young.'

'And Jade?' asked Abbey.

'They've taken Adam down to Wadi Musa police station and Jade has gone with him.' Cat sighed. 'I don't think she entirely understands the system here. I did warn her she might make things worse for him.'

Abbey snorted. 'I suppose we'll have to call the PSD.'

'They're already here,' said Cat. 'The donkey boy, Ahmar, called his father, who told them about Mrs Cox.'

'I see. What'll happen now?'

'They'll take Mrs Cox to Amman for an autopsy. I think they'll want us all to stay here or move to a hotel in Amman. I'll find out.'

CHAPTER 30

PEOPLE WANT TO BREAK BEAUTIFUL THINGS: YOU ARE BEAUTIFUL AND I AM AFRAID

The tourists went to bed shocked. Sandy blamed herself. If Miss Abbey hadn't had this idea she was a journalist and passed it on to Adam, then surely he wouldn't have been so stupid. Poor Mrs Cox, the unfortunate victim of an accident. Elsa had said she might have had a heart attack and fallen. Poor Adam. He was bound to be blamed. People would say she wouldn't have had a heart attack if she hadn't been so scared. Or, if she had a heart attack in the hotel, her pills would have been nearby. Presumably she had a heart condition, although Mr Cox hadn't said anything about it.

Perhaps she could help somehow. Perhaps she could write an article when they got back. She'd have to be careful what she put in her blog; she didn't want to make things worse for Adam. How could she help him? She might ask Cyril as he spoke Arabic and he would know. Feeling much better, she fell asleep and dreamt she was riding a camel with Cyril, but the camel was Elsa and Elsa said she could write Sandy's blog for her. It would be better, Elsa said, more educated. Sandy moved in her bed and moaned.

Abbey lay sleepless in her bed and stared at the ceiling. The whole thing was inconceivable. Adam had been highly recommended. She'd been told his interest in archaeology made him a much better guide than any of the others. Did anyone mention he was part Bedouin? She couldn't remember. There were moments when she thought this was it. She'd never get another job in tourism, or indeed working with the disabled. She had allowed a death to happen. And a hostage situation.

She got up and paced around the room. This was so, so awful! What would happen to her if she couldn't get another job? She'd end up on the streets. She'd die cold and unloved in some dirty doorway.

Mrs Tank was also sleepless. Damn Jade for getting herself mixed up with that boy. She was always like this. She got a fancy for some awful brat. Usually some over-tattooed halfwit with no conversational skills. Admittedly, Adam was different. He was interesting. And educated. And, come to think of it, rather daring. But now he was in prison. However, thought Mrs Tank more philosophically now, if Jade really did care about the boy, it would certainly help that they had lots of money. Justice, Mrs Tank was happy to say, was much kinder to the rich than the poor. Pity those tiresome detectives turned up. What could they be doing here? Negotiators, my foot. That Miranda had the diplomacy of a cow taking ecstasy. They were trying to find her. Bet someone paid them to find her and take her home. Perhaps, thought Mrs Tank sleepily, she could outbid them. Although that damn Cat seemed petty-minded and moralistic, possibly even one of those rare people who couldn't be paid off. Stupid Red Cat.

Jade was sitting in the police station drinking coffee. She had been amazed how nice the young police officers were to her. Many of them, particularly the military policemen, were Bedouin themselves, and worked their animals when they weren't on their government shifts. They understood what the Bedul were talking about and had a lot of sympathy.

However, everyone knew how much Jordan was suffering from the lack of tourists, brought about by the war in Palestine. The words 'after 7ᵗʰ October' flew unspoken around the room. None of the policemen felt Adam could be let go. The potential tourists were scared enough. This would only make the situation worse. Fewer visitors meant less money.

Jade needed to do something to protect Adam, and she would need to involve her grandmother. How lucky then that she had such a good hold over her and, as it happened, how lucky that those excrescences from the SeeMs Detective Agency were here. They could be, unwittingly, extremely useful if her grandmother refused to go along with the plans now forming in her head. Jade smiled and drank some more coffee.

'Tell me,' she said to the friendly man in charge of the police station. 'If you were going to be moved to another prison which one would you choose?'

'Why, Salhoub,' he said, 'north of Amman, but he won't be taken there. You need influence to be put in there. It's a special place.'

'No,' said another man, 'it closed remember, but Muwaqqar is still open but you won't get there either.'

'Thank you,' she said. 'Can I say something to Adam and then I'll go back to the hotel?'

'Sure.'

Adam was sitting on a bench at the back of the police cell, still wearing his handcuffs.

She moved to the bars so he could see her.

'Adam,' she said, 'don't give up on your dream.'

'Jade?'

'I have a dream too,' she said, 'and it includes you.'

He gave her a weak smile. 'Thanks.'

She beckoned with a finger. 'Come closer,' she said, 'give me your ear.'

She whispered something to him and then turned and left.

As she walked back to see her grandmother, she knew he didn't really believe her. Thought of her as just another Westerner who would let him down like so many before. But she wouldn't. *I*, she told him in her mind, *will save you. I can't do it alone, but I know a way of getting help.*

CHAPTER 31

TIME IS LIKE A SWORD; IF YOU DON'T CUT IT, IT WILL CUT YOU

None of the tourists were late for breakfast, although Jade and Mrs Tank had already left for Amman. Mr Jarvis was smiling when he tapped his watch. 'Excellent. Everybody on time. But it is a three-hour drive along the desert highway to Amman, unless...' He paused. '...unless there is a sandstorm. Then we could be stuck there for hours.'

Miss Abbey gave him a furious look. 'Forecasting is extremely good here. We'll meet in the drawing room in half an hour. Everyone happy?'

Roxy made a cynical noise. 'Having a ball, thanks. Nothing like being a hostage and spending time with a dead body for a good giggle. Eh, guys?'

The other guests stared at their plates.

After breakfast they gathered in the drawing room. Cat and Miranda were already seated at a large table when they arrived. No one was surprised to see them but all the guests were feeling disorientated, as though the world somehow lost its direction.

'Will you come and talk to us later?' Jolly asked Cat in a

low voice. 'We did see some things a few days ago that might be relevant. Spice is lying down, not feeling well at the moment, but can we chat when we get to the hotel in Amman?'

'Yes, of course,' said Cat, although she could see Miss Abbey, who had overheard them, rolling her eyes.

Cat stood up. 'Adam has been taken to Muwaqqar Prison, south of Amman. As you may know, Jade and Mrs Tank left this morning in a taxi. However, the PSD wants all the hostages and the Wheelchair Warrior Holiday guests to stay in the same hotel, so you have been booked into a comfortable hotel in West Amman for as long as this takes. Jade and Mrs Tank will be staying there too.'

'Oh yeah?' said Roxy. 'And who's paying for this comfortable hotel in West Amman? Pardon me for being so vulgar but I've heard West Amman is expensive.'

Cat inclined her head towards their leader, but seeing Miss Abbey's distressed face, added, 'The guests will not have to pay for their rooms. The bills will all be picked up.'

'Good!' said Roxy. 'About time WWH put some money in the pot.'

There was a general murmur of pleasure as the guests thought about the comfort of a five-star hotel in a beautiful area of town.

Abbey was feeling incredibly sick. She had informed the WWH office of what had happened and had a very emotional talk with her boss. He had said the insurance company was trying to get out of paying, saying this was an act of war. Her boss had added that it was her responsibility to make sure it wasn't. Abbey's mind was reeling with what exactly she was supposed to do. She knew she would eventually have to take charge of the guests, but she was glad Cat was doing it for the moment.

Looking at the assembled company, Cat said, 'If possible I'd like to have a short chat with each of the hostages before we leave, so I can ascertain what they saw. Once we are back in Amman, I would like to have a chat with the rest of the guests. As Spice isn't feeling well, we'll talk to her and Jolly in Amman.'

'Bit out of your depth, aren't you?' said Roxy. 'Little British detective agency goes global! Besides, aren't you needed down here for negotiations? Or are you redundant now that Adam's in prison?'

'Perhaps, Miss Roxy,' said Cat, smiling at her, 'you'd like to come and chat to me first. Tell me what you think happened.'

Roxy laughed. 'Love to. See you in five.'

A few moments later Roxy bowled into the room at top speed, although she gave a quick curse to the slowness of the chair.

'Crap compared to my chair at home. WWH claimed all their chairs were top spec. Ha. Rose-tinted spectacles indeed.'

Cat waited politely and then asked Roxy to go through her experiences.

'Well, that Adam chap, he shuffled us all into the cave and pulled out a gun on his girlfriend. Yeah! I knew then this was a rubbish deal. But she might have pushed the old lady off the rock. That Jade. She certainly didn't like the Coxes... called him a racist git. Of course, he was.'

'I believe,' said Miranda, 'you yourself had a run in with Mrs Cox.'

'Probably. I forget. That sort of woman is endlessly complaining about free spirits like mine. But I didn't kill her, however much I might have wanted to… Unfortunately my chair wasn't close enough for the opportunity.'

Cat frowned. 'No one is suggesting anything except a natural death. Do you have some reason for suspecting something more nefarious?'

Roxy sneered. 'You dickies! If you're interviewing, Miss Marple, then you think something happened. You don't think it was a heart attack, I'm sure of that.

So, you're looking for a scapegoat and I'm not going to be it. OK?

'To continue, the boy Adam had arranged for us to have food and drink, not that I ate any, I thought he might have drugged it, make his kidnap easier. Anyway, both Jade and Sandy were wandering around giving out these treats. You ask them why they didn't notice that Mrs Cox was poorly. Odd I call it.'

After interviewing Roxy they talked to Mr Cox.

'Did your wife have any kind of heart condition?' Cat asked. 'Would the strain of something like the hostage situation have made it worse?'

He sucked air in through his teeth. 'Not a heart condition. I'm the one who suffers from that, atrial fibrillation, that's my problem, don't need any stress, I don't. I carry amiodarone just in case. I was really worried about that Adam problem… Luckily for me that lovely Elsa held my hand all the way through. We comforted each other. If she hadn't been there, I think it would be me lying in the dust. Both Coxes hit the deck. How would that filthy little kidnapper deal with that, eh?'

Cat frowned. Did he really need to turn this around to his problems?

'And your wife? Any other health issues?'

'Nothing really. She did have a thyroid problem but then many old women do, used beta blockers. Mind you, she was an emotional woman, anything could set her off bleating... She loved being ill, always complaining about her health the way old women do. On and on and on. I blame myself for not having given her a baby earlier. By the time we tried, it was too late. A woman without a child is a sad business. It's not the same for men. And she never could be bothered to lose weight, no matter how often I warned her. Good wife, though. We've been married some forty years and she was a nice little cook if only she wouldn't rabbit on so.'

'Sorry to ask this, Mr Cox,' broke in Miranda, 'but why didn't you notice your wife wasn't with you when you all boarded the bus?'

He sighed. 'I can't really say. I guess in all the hustle and bustle I was just concentrating on getting myself home. It was dark, we could hardly see anything. That Elsa was looking after me, she's a lovely girl. So kind and she really had a way with the wheelchair; pushes it so smooth, she does. It almost feels like a sports car the way she does it.'

Their next interviewee was Sandy. She explained clearly how Adam had told them about the striations in the rock, how he had asked them to move deeper into the cave and had then pulled a gun on Jade.

As Sandy talked, she squirmed in her chair as though reliving the event was making her uncomfortable all over again.

'He asked Mrs Cox to get out of her chair and go and sit on a flat stone at the back. She could walk, you see. She had sprained her ankle in Amman, but basically she was OK and just limping. Then he asked me to get Mrs Cox's chair and tie Cyril to it. He told me to sit on Cyril, but first, Jade and I had to give out all the blankets, crisps, and water. When we'd done that, I came back and sat as carefully as I could on Cyril. I'm not huge but I'm not stick thin like Elsa and I was worried I might squash him.' She blushed.

'Why did he ask you to sit on Cyril?' asked Cat, surprised.

'He didn't say but I assumed it was because Cyril was the only person who might try to rush Adam. All the others were disabled except Elsa, who was clearly terrified and holding Mr Cox's hand most of the time, and Jolly, who isn't young or strong, even though she isn't in a wheelchair.'

'Since you walked around the cave, you'll know who was sitting where,' said Cat. 'Who do you think was close enough to Mrs Cox to push her into the crevasse? I'm not suggesting that is what happened. I'm merely looking at the positions people and wheelchairs were placed.'

'OK,' said Sandy, reaching over to the desk and taking a piece of paper and a pencil.

'Mr Cox was over to the left of the holes with Elsa.' She drew an X and wrote *Cox and Elsa*. 'He couldn't have moved without Elsa knowing. Mrs Tank was in the middle, and Roxy was on the right of the holes.'

She illustrated those points, putting Mrs Tank next to Mr Cox, and Roxy on the far side.

'The flat rock on which Mrs Cox was sitting was between the holes but on the right side, towards Roxy.' She drew a little circle above Roxy. 'Jolly and Spice were on the far side of Roxy, with Spice in the chair and Jolly sitting beside her on the rock. When I took Jolly her blanket, she said, "Thank Heaven because the stone was so cold I was frightened of getting piles." And Spice giggled.

'Jolly and Spice giggle a lot. A first I thought it was a nervous reaction but I think the truth is they were having a lovely time, and they love each other and…'

She blushed again and turned towards the detectives, looking much more relaxed. She took up her pencil again.

'Then there was the chair that Cyril and I were sitting on, which was originally Mrs Cox's chair. It was in front of Mrs Tank, and in front of us were Adam and Jade.'

She marked it with a cross.

'I see. So both Mrs Tank and Roxy were close enough to Mrs Cox to push her off her seat. And Jolly would only need to move slightly to push her.'

'I suppose so,' said Sandy, biting the end of the pencil, not wanting to impute blame anywhere. 'But if Jolly moved, Roxy would have seen her.'

'And, as far as you know, are either Mrs Tank or Roxy able to walk at all?'

'Oh,' said Sandy, 'I don't know about Mrs Tank. Roxy can walk a little but her legs are withered. She can't walk far, even when she's leaning on the chair. I think it hurts her.'

'What do you think of Roxy?' asked Cat.

Sandy paused. She hated criticising people, but this was an investigation into a death. She should tell the truth. 'Well, she can be charming, lovely and kind, but then sometimes…' she wasn't sure how to phrase this, 'it's like she has a change of personality… she says things. Rude things.' Sandy sighed. 'The thing is, on a holiday like this, you only see someone in a short period of time and you can't know all the pain and suffering, or even the good times, in their life, so you don't really understand what drives them. To me, it seems that Roxy is a very complex person and I haven't been able to… to… well… fathom her depths.'

She wondered if they thought she was being pretentious; certainly she hadn't really begun to explain what she felt. However, it seemed their investigation was moving on.

'How dark was it in the cave?'

'Very. Sort of late twilight, when you can see a bit but everything takes on a different shape and sometimes you confuse people with each other.'

Cat nodded.

'So when Cat told Adam to take everyone to the van and drive back to the hotel, what exactly happened?' asked Miranda. 'Did you push the wheelchairs out or did people take themselves out?'

'Well... actually,' said Sandy, again blushing, her skin like a beacon flashing out her emotions, 'when Adam said we were free, I did kiss Cyril. It was the pent-up emotion. I was so relieved. I'd felt so bad about tying him up and sitting on him. I was so happy we were OK. I know I shouldn't but... but it was lovely and he kissed me back.' Sandy's face was now so red it looked sunburnt. 'Anyway, I untied him, and then he and I went to the bus... I would have gone to get Roxy but she had already wheeled past me, yelling, "Let's go". I think she wanted to be out of there as soon as possible. I don't think she likes confined spaces.'

'I see. Who took Mr Cox?'

'Oh, I suppose Elsa wheeled him out. I'm afraid I wasn't really concentrating on anyone except Cyril and Roxy... I should have but...' She spread her hands. 'Sorry.'

Elsa came in next. She looked tired and obviously hadn't slept well last night.

'Oh, what an awful thing this all is,' she said. 'Poor Mrs Cox, I feel so bad about leaving her behind. I was pushing her husband and we were talking and I suppose I thought

Cyril would bring her... I'm afraid I was concentrating on Charlie...'

'Charlie?'

'Mr Cox. And I just didn't notice. If I thought about it at all, I would have thought that since she only had a sprained ankle, she would be able to limp out.'

'What happened to her chair?' asked Miranda. 'There weren't any chairs left in the cave.'

'Oh,' said Elsa. 'I don't know. Maybe Jade took it. I didn't see.'

When she had gone, Cat and Miranda looked at each other. 'Good point about the chair,' said Cat. 'Someone must have folded it up and that person presumably should have realised that Mrs Cox wasn't in it.'

'Indeed.'

The last person in was Cyril. He looked calm and relaxed, completely different from all the other people.

'Hello,' he said. 'What would you like to know? I'll do anything I can to help.'

'Do you know who took Mrs Cox's chair out of the cave?'

'Yes. I did.'

'Oh, didn't you wonder why Mrs Cox wasn't in it?'

'To be honest, no. I'd been sitting in it. By the time Sandy untied me we were the last people in the cave. Roxy had already wheeled herself past and if I thought about her at all, I assumed Mrs Cox had walked out. She only had a sprained ankle. So, Sandy and I folded up the chair and put it in the van, then we got in and we were chatting.'

'Did you look around the cave to see if anyone was left?'

'I'm afraid I can't remember. I think I would have had a look around to check, but maybe I didn't. You have to understand, we were all pretty emotional by the time we were released. We weren't acting like normal, rational people – we just wanted to be out of that cave.'

He looked at them steadily. 'It's a pretty horrible experience being a hostage. You have no control. I know that sounds obvious but when it happens to you it is much, much worse than anything you can imagine.'

'I see,' said Cat. 'In that case, why did you offer to go back with Elsa when she wanted to examine Mrs Cox's body and bring her back?'

Cyril shrugged. 'I guess I wanted to be helpful. Elsa isn't strong enough to lift Mrs Cox, who was a big woman, onto the donkey, let alone out of that hole, and I thought Ahmar and I would be able to lift her between us.' He half smiled. 'Even for us, using the rope and the rocks as a pulley, it was a struggle to get her out. As you saw, she wasn't a light burden.'

There wasn't much more he could tell them as he couldn't see past Sandy into the back of the cave, and Adam and Jade were behind him. He didn't mention Sandy had kissed him, but Cat thought that was probably because he was too chivalrous.

After he left, Cat said, 'You know it could be he went back because he wanted to make sure she was dead. I do think it's odd he just folded up the chair and put it in the van without even looking to see where its previous owner was.'

Miranda gave a hollow laugh. 'That, my friend, is because you're living with a man who cooks for you and does your washing, looks after you and generally behaves like a gentleman. I assure you, my beloved Phillip could quite easily leave our children behind if his mind was on work, and we've already had an indication that Cyril's mind was entirely on Sandy.'

Cat nodded thoughtfully. 'And it's hard to imagine what motive Cyril could have had for killing her.'

'Which does make it look like she had a heart attack and fell into the hole,' Miranda said. 'We still don't know if she died of natural causes. Maybe she did, and so, even though we are murderer hunters, we shouldn't jump ahead. But one thing I will say is, speaking from my instinct, that if Cyril pushed her in, he is the most relaxed criminal I've ever seen.'

Cat put her hand to her cheek and lent on it. 'Yes, but I'm not as instinctive as you. I need facts. Mrs Tank was in the best position to do it, but what could possibly be her motive?'

Miranda shrugged. Right now her intuition was telling her nothing.

'Roxy was also in a position to push Mrs Cox,' said Cat. 'But again, why would she?

What was her motivation for killing Mrs Cox? It's got to be more than the odd shouting match.'

'And Jade, she had opportunity but absolutely no motivation. In fact, unless she is playing a very deep game, she had counter-motivation. Mrs Cox's death is extremely bad for Adam.'

'And then there's Sandy. Why would she push Mrs Cox into a hole?'

'Yup. And Sandy doesn't strike me as the type to kill in cold blood. Given what we're hearing about her liking for Cyril, perhaps if he had been threatened. But no one is suggesting that.'

'Indeed. We'll need to do some research into Mrs Cox.

Who was she? What was her past? And had she met any of these people before, or had any interaction with them?'

'What about Elsa?'

'Same thing. No motivation as far as we know.'

'How about Mr Cox?' said Miranda. 'It's often the nearest and dearest who do it.'

'Yes, well, we can check his background. He may well have an insurance policy on her life that would give him lots of money, but given that he's a businessman, he might have had one of those even if he is innocent. Problem is, he was too far away from her to push her, and unless Elsa was in on it with him, she would have noticed. So, no opportunity.'

Miranda wiggled her nose. 'It does rather look as though she just had a heart attack and fell. We'll see what the autopsy brings up. Maybe we're redundant here and should just find our absconder and go!'

'Maybe,' said Cat. 'But if so, Adam will be blamed and... who knows what kind of penalty he'll get. We'd better wait until we see the autopsy results. I wonder how long it will take.'

CHAPTER 32

GOOD INTENTIONS ARE THE MOST BEAUTIFUL OF SECRETS

After all the faffing about, and then lunch, the van did not leave for Amman until quarter to three, with Mr Jarvis muttering about sandstorms being worse in the dark. The bus had only just left when it drove back into the hotel grounds and stopped outside the front door.

Miss Abbey came down the stairs, her walk stiff with emotion. 'Mavis's handbag,' she said in answer to Cat and Miranda's surprised looks. 'She does this all the time – leaves it somewhere. I know it's attention-seeking. I should have watched her.'

Furiously she strode into the hotel and returned a moment later, the bag swinging from her arm.

'I hope she's not going to hit Mavis with that,' said Cat as she and Miranda watched the bus finally depart.

'OK,' said Miranda, 'it's three o'clock here, so it will be 6 a.m. in South America. Stevie will be awake and we can ring her. I've sent her an email with what's happened so far so she's up to speed and no doubt longing to know what's happening.'

Stevie answered on the first ring. 'Hi, how's it going? Have you apprehended my former girlfriend yet?'

'Yes and no,' said Cat. 'She's here, but there's been so many other things that we haven't had time to formerly identify her.'

'Be careful,' said Stevie, 'you know she's a will-o'-the-wisp. She'll have disappeared before you know it. Keep your eyes on her.'

She switched to video call and they saw she was already up and dressed but in jeans, not her uniform. 'So, I'm guessing the phone call means you want my help. I'm not flying until later today, so I can do a good bit of research this morning. What do you need?'

'Well,' said Cat, 'at the moment we don't know if we're investigating or not. It could be the "victim", a Mrs Cox, had a heart attack but it also might be something else. We won't be certain until we get the result of the autopsy but we're behaving like detectives just in case. So, first, we need as much background research as you can find about Mrs Cox and her husband. I've got pictures of their passports, which I can email you. Secondly, you'll need to look at all the other guests, some of whom I fear are not who they say they are... I'll send you a list and the few details we know.'

'OK, I can do all that,' said Stevie. 'How about you take photos in the cave where the hostages were held and around the area with all the exits and entrances. That will help us get a kind of angle on the place, its potential, and then we can fit it in the plan of where people were sitting, and look at the potential for anyone else sneaking in another way. Oh, and can you also collect anything that looks suspicious? While you're doing that, I'll find a place in Amman that can analyse anything you find in the cave.'

'OK,' said Cat. 'We'll pop up there now before it gets dark.'

Miranda groaned. 'Pop! Pop indeed. Flipping mountain climber.'

Although it was full sunlight outside, the cave was dark and gloomy inside, particularly at the back where the daylight hardly penetrated, making it hard to see even when their eyes had adapted to the lack of light. Cat took a video of the whole site, starting from one side and sweeping slowly to the other, making sure she got every part of the cave from floor to ceiling. She went up to each hole and took videos, then went outside to get pictures of the overall area.

'What are we looking for?' asked Miranda, arriving at the cave some minutes after Cat and panting due to the long climb. She had had quite enough of this rushing up and down steep hills. Her body type was not made for this kind of activity. More, she thought wistfully, for sitting on beaches, sipping champagne and flirting with handsome men.

'I don't know,' said Cat, striding back into the cave and waiting for her eyes to adjust again, 'but if you shine the torch just in front of me on the floor, I'll keep looking. I can't help feeling we're going to find something hidden in the debris.'

'Oh yes, who's being instinctive now? OK, let's go.'

They walked up and down the cave, quartering it, and examining everything that struck them as even slightly out of place: a crisp packet that seemed to be hardly open, or one that seemed to be shredded; particles of hard plastic that lay, seemingly unconnected to anything else, on the dust floor; random gloves that had been shed by their wearers; blankets that had been shrugged off and not collected by the group.

At the end of the investigation Cat was holding a big bag of things she felt were important.

'I wish we'd brought up a donkey.' Miranda sighed. 'Now I suppose you'll want me to share carrying that load down the hill.'

Cat grinned at her. 'I was thinking of carrying it all myself, but now you mention it, we could divide it into two loads and carry one each.'

Miranda wrinkled her nose at her friend. 'Except, we only brought one bag with us. Oh bother. What a shame, I would have loved to have helped you...'

Cat laughed and threw the bag over her shoulder. 'OK, you take some more photos and I'll get out the way. We should have everything Stevie needs.'

'Oh? This is for Stevie... is she feeling cold? Needs more blankets and gloves?'

'Ha ha. Now hurry up before it gets dark.'

Once they got back to the hotel, Miranda and Cat uploaded the photos and sent them on to Stevie. The bag of stuff they put in Cat's suitcase (which was not as full as Miranda's), preparatory to dropping off at the laboratory in Amman that Stevie had found and was ready to analyse their treasures. And then they started the three-hour drive to the hotel in West Amman.

CHAPTER 33

ONCE THE SEA CASTS ITS SPELL, IT HOLDS YOU IN ITS NET OF WONDER FOREVER

W hen the detectives arrived at the hotel in Amman it was late. The guests had all finished dinner and some of them were sitting in the drawing room discussing the events of the past few days.

Mr Cox, who was sitting next to Jade on the sofa, was adamant that he wanted to take his wife's body home as soon as possible.

'I want to bury her in a law-abiding Christian country,' he said, glancing at Jade then quickly averting his gaze, as though it hurt him to look at her.

'Good luck finding one of those,' spat Jade. 'There might be some small island in the Pacific, but by now it probably belongs to China.'

He snorted. 'You just tell your boyfriend to admit it was his fault and we'll let it go. I won't insist on a blood feud.'

Jade scoffed. 'Blood feud! You've been watching too much *Lawrence of Arabia*. They have sharia law here and your fat wife's heart attack doesn't count much in the scheme of things, even if you try and blame it on Adam.'

'The point is,' said Abbey, hoping to calm all the parties, 'the police forensics are doing an autopsy and we have to wait for the results. There's no use arguing about theoretics. Autopsies take time.'

She greeted the arrival of the detectives with relief. Normally, she would have thought detectives as tiresome as journalists but on this occasion she felt certain they would be on her side, and the side of the law, and against the tiresome clients and their anxieties.

'Did you find anything in the cave to help?' she asked the detectives, smiling invitingly.

'Ooh,' said Roxy, 'they've been snooping again, have they? What did you find? Lots of crisp packets and plastic bottles. Well, none of those are very good for the environment, are they? Criminal, what gets left around.'

Abbey went to order some refreshments and Cat followed her.

'Miss Abbey,' she said quietly, 'you said something earlier about Harry talking Arabic to Adam.'

'Yes.'

'I wonder, can you remember if Adam told you Harry's Arabic name?'

Abbey smiled. This at least was an easy question. 'Indeed I can. It's the sort of name you never forget: Messiah.'

Cat nodded, rubbing her jawbone. 'Thank you. That's very important. Very helpful.'

While the older members of the party argued, Tony sat down beside Cyril. 'How about a few jars in the local watering hole?' he said in a quiet voice. 'Don't think we checked out this side of town much last time.'

To his amazement, Cyril glanced at Sandy and shook his head. 'No thanks, mate. I think I'm starting to find other things more interesting than drinking all night.'

Tony ground his teeth and turned to Sandy. 'Blimey. How about you, lovely? I bet if you say yes, Cyril will tag along.'

Sandy looked at him, surprised. 'No thanks, Tony. Kind thought but I don't drink alcohol much. I did try it a while ago, but it just wasn't my bag.' She smiled at Cyril. 'Like Cyril, I've got other things I'd rather do than stare drunkenly at a disco ball.'

Tony huffed. 'Come on, Elsa, how about it?'

She yawned. 'No thanks, Tone. I think I'll give it a miss tonight. I'll have one at the bar here if you like, but I'm not really in the mood for a sesh.'

Tony looked at his watch and wondered how long they would hold them here. This was really boring. When he saw Cat going outside, he followed her.

'Cat?'

'Yes, Tony.'

'Do you think the police need me to stay here? I wasn't in the cave when Mrs Cox was killed. I'd never met her before and, frankly, I can't think of a single reason why I might have killed her.'

'I'll ask the police tomorrow, Tony, but I don't hold out much hope. Even if you weren't in the cave when she was killed, you could have been an accomplice. I do understand your frustration, but I'm afraid this is a very rule-bound country and it's better to keep you here now, than have to try and get you back later.

'But if you want a bit of distraction I could ask if you and some of the others could go and float in the Dead Sea. It's only an hour away and at least then you won't be hanging around the hotel getting bored.'

Tony rolled his eyes. Floating in the Dead Sea and plastering himself with mud was not his idea of fun, but to his surprise, Cyril, Elsa and Sandy, who had followed him out of the drawing room, were all very keen on the idea.

'Wow,' said Sandy, 'that sounds brilliant. I've heard of the Dead Sea but I never thought I'd get to swim in it.'

'Float,' said Cyril. 'You can sort of swim, but it's really hard to get your legs down into the water, so it's more a body float with the arms in charge. You'll see tomorrow. I'll help you; it can be quite difficult until you get used to it, but it's fun.'

Sandy looked at Cat. 'Will someone else be able to help Roxy if I go down to the Dead Sea? I don't want to leave her in the lurch.'

'Sure,' said Cat. 'Miranda and I want to talk to her about various things. We'll be happy to get to know her better and keep her from getting lost.'

Sandy considered Cat in surprise. There had definitely been an odd tone in her voice when she said that. It almost sounded as though she was stifling a laugh. What could Cat know about Roxy? They'd only just met.

CHAPTER 34

A PARADISE WITHOUT PEOPLE IS NOT WORTH STEPPING IN

I t was over a week before the autopsy was finished. Abbey wasn't sure if the autopsy was very compli- cated or if the desire to have so many elderly tourists staying in one of the most expensive hotels in Amman, and spending freely, was just too much of a counter to getting the evidence quickly. Amazingly, her boss had managed to get the insurance to agree that this *particular kidnapping* was not an act of war and it would be paying for the hotel, daily expenses and all of the guests' return flights when they were finally released. Abbey didn't know if this meant her job was saved but at least she wouldn't find herself responsible for thousands of pounds in bills.

Eventually, Cat was asked to go to the police station in West Amman to hear the results of their investigation. When she returned she was wearing a resigned look. She asked Miss Abbey to gather all the guests in the drawing room while she had a quick chat with Mr Cox. Once done, she found the group assembled around the room, some of them still in their wheelchairs, others on chairs. Everyone was there.

'You're a right little Miss Marple, aren't you?' said Mrs Tank as Cat walked in. 'Gathering us in the drawing room to get us to spy on each other.'

'That was Poirot,' said Roxy. 'Miss Marple was the one everyone thought was just a silly old deaf woman but turned out to be a master criminal.'

'Is that so?' said Mrs Tank. 'I think you must have been reading an odd version of Agatha Christie's book. Perhaps you wrote it yourself.'

'Says the expert!'

The other guests looked at the two sparring women with relief, letting them act out the tension that was affecting everyone except Cyril, who was still moving around the hotel and helping where he could. When he wasn't busy, he sat alternately with Sandy or Elsa, trying to keep their spirits up.

'So,' said Cat, standing up and, now she was wearing her Louboutins, towering over everyone, at six foot four. 'We've had a lot of information from the police and I'm afraid it does mean that they, too, will want to come and interview some of you. Because of the likely cultural differences, they have suggested I interview most of the guests first and afterwards they would like to talk to one or two of you.'

'Oh! Poirot the Cat isn't good enough then,' said Mrs Tank.

Cat ignored her. 'The major discovery is that Mrs Cox had a large ingestion of digoxin shortly before she died. This, as you probably all know, is a drug related to heart problems.

'I've asked Mr Cox,' she stopped to smile politely at him, 'about Mrs Cox's health and apparently she didn't have any heart issues, so it was not her own digoxin. However, she did have an overactive thyroid and was taking beta blockers, a drug which can work adversely with digoxin and may possibly have made its effects worse.'

She paused, waiting for all the guests to take in what she said.

'But beta blockers and digoxin are often prescribed together,' said Elsa. 'Are you saying that that could actually be deleterious?'

Cat looked at her thoughtfully before replying. 'I'm not a medical expert, Elsa, but Mr Cox tells me his wife was specifically warned not to take digoxin without medical assessment, so it seems in her case the two drugs together were dangerous.'

Elsa nodded and said nothing more.

'But,' said Cyril, 'you *are* saying that Mrs Cox was killed. And that it could be any one of us here.'

'I'm afraid it does look that way.'

The guests all looked at each other. Suddenly no one felt like making flippant comments. One of them was a killer. Cat wondered if they were still hoping it was Adam, and thus some kind of local issue that meant they could be released to go home quickly and never think about this episode again.

However, finding out that Mrs Cox had been killed did seem to put Adam in the clear. Mrs Cox was still alive when he asked her to go and sit on the seat at the back, and he hadn't been anywhere near her after that. He could be an accomplice, but he could not have killed her himself, which possibly meant they were all hoping Jade did it. Even Mrs Tank was looking a bit green.

'Where's Jade?' asked Roxy.

'She's at the prison with Adam. The police are interviewing her now.'

The atmosphere lightened considerably and some of the guests began muttering they knew it; Jade struck them from the beginning as having very dubious morals.

'Yes,' said Roxy, 'I believe murder runs in families, and I think we all know who Jade's grandmother was.'

Mrs Tank stood up furiously and walked up to Roxy, towering over her. 'If you think my gran... my friend's granddaughter is a murderer, you'd better say so now and let my lawyers deal with your totally unfounded suspicions.'

No one spoke, either because of what she said or because they were stunned by the realisation that Mrs Tank clearly didn't need a wheelchair at all: her walk had not been an effort or even a limp, but as strong and purposeful a stride as anyone else over eighty.

'Hmm,' Roxy said, sniffing the air. 'I smell a rat somewhere...' She smiled, showing her teeth. 'And I'm pretty sure it's a celebrity rat.'

'Please, please,' said Miss Abbey, 'let's not start accusing each other. We have the police and these detectives working on the matter. Please.'

Mrs Tank shrank into an old woman again and hobbled back to her chair, collapsing down in relief and apparently falling asleep.

Cat said, 'If you don't mind, I'd like you to go into the library, where the hotel staff will bring you refreshments, and then come talk to me in turn. I'd like to start with Harry.'

Harry, who had been staring out of the window and apparently not following a word, jerked back into reality when he heard his name. His eyes widened and he pointed at himself. 'Me?'

'Yes please, Harry.'

He nodded and waited as the others wheeled out of the room, Elsa again pushing two chairs as Harry was not available to push Mrs Williams. Only Cyril stayed behind.

'Would you like me to translate? I know Harry speaks at least some Arabic, so I might be able to help.'

Cat swivelled round to him. 'Do you speak Arabic?'

'Yes, you might say it was my first language. I was born here, my whole family speaks Arabic and French, as well as English, of course. I believe Harry speaks French too, although I haven't tried him out.'

Cat nodded thoughtfully. 'But you have chatted to him in Arabic?'

'Yes. Not a lot, but we've had some conversations in MSA... modern standard Arabic.'

Cat, like Miss Abbey earlier, thought there was an awful lot of non-communication going on. Someone might have mentioned this before.

'Thank you,' she said. 'That would have been very kind but actually Messiah and I have met before, and we were able to communicate then, so I think we'll manage this time too.'

She gave a smile of dismissal and although Cyril looked at Harry/Messiah curiously, he left the room silently. Harry sat down on a chair across the table from Cat. He was holding her voluminous handbag, which he passed over to her. 'Sorry, but this was on the chair.'

Cat frowned. Was he trying to distract her? She was certain it had been on the table when she turned to talk to Cyril. She shook her head.

'So, Messiah,' said Cat, 'do you remember me?'

Messiah took off his glasses, rubbed his eyes, put his glasses back on and sighed. 'Yes, Mrs Red Cat, I remember you from Vietnam. Perhaps you and I are here for the same purpose.'

Cat looked at him. 'And what purpose would that be?'

He looked from Cat to Miranda before speaking. 'I'm looking for my mother's killer.'

Cat inclined her head. 'Please continue.'

'Well, as you know, my mother was killed by Lady Bumstead, who was then convicted of manslaughter and sentenced to life in her palatial mansion. I didn't think it was an appropriate punishment. However, it was what the judge decided, so I went along with his decision.'

He sighed again. 'And then I heard on the grapevine that Lady Bumstead was no longer incarcerated, nor was she, as she claimed, going to be treated in hospital, but had in fact done a bunk and gone on holiday. My sources managed to narrow it down to the fact she had disguised herself as someone needing a wheelchair, even though she is perfectly able to walk, and so I applied to be a pusher at Wheelchair Warriors Holidays, hoping I would find her on one of the trips I chose.

'When I was asked if I could push the eighty-two-year-old Mrs Williams, I happily agreed. Lady Bumstead will be eighty-two by now and I hoped it was her. I realised she would be disguised, so when I first met Mrs Williams, I thought she might well be Lady Bumstead.

'I decided to pretend I couldn't understand English because I thought that would give me a much better chance of watching all the guests without interruption.'

'But you spoke to Adam in Arabic,' said Cat. 'Why was that if you were pretending not to be able to communicate?'

'I didn't think anyone else spoke Arabic,' Messiah said. 'I wasn't at that time aware Cyril spoke our language, so I didn't think it would be relevant, and I hoped Adam might be helpful in finding my mother's killer.' Messiah sighed wistfully. 'But I hadn't envisaged his kidnapping plans. Adam was not the reliable person I had assumed.'

Cat gave a disappointed moue to encourage him. But Messiah was still talking. 'Since nobody spoke Arabic to each other, it was more useful to be able to understand English while pretending not to. When I heard Adam telling Tony what he was going to do—'

'What?' Miranda broke in. 'Are you saying Adam had already told Tony about the kidnapping before he did it? That Tony knew?'

'Yes.'

Cat made a face at Miranda. 'Sorry, Messiah, what were you going to say... when you heard Adam telling Tony...'

He studied her for a moment, then continued. 'I had already discovered Mrs Williams was not Lady Bumstead. Mrs Williams has a huge family, all of whom seem to dote on her and ring her often, worried that she might get caught up in the turmoil in Palestine. So, knowing what I did, I persuaded her to go back to the hotel early. I didn't want her to get caught in the kidnapping plot and possibly get hurt. She's a kind woman.'

'I see.'

'I didn't know what was going to happen with the kidnapping, so I paid one of the donkey boys to hide a couple of mules in a cave for a few days. I thought I might be able to help steal away the guests, and I knew many of them couldn't walk.'

Cat thought they had missed something here but she asked the relevant question.

'So have you identified which one of the guests is your mother's killer?'

'I'm not sure. I thought Spice might be the one I was

looking for – she wears a lot of make-up that she claims Jolly applies for her as she can't see very well, which could be a disguise. But her whole manner is completely different. If she is Lady Bumstead, she's a brilliant actress.

'Then I wondered about Mrs Cox. She and Mr Cox are... sorry, were... so much of a typical, unhappily married couple that I thought it might be an act. And although Mrs Cox was much larger than Lady Bumstead, a fat suit is an admirable disguise. But when I saw them physically fighting in the Amman amphitheatre, I felt certain that Lady Bumstead would never get herself into a situation like that. I have now heard they were married for some forty years.

'I was down to Roxy and Mrs Tank, and then Mrs Cox was killed and everything changed. I had no time for rumin-ations.'

'So you're still not sure if your mother's killer is here, if she is one of those two women, or if she's somewhere else completely?'

'That is correct.'

'And what are you planning to do if you find that one of those women was your mother's killer?'

Messiah rubbed his eyes. 'I was planning to alert the authorities that she was here and have her returned to the UK, hopefully to do a proper sentence. To pay the penalty for the crime she did.'

Cat scratched her chin. 'You won't take the law into your own hands, will you, Messiah? To kill or hurt anyone, even for good reasons, is a crime.'

Messiah nodded, but Cat wondered if he had really heard her.

CHAPTER 35

THERE ARE NO SHORTCUTS
TO ANYWHERE WORTH
GOING

Mrs Williams came next, pushed in by Tony who saw that Harry was wandering around looking lost and did the duty instead.

'Do you want me to stay, or go and return?' he asked. 'I can sit outside and when you want me, just come and open the door. Or, if you like, I could be interviewed at the same time, although of course I wasn't in the cave, but I'm willing to help any way I can. I'm very observant and I may see things you miss.' He grinned at them happily.

Cat wondered if he would listen through the door, but, seeing him get out his phone when she ushered him out, guessed he probably wouldn't bother.

'Stick around, Tony,' she said, 'we'll talk to you soon. Don't go off into town, will you?'

'No. Sure. Great. Looking forward—'

'Thanks.'

Mrs Williams was deaf but she had a good hearing aid and said she could hear perfectly well without Cat and Miranda needing to shout.

'Why,' asked Cat, 'didn't you go with the others on the monastery trip?'

She laughed. 'Principally because there wasn't room. Mrs Cox had already made a hell of a racket about being left behind – poor fool, if only she'd have been a bit more sensible she'd still be alive, but there you are, we all have our time limit and I guess hers was up. So, mainly because of that, but also because I was tired of looking at old buildings and ready to go back and have a ziz.

'Lucky, I did too. Mostly for you lot. My family have been over-protective to say the least, ringing me up every five minutes to check I'm OK. They're so worried about the Hamas hostage taking that if they'd discovered I'd been in a kidnap situation, they'd be over in their plus fours carrying their twelve-bores.' She roared with laughter. 'You'd never hear the end of it.'

After Mrs Williams had left, Cat and Miranda were about to discuss what they knew when Mr Jarvis burst into the room.

'Hello, detectives, I need to speak to you urgently.'

'Of course,' said Cat. 'Please sit down.'

Mr Jarvis pulled out the chair and sat on the edge of it, but he couldn't sit still and kept almost jumping up and sitting back down again. He drummed his fingers on the table.

'I've something I have to tell you.'

'Go ahead.'

'It's Mavis. She's only a child. She isn't yet fourteen. She may look older because she's been ill her whole life, but actually she's only just a teenager.'

Cat and Miranda exchanged a discreet glance. Did Mr Jarvis think his daughter had killed Mrs Cox? She wasn't one of the hostages, and it was hard to imagine how she could have given Mrs Cox an injection of digoxin when she hadn't seen her for several hours. They waited.

'Of course, partly she does it to annoy me. It's hard to be a rebel when you're unwell. When you spend so much time in a wheelchair. She can't get up to all the high jinks of her brothers or other children her age. It isn't her fault. I understand why she wants to cheek me, to show her independence.'

Cat was confused. 'Yes, of course. And how does she show this independence?'

Mr Jarvis stared at them for a moment. 'Did no one tell you?'

'No,' the detectives chorused.

'Oh, well, she leaves her handbag everywhere. Anyone could have touched it, anyone could have helped themselves to the things inside.'

Cat was even more puzzled. When her daughters were teenagers, the sort of things they kept in their handbags were not the sort of things anyone would want to steal, and certainly nothing relevant to a murder investigation. Still, Mr Jarvis would not be here and in this nervous state if his daughter's handbag was full of make-up and tampons.

'And what's normally inside?'

Again he stared at them, as though he thought they should have known. Perhaps, Cat thought, all that talk of Poirot and Miss Marple had confused him into thinking they had more insight than they did.

'Her drugs, of course. Mavis has osteogenesis imperfecta with cardiac complications. What you and I would call brittle bone disease. She carries Lanoxin, which is the brand name for digoxin. The doctor warned me that the digoxin is not good for her bones, but because of her cardiac complications, she carries it in case she needs a quick heart reset, if you see what I mean.'

'Ah,' said Cat, 'you mean Mavis has been carrying digoxin and leaving her handbag lying around, so anyone could have helped themselves to the drug at any time. Is any of it missing?'

'Yes. Because we don't use it, I don't check it every day, but Mavis carries it with her all the time, just in case. But when you came back from the police and said that digoxin was used in the murder case, I immediately went to Mavis's bag. Because we are away from base, as you might say, and we didn't know where the nearest chemist might be, we were carrying 140 mgs of the drug with us. Half is missing. That's enough to kill a grown man, let alone an overweight woman like Mrs Cox.'

When Mr Jarvis had left, Miranda said, 'Funny thing to say "an overweight woman like Mrs Cox" in relation to the drug use. I thought smaller people got a bigger effect from drugs.'

'Yes, I think they do, but perhaps because his daughter has a heart problem and is overweight, he thinks it works that way. And, even though he has to give drugs to his daughter, he doesn't necessarily know a lot about their further effects.'

'No, probably not.'

'Shall we have Mavis in next?' said Cat. 'Her father will need to come in with her as she's under sixteen. Do you want to go and ask them?'

'Sure.'

Miranda returned with Mr Jarvis and Mavis. Mavis was walking beside her chair but pushing it.

'Good exercise,' she said, and flopped down on the seat, looking tired.

'Thanks for coming, Mavis,' said Cat. 'Your father has told us about the Lanoxin in your handbag. Can I ask if anyone knew you were carrying drugs and that they were in your handbag?'

'Yes, Sandy did. We had a long chat in the garden after we all returned from Jerash. Dad was having a nap and I was bored.' She glanced at her dad. 'I told her lots of things, including all about Mum's acronyms.' She giggled.

Her father frowned, glanced at his watch but didn't speak.

'She'd call you DC and SP!'

Cat looked pleased. 'Is that DeteCtive and SideKick?'

'No. Don Chicky and Sancho Panther.'

Cat snorted. 'Don Quixote and Sancho Panzer. That's funny, your mother has a great sense of humour.'

'That's enough, Mavis,' said her father. 'Just answer her questions.'

'Yes, Dad!' Mavis stuck out her tongue behind her cupped hand.

'OK, so you told Sandy you were carrying prescription drugs. Were you specific?'

'I can't remember.'

'OK. Anyone else?'

'No. Sandy was the only one who chatted to me. None of the others can be bothered with children.'

'That's enough, Mavis.'

'Yes, Dad! But Sandy's nice. She wouldn't kill anyone, and if she did, it would be Elsa.'

Cat blinked. This was a new line. 'Why would Sandy want to kill Elsa?'

'All's fair in love and war, Mum says, and Elsa is an SP.'

'An SP?'

'Sexy piece.' Mavis giggled.

'That, Mavis, is definitely enough!'

'Any wiser?' asked Miranda, shutting the door behind them and coming back to sit down.

Cat pinched her chin thoughtfully. 'We'd better have Miss Abbey in next and ask her if she's seen anyone handling Mavis's handbag. I find it hard to think of Sandy as a killer, don't you? What does Stevie's list say about her?'

Miranda read it out. 'Left school early to look after her mother, who subsequently died in a hospice. Lives with elder brother who works as a mechanic. Sandy works for Percy's Bifold Doors in Guildford and commutes from the suburbs. She wants to be a novelist and has a blog under the name Sandra Dee!'

Miranda laughed. 'So she's owning it then. I heard Jade singing that virginity song at her... I'm glad the girl can wear it.'

'Maybe.'

'Of course,' said Miranda, 'if she's a writer, she probably has a brilliantly devious imagination. Maybe she killed Mrs Cox and then planted the evidence on Mrs Tank to get at Jade for singing songs at her.'

Cat sighed. 'Yup. I can see why you're a detective. Very funny.'

When Miss Abbey walked in, Cat felt a huge jolt of sympathy. There were dark circles under the woman's eyes and her face looked drawn and haggard. It was clear she was not sleeping.

'You wanted to see me?'

'Yes, please sit down.'

Miss Abbey collapsed on the sofa slightly away from the detectives. She tried to get comfortable but didn't seem able to find a good spot.

'Are you having any luck? Honestly, I can't believe what has happened. It was bad enough when it was an accident, but a murder. Who would want to kill an elderly woman? As far as I remember, she doesn't even work, so it can't be an enraged colleague.'

Cat decided to get straight to the point as Miss Abbey looked very close to breaking point. 'Mr Jarvis has told us his daughter had digoxin in her handbag and half of it is missing.'

Miss Abbey's mouth flopped open. 'What? Mavis's handbag... that half-witted girl! Why was she carrying a virtual poison around... and... oh my God... she left that handbag everywhere. Oh jeez! If you were carrying... wouldn't you...? Oh my goodness... teenagers!'

'We wanted to ask,' said Miranda, 'if you'd seen anyone looking inside the bag, taking anything out? At any time.'

Miss Abbey closed her eyes. Miranda wondered if she'd gone to sleep. She looked tired enough.

'Well,' she said, 'I remember Cyril looking inside it... She left it behind so often everyone knew it was her handbag, can't think why he needed to look in it.'

'I see. Did you see him take anything out?'

Miss Abbey scrunched up her face in thought. 'No. Not actually. No.'

'Anyone else?' asked Cat.

Miss Abbey snorted. 'Almost everybody, even a few waiters... perhaps someone bribed one of them... I'm sure one time, Mrs Tank and Jade brought it back... certainly Sandy – she even started to look out for it. But whether they opened it, I doubt it. That handbag was legendary.'

CHAPTER 36

IT DOESN'T MATTER HOW SLOWLY YOU GO, AS LONG AS YOU DO NOT STOP

When Cyril came in, he admitted it immediately. 'Yes, I opened it and looked inside. And yes, I'm not for a moment pretending I didn't know it was Mavis's handbag, but I thought it might make a nice present for my sister. It's not long until Christmas and my sister is a doctor. Doctors often need to have their hands free and yet carry things, and, when she wasn't leaving it around, Mavis had it slung across her body very neatly, so I thought I might see if I could get something similar for ... for my sister, and I wondered who made it.'

'Did you take anything out?'

Cyril looked surprised. 'No,' and then raising an eyebrow thoughtfully, 'hang on, was there something in the handbag that's gone missing?'

'Yes,' said Cat.

Cyril nodded and slowly smiled. 'I'm pretty close to my sister and I know what sort of rubbish she carries in her handbag. I'm almost feeling queasy at the idea someone might steal some of it... make-up? Toiletries? Love notes? Oh boy, I would have to be desperate.'

'Since you speak Arabic, did you have any idea about what Adam was planning? Did you overhear anything?'

'No, but when Adam said he was going to drive us to the monastery, I knew something was up. It isn't possible. Not the whole way. You can take a van and a four-by-four to get close to the back entrance but even then, you must walk or ride a donkey up the last bit of the hill. My sister and I have climbed up there many times and if we could have had a lift, we would've.'

'But you didn't think to say anything?'

'No. I thought it was a bit of a game. Some of the tourists were getting a bit restless and I thought Adam might have thought of a *blague* to keep them entertained.'

'Why do you think Adam had you tied up?'

Cyril grinned. 'I think he guessed I would jump him. I might have, even though I wasn't taking any of it too seriously. You know, my sister calls me a home-grown hero...'

When Cyril had left, Miranda said, 'He still doesn't appear to be taking the situation very seriously.'

'True. Do we know what he does for a living?'

Miranda giggled. 'Why? Are you thinking he might be a spy and murder is an occupational hazard?'

Cat frowned. 'Don't let Miss Abbey hear you laughing, she'll think *we* aren't taking things seriously. You got Stevie's list of people and their details?'

Miranda fished it out of her bag. 'Cyril Curtis, he works in corporate finance. It says he has experience in raising money for charities and small businesses. What do you think? Cover for 007?'

'Probably not.'

Cat sighed. 'Boys! You know, Miranda, I understand Tony might be blasé about the kidnapping, thinking as he does from a rich Westerner's viewpoint, but Cyril was brought up here. Shouldn't he know the leeway you get in a democracy isn't the same in a dictatorship?'

Miranda spread her hands. 'Guess not. But even so, I find it hard to think of him as a killer. Who shall we interview next?'

'How about Elsa? We don't know much about her except that she's a doctor—'

'And an SP,' broke in Miranda.

Cat gave her friend a quelling frown. 'Ha ha... and so, as a doctor, she would know about digoxin and how to administer it. Incidentally, do we know what form the digoxin was in? We didn't ask Mr Jarvis if his daughter's drugs are in pill or liquid form but pills would be harder to administer. Can you imagine trying to force a woman to take tablets?'

'I suppose they could have been popped into the water bottles. Water was given to the hostages. Any idea if digoxin will dissolve in water, or how quickly?'

'No, but even if it does, it wouldn't be quick enough. Besides, how could anyone be sure it would be the right bottle or that it wouldn't sink to the bottom?'

'Good point,' said Miranda. 'We'll ask him later about the pills. I assume it must be in injectable form because he said it was only for emergencies. If she collapsed from a cardiac complication and needed "a heart reset" then it would have to be an injection.'

'Yes. Which also points to some kind of medic like Elsa. How many people can give injections without the victim noticing?'

Miranda nodded. 'Let's see Elsa next.'

Elsa was shaking when she walked in, her steps juddering

across the floor. She collapsed onto the chair and Miranda offered her a glass of water.

'Are you OK?'

'Yeah, I'm sorry. My brother and I are completely different. It's like I got all the nerves and he didn't get any. It's lucky I'm not planning to be a surgeon.' She laughed wistfully. 'I'm OK once I get going, but it's thinking in advance that throws me. Sorry, that wasn't very clear, but I'm fine, ask away.'

Cat smiled at her, trying to calm the girl. 'You're a practising doctor, are you not?'

'Yes.'

'But you don't carry drugs with you?'

'I would if I was on duty, but I'm on holiday. Obviously I have all the over-the-counter stuff in my washbag, like paracetamol, ibuprofen, and bandages and dressings, but nothing you need a prescription for.'

'So no digoxin.'

Elsa laughed. 'That was a joke, right?'

'Tell me, would it be possible to inject someone without them noticing?'

She laughed again. 'Like in the movies? Right! Pretty difficult, especially for a doctor – some of them are the worst injection givers I've ever known. Patients usually ask for a nurse or a phlebotomist.'

'Did you know that Mavis carries digoxin in her handbag in case she needs it?'

'No kidding, the handbag she leaves everywhere. No wonder her dad is so protective. She is a bit of an airhead but then I guess we all were when we were young, and she's got all those additional problems. Mind you, it doesn't always work that way. When I was in the paediatrics department some of the dreadfully sick kids were more like adults in their behaviour. I thought it was the result of years of being in and out of hospital.'

'Did you see Cyril looking in Mavis's handbag?'

Elsa stared at them, her eyes flying open. 'Cyril? What my... I mean Cyril?' She sat back in the chair, her eyes wide under lowering eyebrows. 'You're not looking at Cyril as a suspect, are you? Cyril! Now that really is laughable.' She shook her head. 'Have you told him you think he's a suspect? He'd love it!'

Cat wrinkled her nose. 'We're looking at everyone as a suspect. Even you. We have to look at the facts and then make a decision.'

Elsa shook her head incredulously. 'Yes. Me, fine. If I got wildly nervous and out of control, lost my mind, I expect I could murder someone. It's hard to think of anyone fearing Mrs Cox – she was just a silly old woman who spouted out lots of rubbish. Or are you saying she knew someone's deadly secret? Maybe that I'd killed a patient when I was training or something. But Cyril. Blimey, that boy is so chivalrous he'd probably ask the person to kill him first. The only thing Adam did right was ask Sandy to tie Cyril up, because he's exactly the sort of home-grown hero who would have a go at the villain. You know, when I was going through my training and we were learning about such awful things, I sometimes didn't want to tell Cyril in case he tried to stop me being a doctor, worried it was bad for my mental health.'

Cat and Miranda exchanged glances.

'How long have you known Cyril?' asked Cat.

Elsa put her hand to her mouth. 'Oh!' She winced. 'I forgot. You won't tell Miss Abbey, will you? Relatives aren't supposed to sign up for WWH at the same time – some rubbish about a previous trip where two brothers got drunk every night and didn't do their duty. Since I've got a different surname on my passport...' She paused. 'Look, I'm married but my husband was working this week so Cyril and I... well, we've always got on well and it's fun to be able to spend time together before the...' She sighed slightly and shook herself. 'Sorry, anyway, I was saying that since I've got a different surname it was easy for us to sign up without Miss Abbey and WWH realising we were related. But of course I've known him since he was born, and we've always got on.'

'He's your brother?' asked Miranda.

'Yes. Did you think he was my husband?' She doubled up with laughter, her body convulsing on the chair. 'That's funny. You wait till I tell my husband about that. He thinks Cyril and I are opposite sides of the same coin already.'

After Elsa had left, Miranda shook her head. 'Nobody is exactly who they seem, are they? She could have done it, but would she?'

Cat shook her head. 'Too straightforward. One of those clever scientists who can't understand the devious thinking behind jokes. And too nervous – she couldn't even keep the secret of her brother for long.'

Miranda half shrugged. 'Shall we have the rabid journalist in next?'

Sandy slipped quietly in, walked quickly across the room, sat on the chair and waited attentively. Her hands were folded in her lap but she was obviously nervous as her thumbs kept twiddling before she realised what she was doing, stopped, and then started again. Miranda offered her some water.

'Oh, yes please,' she said, taking it with a hand that shook. 'Look, I have to say I feel so guilty. I can't help thinking this is all my fault. I put writer on my form and Miss Abbey thought I was a journalist. Then Adam got the idea that I was going to write amazing pieces in the national and international press about the Bedouin and their fight. And then Mrs Cox was killed and of course...' she finished disjointedly, 'really I'm no one.'

Miranda knelt down by her chair and took her hand. 'Everyone is someone, and you are a wonderful, enthusiastic person, but don't worry, Mrs Cox's death has nothing to do with the kidnapping. I'm sure it would have happened anyway, just somewhere else.'

Cat looked drily at them both and rubbed her neck.

'Sandy, do you know what Mavis kept in her handbag?'

Sandy screwed up her face. 'Hmm. I'm trying to remember if she told me. We did talk a lot about various things, about her little brothers, about her mum and the acronyms. That she and her dad were on a bonding trip. I can't remember if she told me what was in her handbag, but I guess the usual things. You know, make-up, money. She's probably too young for credit cards. Does she have a phone? She must do, I guess. And then the rubbish we all accumulate, you know. Was there anything special I ought to know about?'

'She had her prescription drugs in there, which included digoxin.'

'Ah,' said Sandy, nibbling her thumb. 'I see.'

The detectives watched her thinking through the implications of that, sitting with her head bent, not speaking.

'Sandy, did you know Mrs Cox before you came here? Had you ever met her before?'

Sandy raised her head in surprise. 'No. Does she, did she... do they live in Guildford? I never thought to ask.'

Cat, who had just thrown out the question to see what

reply she might get, realised she had no idea where the Cox family lived. She gave a quick glance at Stevie's list.

'No, they live in London. Mr Cox has a business in the industrial use of plants, and Mrs Cox was recently on the jury...' Cat's voice faltered and then continued quickly. 'She didn't work, I believe.'

After Sandy had gone, Cat turned to Miranda. 'How well have we read Stevie's list?'

'What do you mean?'

'Mrs Cox was recently foreman of the jury in a celebrity court case. Stevie has added "yes, it was our pal, Lady Bumstead". We'd better have Mrs Tank in.'

'Yes,' said Miranda, 'but before we do, let's have a quick chat with Tony. He told me Mrs Cox was bragging about being the foreman on a celebrity trial and Mrs Tank was there when she was doing so, although he thought she might have been asleep. And we need to ask him about what Messiah told us; about Adam having told him about the kidnapping.'

'Yes.'

Tony came in jauntily and happily shook both detectives' hands.

'How's it going, Marlowes, found our killer yet? Anything I can help you with, I'd be delighted.'

He remembered the conversation with Mrs Cox and confirmed that Mrs Tank had been there, but other than that he remembered little of what Mrs Cox had said.

'Neither of them were particularly broad-minded,' he said. 'Mr Cox argued with Jade all the time. He seemed to have a thing about her tattoos and stuff. But I don't remember Mrs Cox saying anything to her, although she had a go at Roxy a couple of times. Can't remember why.'

'One more question,' said Cat. 'Messiah says he over-heard Adam telling you he was going to kidnap the guests and take them up to the cave as part of the Bedouin complaint. Is that true? Did you know about the kidnapping in advance?'

Tony bit his lip ruefully. 'Yes,' he said, sighing slightly. 'I did.'

'You didn't think to tell anyone? Or to dissuade him?'

Tony rubbed his nose. 'No. To be honest, I thought it was a bit of a laugh. A joke. You know, all part of the holiday… bad luck, you're kidnapped! Whoopee, you're free! Like those detective holidays you go on. Of course, I had no idea Mrs Cox was going to die. If I'd had that level of forward vision, I'd have told him to pack it in, but as it was… well, you know.' He shrugged. 'A bit of fun.'

Cat bit her lip. She felt like asking him how old he was. Was he a child not to have thought through what might happen? What was he thinking? But at the same time, she knew her own son might have considered the kidnapping of a few old people a bit of a laugh, not thought of any conse-quences. People look at things in different ways. And perhaps, if everyone had returned safely, that's what it would have been; something to talk about in the pub.

But the same could not be said for Adam. He was not a protected Westerner having a laugh. He was never going to be OK, even if the old lady had remained alive. Silly, silly boy.

'Why did he tell you?'

Tony grinned at them and flexed his biceps. 'I was the only physical threat, that would be my guess. The rest of the men were in wheelchairs except Harry, who couldn't follow a thing, and Cyril, who's a thinker, not a doer. No, I'm pretty sure he could see I was a possible hero. I was going to tell Cyril, even so.'

'Did you?'

'No, I was going to when we got up to the monastery, but they never arrived. I hadn't realised Adam was going to do it then, he just said sometime soon. I was a bit pissed off when Elsa didn't arrive, she's a lot of fun. I wanted to get to know her better.'

After he'd gone, Cat raised her eyebrows at Miranda. 'He has no idea what trouble Adam is in, has he? He still thinks it's a bit of a laugh.'

Miranda shrugged and glanced at Stevie's list. 'He's just left Cirencester, looking for a land agent job. I guess his world is rather different. He's still in the stage of getting drunk and driving cars the wrong way up the motorway!'

'Oh dear,' said Cat. 'Do young men do that?'

Mrs Tank was pushed in by Cyril, as Jade was still at the police station.

'Thank you, my darling,' she said, rewarding him with a tremendous smile. 'It's so nice to have proper men around; men who treat their women like the poor, weak beings they are. I do love a chivalrous man.'

Cyril's lips twitched but he bowed gently to both Mrs Tank and the detectives, then showed himself out, closing the door quietly.

'So, my lovely Red Cat. You don't mind me calling you that, do you? You have such a... well... *red* feel about you. What can I do for you?'

Cat gave her favourite Cheshire Cat smile. 'I don't mind

at all. In fact, your forthright speech makes everything a little easier.'

Mrs Tank smiled.

'Tell me,' said Cat, 'how long have you known Jade?'

Mrs Tank examined Cat thoughtfully and then turned her gaze to Miranda. 'I am a great friend of her wonderful step-grandmother, Lady Bumstead. A woman who was treated so badly by the law... as indeed women often are. I say that the law was made by men, for men.'

'Thank you. Please explain how you are related to Lady Bumstead's second husband, Phillip Tank?'

Mrs Tank snorted impatiently. 'Oh dear. I suppose you SeeMs Detective women are going to be clever clogs again. Yes, all right. Darling Phillip Tank was my second husband and definitely the best of the bunch. I wish I could have remained Mrs Tank. But there we go.

'I am Lady Bumstead, and I'm sure you feel a sneaking admiration for me having arranged everything so cleverly so I could go off on holiday. And yes, Jade was marvellous in covering for me. Despite her strange looks, she is a wonderful granddaughter. Frankly, I blame that stupid Cox woman. Once she got herself killed, I could see you were going to ruin my holiday.

'Why are you here? You SeemLess Detectives! You couldn't be looking for me. I covered my tracks perfectly, as only I know how. And you certainly didn't come as a government negotiator, however *cheap* you may have been.'

'Perhaps we were just on holiday,' said Cat. 'But the point is, Lady Bumstead, we do now know who you are and will be alerting the authorities that you're here. You'll be returned to the UK, and I doubt your punishment will be so easy this time.'

'Ha! You have no idea! House arrest is a terrible thing. How I suffered for my innocence. How I—'

'Thank you. Now, Lady Bumstead, can you tell us what you knew about Mrs Cox?'

Mrs Tank snorted. 'Certainly. She was a silly little woman, full of herself and sure of her own importance when actually she was a nooooobody, and a fat nobody at that. Lots-of-fat body, but still no-body.' She gave a ringing laugh.

'And had you met her before, or perhaps seen her in some official capacity?'

Mrs Tank sneered. 'Ooh, still the so-clever detective, Red Cat. Are you trying to trick me into saying I didn't recognise Mrs Cox as the foreman of the jury on my corrupt and unfair trial? Of course I did. But it also cannot have escaped your notice that her death is a bad thing for me. Now my little holiday has been discovered, I'll be sent back and, as you rightfully point out, given an even more unfair sentence for someone else's crime. No, the stupid woman was annoying, but not annoying enough to kill her.'

When Mrs Tank had left, Miranda said, 'She has a point. If no one had been kidnapped and no one had been killed, she would have just gone in and out of the UK using a false passport. No one would have noticed her absence and she would have returned to her nice life under house arrest. Now she's facing a much bigger problem.'

Cat shook her head. 'No, that's not right. We were here before Mrs Cox was killed. And even though we are looking for someone else, not her, she wasn't to know that. She could have seen us and assumed we were here to take her back to London and then freaked. Decided this was her only chance to kill Mrs Cox right away and did the deed.'

'You think? She's clever and manipulative – she wouldn't panic and do that. She would have waited.'

'I don't know, Miranda. She had motive and opportunity.'

'Motive, yes for sure, but how would she have been able to inject Mrs Cox, or persuade her to take the pills, if pills it was?'

'She can walk,' said Cat, 'as we know, so she doesn't need the wheelchair.'

'True, and of course she has a deep knowledge of Quaaludes and may know about other drugs, but even so. It's one thing injecting yourself, quite different injecting someone else.'

Cat rubbed her chin thoughtfully. 'True. To slaughter one person could be an accident, but two looks unfortunate, as Oscar Wilde might have said. We shouldn't strike her off the possible list though.'

'Thanks, Creative Cat!'

'And now,' said Cat, 'how about Roxy? What does Stevie say about her?'

Miranda looked at the list. Imitating Stevie's voice, she said: 'Roxanna Victory, I would take a close look at her. Could this be her joke name for Victoria Bell alias Bella Chantry – two names she used in prison? Roxy is a slang name for one of the opioids that are available in prison and can also mean new dawn! Talk about hiding in plain sight! Typical Victoria. Playing with things that might give her away would be her attitude. Testing us to see if we're clever enough to find her. And, I'd be prepared to bet, she's wearing false teeth. All in the name of art!

'Hmm,' said Miranda, speaking in her own voice, 'she knows her former girlfriend well.'

Using Stevie's voice again, she continued. 'Personally, I'd

say there are several things that point to her being our absconder. Firstly, she doesn't deny she was in a car accident and that she was the victim of a nasty deceit. Secondly, she says she has fallen out with her family who moved to Hong Kong and didn't speak to her any further.

'While these things would mean nothing to anyone else, Miss Abbey, for example, or the WWH, to us it seems impossible that anyone else could also have experienced these events. Roxy is Bella Chantry and thus is our absconder. Tread carefully. We know what a difficult and manipulative person she is, and if, as I think, she is Bella Chantry, for heaven's sake don't let her know that you know who she is or she'll disappear again.'

Miranda shook her head. 'Poor Stevie. That horrible woman. But I expect she's right – one often has an instinct about ex-lovers.'

Cat shrugged. She had been married for forty years before her husband died and now had a younger boyfriend and there were no ex-lovers to worry about.

'OK, we're forewarned. Let's have her in.'

CHAPTER 37

BE THE CHANGE YOU WANT TO SEE IN THE WORLD

When Roxy arrived in the drawing room, wheeling herself, she sneered at Cat. 'Sorted out who killed Mrs Cox yet? Bet it was her husband! You should see the way he canoodles with that Elsa girl... he's got money and she's got youth. You mark my words, either he did it or she did. She looks like a little cat to me... ooh... current Cats omitted!' She snorted. 'Have you noticed the way Elsa has all those boys around her little finger? That Tony'd like a go there, and as for that Cyril, he can't keep his hands off her, always patting her arm and looking into her eyes... mind you he's a one too. Look at the way he's leading my naïve little Sandy up and down with his sly glances and promises of love. I'd put money on him being a killer... killed for love?

And then we come to Mrs Tank. You know who she is, don't you?'

Cat raised her eyebrows. 'Tell me.'

Roxy looked down her nose and nodded her head. 'She's Bella Chantry! I expect you've heard of her, haven't you? You read the papers like the rest of us and there were many column inches about her when she escaped from Ford Open Prison.

A rather clever and misunderstood mind, she escaped by simply calling a taxi and thus evaded the law. She's been missing six months, and no one knows where she is. And then we find her here, disguised as Mrs Tank, with a fatuous relationship to a girl called Jade, who we all know is Lady Bumstead's step-granddaughter and, no doubt, bent on avenging her grandmother by killing the foreman of the jury in her murder case. The foreman who was Mrs Cox.

'So! There you are. I've solved your problem for you. Jade did it and Mrs Tank is an escaped criminal. Red star for Roxy.'

'Thank you,' said Cat drily. 'I'll keep your suggestions in mind.'

'Good. Now what else do you lot want to know? Or are you busy ignoring the facts and looking for a scapegoat? You prefer that method, don't you?'

'How well did you know Mrs Cox?'

'Hardly at all. Even if I'd felt like pushing her off a rock, which she was annoying enough to do, those were hardly the circumstances for it, with a strange man with a weapon at the front of the cave. And as for giving her an excess of digoxin, if that's what we're looking at... have a think, my friends! Where would I have got it from and how would I have administered it? You tell me that.'

'You could have got it from Mavis. Apparently she left her handbag lying around and it was full of the drugs she needed.'

Roxy sneered. 'And I was supposed to divine that how? I'm cleverer than you lot but even I can't see inside the stupid girl's handbag.'

Cat sighed. 'Tell me something about yourself, Miss

Roxy. We know from your holiday form that you were hurt in a car accident. Could you tell us something about it?'

Roxy gave a half smile. 'Well, I was driven by a drunk, a man so drunk that he spun off the road and injured me so badly I've spent the rest of my life in a wheelchair. While he himself was not only unhurt, he didn't even stay to see what happened to me. Then, when years later he committed suicide, I was blamed for his death.

How fair does that sound to you, my lady detectives? Talk about using the victim as a scapegoat.'

'And what happened next?' said Miranda. 'Do you remember a man called Rupert?'

Roxy raised an eyebrow. 'I don't say I do. Anyway, I'm bored of this conversation. Are you going to ask me anything to the point or shall I call your next victim?'

When she'd gone, Cat said to Miranda, 'Was that wise? Bringing up Rupert. Yes, she killed him too, but you must have alerted her that we know who she is.'

'Nah! She's so full of herself she thinks we're idiots. She reckons she's convinced us that Mrs Tank is the real Bella Chantry.'

Cat stared at Miranda thoughtfully. 'I hope you're right. We'd better make sure we always know where she is. Just in case. But she obviously is Bella Chantry. Only Bella would know those details about her escape from Ford and the piece in the paper was miniscule. We missed it. If it wasn't for our friend in UIO we would think she was still in prison. I doubt if any of the other guests have even heard of Bella Chantry. I think she knows we suspect who she is and she's playing with us, which means she's about to escape again.'

'Possibly,' said Miranda. 'But you know what? I think she's running out of money and wants to go home. It can't be as exciting as she thought, moving listlessly around the world.'

'Again, I hope you're right. But don't forget she was working with some corrupt policemen... she has friends in useful if not high places and she's a very slippery customer. Plus, our employer told us they were sure she was planning to meet someone here. To do some kind of exchange or something.'

Miranda shrugged. 'Who? Perhaps it was Mrs Cox and the exchange went wrong. In fury she fed her digoxin and pushed her into a hole.'

'Ha ha. Too far-fetched. But one thing we can be sure of is that she doesn't want to return to prison. She'll know that once they've got her back, they'll keep a much tighter watch on her. The ignominy of finding out a murderer has gone on holiday in another country rather than staying put in prison is going to stay with the UK government for a long time.'

Mr Cox was next. He was pushed in by Elsa, who offered to stay. He looked at her lovingly.

'Thank you, my dear, there is certainly no need for you to go on my behalf. I've nothing to say that you shouldn't hear.'

'Even so,' said Cat, 'I think you'd better sit outside, Elsa. We've interviewed everyone else alone, so we must do the same with Mr Cox.'

Elsa left and Mr Cox watched her go before turning to the detectives. 'A bad business this, a very bad business. I'm not going to pretend Mrs Cox and I didn't have some disagreements, but she was a good little wife and she made a cracking shepherd's pie. I ask you, who's going to cook for me now?'

Cat murmured how sorry they were for his loss. 'Do you have any idea who might be responsible for her death?'

A strange look flashed briefly across his eyes, but Cat thought it might just be indigestion. She remembered from when her husband was dying that sitting in a wheelchair did terrible things to your internal organs.

'Well,' he said, 'at the beginning I thought it was that Adam fellow, with his pincushion girlfriend. You can't trust those types. I mean, locking us up in a cave and what have you. He'd even made preparations for keeping us there all night. Honestly, what kind of guy does that? And as for that silly cow with the piercings and tattoos, well a woman like that can't be trusted at all. I wouldn't believe the pair of them if they offered me a hog roast on a Sunday. But after a while I changed my mind about Adam. I realised he was just a fool like so many of my employees. I'm a thinking fellow myself. If I wasn't, I wouldn't have made all the money I have... And I can tell you, back home I drive a very pretty little number, had to be converted for disabled driving, of course, but the smoothest little baby... a nice little goer she is.'

Miranda coughed and he stopped.

'How nice,' said Cat. 'So, Mr Cox, you said you changed your mind about Adam being guilty. Did you have any other thoughts?'

'Well, that la di da Mrs Tank for starters. You know she actually hit my Ophelia. Did anyone tell you that?'

'No,' said Cat. In all the interviews they'd had, no one had mentioned it and she wondered why. 'When did that happen?'

'Ah. We were in the amphitheatre in Amman and my Ophelia thought she'd seen a ramp to get me down to the bottom of the theatre. I must say it was pretty poor planning from WWH and Miss Abbey not to have realised there weren't any ramps in the place, but I'll reserve that for my feedback form. Well, there we were at the top of the steps, wondering what to do next and how to get down. When that Mrs Tank floats up, walking. Yup, walking. So clearly she didn't need the wheelchair. She says something to my darling about when Ophelia was foreman of the jury in that celebrity trial case... you know, the one when that desperate murderess, Lady Bumstead, tried to get away with saying it was the CIA that did it. As though the CIA cares two hoots about go—'

Miranda made another throat-clearing noise. Mr Cox frowned at her.

'...and, as I was saying, she thumps my wife on the head. Well, naturally, Ophelia lets go of the chair and off I go, sailing down to the bottom. Was I worried about her or what? Called her name, I did. "Ophelia, Ophelia", and when she didn't answer, I felt sick with fear. When we got back to the top, and that, to give him his due, was thanks to Adam and Miss Pincushion carrying me, I was never more relieved in my life to see Ophelia was OK, just a little bruised.'

'I see. And what happened then?'

'Well, nothing much. Miss Abbey smoothed over the whole thing. Tried to pretend it didn't happen. I'll be putting that in my feedback form too. My lovely Elsa gave Ophelia some first aid. And after that, Ophelia had to go in another chair, which Cyril agreed to push, and Elsa pushed mine, which was a benefit when you come to think about it, but I can't give Miss Abbey any credit for it. If anything, it was that Roxy woman, Poxy Roxy I call her, who suggested it.'

'I see. And in the cave? Did you see Mrs Tank get up and do anything there?'

He gave a heartfelt sigh. 'Well, it was dark, you know, but the very fact Mrs Tank can walk makes it quite possible she moved over to Ophelia and injected her. Could easily have done it.'

'Thank you. I do have one other question, if you don't mind?'

'Sure. Honest and open as the day, me.'

'You and your wife both have large insurance policies on each other. Why is that?'

'Huh! You trying to blame me, are you? You've a cheek. But to be honest, Ophelia and I took those out years ago – you'll see that's true if you check it. And with those blooming policies, once you start them, you have to keep paying the extortionate premiums or you lose the lot. I'd actually forgotten about that, but now that you've reminded me, I'll get on to the insurance company and get some compensation for this great mess.'

After Elsa returned and wheeled him out, Miranda sighed. 'Are we getting any closer? Everyone wants to blame someone else.'

'Yes, but we'd better get Mrs Tank in again and ask her about that. Did she really hit Mrs Cox? Or was that him just playing up?'

Miranda moued. 'She'll no doubt deny it. How about Jolly and Spice? You know they told Miss Abbey they thought they saw someone hitting Mrs Cox, but because Spice can't see very well, and anyway, since everyone was wearing the same headdress – the keffiyeh – they admitted they weren't sure exactly who it was. Miss Abbey thought they were just trying to get attention.'

Cat frowned. 'More likely she didn't want to get any

adverse publicity. But now it's a lot worse than just a domestic dispute and a bruise on the head.'

'OK, let's get Jolly and Spice in and hear what they saw. It may at least confirm what Mr Cox said, although I find it hard to believe Lady Bumstead, who is no fool, would have done such an emotional thing with such sparse reason.'

CHAPTER 38

I TELL HIM IT'S A BULL AND
HE REPLIES IT WILL STILL
GIVE MILK

It took Miranda a while to find Jolly and Spice. They had apparently thought that, since they hadn't really known Mrs Cox, they wouldn't be needed for a while, and had gone shopping. When Miranda finally found them, returning on the hotel's shuttle, they were over the moon about the shops in West Amman.

'My goodness,' said Jolly, 'they have everything here. All the shops we have at home and far, far more. Horrible prices, of course, but such interesting stuff. I could stay here all day, couldn't you, Spice?'

'Yes, Jolly, I could,' said Spice. 'We only came back because we thought it might be time for lunch. Shopping makes you terribly hungry, and of course, it's all free in the hotel. Wonderful place. I'd like to stay in Jordan for the rest of my life. Although not perhaps where Adam is.'

The girls giggled and Miranda led them into the drawing room.

'Hi, Mrs Cat,' said Jolly cheerfully. 'So sorry to be late. We knew we'd be last and just popped off for a while. It's lovely here, lovely, lovely, lovely.'

Cat smiled. 'Yes, just a couple of questions. I believe you told Miss Abbey that you saw someone hit Mrs Cox, is that right? In the amphitheatre in Amman.'

'Oh yes, we did,' said Spice. 'Or at least Jolly did. I, sadly, have reduced sight but that wasn't just a sight problem as you might say... I mean, there was a bit of swearing too, wasn't there, Jolly?'

'That's right, but then at the end, and with Miss Abbey not really wanting to make a thing of it and both Coxes being unhurt, it didn't seem worth dwelling on, did it, Spice?'

'No, that's right, Jolly.'

'So, what did you see?' Cat tried not to sound impatient.

'Oh,' Jolly gave a sort of embarrassed giggle. 'Well, I don't suppose it's very important, but Mrs Cox wheeled Mr Cox to the top of the steps and she said, "I thought I saw a way down, but there isn't anything. I guess I'll just leave you here and go down myself. No point in us both missing out because you're such a gimp!"

And he replied, "How dare you!" and lifted himself up in his chair and hit her with something he was holding. I couldn't see what it was at the time but it gave a clunk! Later, I saw something in his hand that looked like a pair of pliers, so I reckoned he'd been trying to fix something on the chair and forgotten he was holding them when he hit her. They were always hitting each other, must be that sort of marriage.'

'Right, Jolly,' said Spice, 'that makes sense, now you say it.'

Jolly smiled lovingly at her. 'So, she, Mrs Cox that is, staggered back and the chair took off with a life of its own, and careered down the steps. Boom titty boom titty boom. Didn't it, Spice?'

'It certainly did and with Mr Cox yelling blue murder and that he was going to get her for that... Actually, it was quite funny, wasn't it, Jolly?'

'It was, Spice.'

'So, was Mrs Tank anywhere nearby?' asked Cat.

'No, I don't think so. I know outside they are saying that she can walk, but I've not seen it. I think Jade put her in the shade and then galloped down to see if Mr Cox was OK. At least that was what we thought then, didn't we, Spice? But now we know she was going down to help Adam. We think she's obsessed with him.'

'Obsessed with him,' echoed Spice. 'After all, what kind of girl lets a man hold a gun to her temple? Even if there aren't any bullets in it?'

Miranda's nose twitched. 'What are they saying outside?'

'Oh,' said Spice, 'remember we weren't there for most of it, but when we got back, Mr Cox was telling everyone that he saw Mrs Tank with Mavis's bag. That gave us a good laugh, didn't it, Jolly? Why would Mrs Tank, who has a Gucci handbag herself, want to steal Mavis's little cloth number? Honestly!'

'Yes. And it was hilarious the way Harry suddenly jumped up, as though he partly understood the conversation because, you know, he doesn't understand a word of English. We both tried to talk to him and he looked at us as though we were nuts, didn't he, Spice?'

'That's right, Jolly.'

Miranda and Cat exchanged glances. 'Don't move,' said Miranda. 'I'll go.'

Jolly nudged Spice. 'What's that about? Did we say something?'

'No idea, or as you'd say, "blind venison!" No eye deer, dear!'

They collapsed into giggles.

Miranda came back, running.

'Cat, have you moved the car?'

'No.'

Cat grabbed her handbag and searched through it. 'The keys... they've gone. Oh hell! Messiah must have taken them when he moved my handbag.'

'Oh my God,' said Miranda. 'Messiah and Lady Bumstead are gone.'

Jolly and Spice watched amazed as the two detectives ran out. 'Did you fart, Jolly?'

'No, did you?'

'One of us must have.'

They collapsed into giggles again.

CHAPTER 39

UNTIL YOU HAVE WALKED ACROSS SANDS, DO NOT SLEEP IN SHEETS OF SILK

Outside the room, the detectives found Cyril and Sandy, who were coming to find them.

'Harry grabbed Mrs Tank's chair and wheeled her out to the car park,' said Sandy. 'He spoke in English. I thought he said that you'd asked him to fetch something. But I was mesmerised to think he could speak English all this time. And then he put her in the car and drove off. Her chair's still there.'

'Oh my God,' said Miranda, 'he's making a great mistake. Where's Miss Abbey? We'll need to take the van.'

'She's in the library with the others,' said Cyril. 'I'll get her.'

A moment later Miss Abbey came in with Cyril. She passed the van keys to Cat. 'Cyril tells me Harry took your car and you want the van, is that right?'

'Yes,' said Cat. 'I can't explain now, but I think Harry is making a huge mistake. He's realised that Mrs Tank is someone else – a murderer – and he thinks she probably killed Mrs Cox too.'

Miss Abbey's mouth fell open. 'Mrs Tank! Did she...?'

'No, I don't think so, but we've got to follow them before he does something stupid and makes things much worse.'

'Do you have any idea where they went?'

Cat nodded. 'Almost certainly he'll drive her back to the cave. I don't think he really wants to do what he thinks he does, but this is a sort of blood feud.'

'I'm coming with you. I speak Arabic and if we're going to break the speed limit, you'll need me. Sandy'd better come as well,' Cyril said, grabbing the girl's hand. 'Her blog has already got several thousand followers; they'll want to hear about this.'

'Oh no,' cried Miss Abbey, 'you were a journalist after all.'

But no one was listening. Sandy and Miranda were already climbing into the back of the van. Cat stopped and turned around.

'Miss Abbey, don't let Roxy out of your sight, and when she goes to bed, can you take away her wheelchair? Say you want to give it a quick service or something, OK?'

'OK,' said Miss Abbey slowly, baffled. 'Why...?'

But Cat had gone, jumping into the driver's seat with Cyril at her side.

'Tell me,' Cat said as they raced out of the hotel car park, 'exactly what Mr Cox said to Harry that made him grab Mrs Tank.'

'Turn left here,' said Cyril. 'I know a shortcut. I've done this drive between Amman and Petra a million times.'

'Fine, but tell me about Mr Cox and Harry,' said Cat as she swung down the shortcut, praying they would get to Petra before Messiah reached the donkeys and started on the trip up to the cave. *Don't do it, Messiah*, she thought. *Please!*

'Well,' said Sandy, 'when Harry came back from talking

to you, he was looking very serious. He wandered around for ages, deep in thought. I wondered if he was feeling OK and was going to ask him – in Spanish – if he wanted a paracetamol or something and I was just working out how to say it. But then, when Mrs Tank came back from talking to you, she started laughing as though something struck her as funny or clever, and Harry began watching her every move in quite a creepy manner.

'Suddenly Mr Cox said, really very loudly, "Of course, not everyone here is who they say they are."'

She stopped talking and Cyril took over. 'Roxy, who as you've seen loves a fight, said, "Is that so. So you mean I was right in smelling a rat. There is a celebrity rat amongst us, is that it?"

'And Mr Cox turned to her and said, "Spot on."

'Sandy and I looked at each other, puzzled, but Mr Cox started talking, in a really loud voice as though he was trying to tell someone who didn't really speak English, about Mrs Tank and how she had been walking, and that she took Mavis's handbag. Before I could fathom what was happening, Harry jumped up and wheeled out Mrs Tank. Well, you know the rest. So who is Harry? Didn't you call him Messiah a while ago?'

Cat didn't speak as she concentrated on driving, but Miranda said, 'Sandy, what exactly is in your blog?'

'I just talked about the problems here between the government and the Bedouin, about the shuttle and the animals. I didn't say anything about the kidnapping – I didn't want to get Adam into any more trouble.'

'Thank heavens for that. OK, well if I tell you about Mrs Tank and Harry, will you promise not to put that in the blog either, at least not until we know what's going to happen here? We don't want things to get worse for anyone.'

'Sure.'

'Mrs Tank is really Lady Bumstead, celebrity murderess, in disguise. Have you heard of her? She was convicted of the manslaughter of a woman in Vietnam.'

'I have,' said Cyril. 'It was a contentious case and she says she was framed to make it easier for the hawks of the USA government. She wrote a book. I haven't read it but my sister has. She said it was well written – she thought it was a ghost writer or AI – but the story was rubbish, just didn't add up. That the one?'

'Yes. Well, Harry, whose real name is Messiah, is the son of the murdered woman. He originally told us he just wanted to get her back to the UK and into police hands, but now... Did anyone say anything that might make him think she'd killed Mrs Cox as well as his mother?'

'Mr Cox said he saw her taking something out of Mavis's handbag,' said Sandy. 'He said it was some kind of ampoule.'

Miranda whistled. 'An ampoule, indeed.'

'And he said he wasn't one to make aspersions,' Sandy snorted, 'but that it looked pretty suspicious to him.'

'Oh,' Cat said, 'we're being flagged down by the police checkpoint.'

'That's fine,' said Cyril. 'Pull in, it's just routine. I'll talk to them. Have you got your driving licence?'

'In my bag. Can you get it, Miranda?'

Cat pulled in and wound down the window. Miranda gave Cyril the licence. He talked to the policeman and after a few minutes they were cleared to drive on.

'A 70 hire car with a Moroccan man driving and an old woman beside him pulled in here about fifteen minutes ago.'

'Fifteen minutes! They're pulling ahead.' Cat sighed.

'The problem is all these sleeping policemen where we have to slow down to almost nothing. It takes longer to get back up to speed in a van than in a car. Know any other shortcuts, Cyril?'

'Not on the desert highway. I'm afraid our only chance is once we're at Petra the donkey boys will have closed shop and Harry will find it difficult to find anyone to take him up to the cave. We should catch up with him there.'

'Oh no,' groaned Cat, 'not if he's already bribed a donkey boy to stash a couple of mules in a lower cave.'

'What?'

'Oh hell, Miranda, do you remember? Messiah said something about getting the donkey boys to stash a couple of donkeys in a low-level cave at Petra in case he needed to save anyone from the kidnapping. I didn't really take it seriously. But, of course, I saw him riding up there but didn't recognise him with the keffiyeh wrapped around his face. He went down slightly from the path. Do you think we can find the cave?'

'Why would he do that?' asked Sandy. 'Did he kill Mrs Cox?'

'No,' said Cat, 'but he thinks Mrs Tank did, and, because she also murdered his mother, in his mind she has become a dangerous killer. I think he might be planning to kill her and sacrifice himself to save the world.'

'Oh my goodness,' said Sandy. 'Poor Messiah. But how did he know she was here?'

'He didn't. But someone told him Lady Bumstead had escaped her "prison" and gone on holiday disguised as someone needing a wheelchair and this is a holiday company for wheelchair users. After he had discounted the other guests, the only two possible Lady Bs left were Roxy and Mrs Tank.'

'Perhaps,' said Miranda, 'he stashed the donkeys because he was already thinking in terms of taking both women somewhere to get a confession out of them.'

'You might be right,' said Cat doubtfully, changing gear for another bump in the road.

Once they arrived at Petra, it seemed that Cat was right. The hire car had been dumped by a cave on the road between the shuttle base and the new Bedouin village. They jumped out and hurried into the cave, hoping that Messiah and Mrs Tank were still there.

Inside, there was plenty of evidence donkeys had been living there; stalks of hay thrown into the dust, half-drunk bowls of water, an Arabic newspaper, and a couple of tethers sitting in an untidy pile.

'Do you know the way up to Adam's cave from here, Cyril?' asked Cat.

'I do, but it's a steep climb, especially in the dark.'

'I'll stay here and guard the cave in case they come back,' said Miranda. 'You can take my head torch. Cat has her own.'

'I've got one too,' said Sandy. 'I often take the dog out at night and I always carry it.'

Cyril blew her a little kiss. 'Girl guide,' he whispered.

The two women climbed quietly up the rocks behind Cyril. Cut into the stone were the Nabatean steps that Sandy and Cyril had used on Camel Rock, but this was a much longer and steeper climb, and all three of them were panting heavily by the time they reached the top.

Standing outside the cave were two donkeys. They looked up as the group reached them and swished their tails, but made no noise.

'There's a light in the cave,' Cat whispered. 'It must be him. You stay here and I'll go in quietly and talk to him.'

'OK,' said Cyril. 'But we're just here if he pulls any heavy stuff. We'll be watching. Take care.'

Cat nodded and her head torch did a little dance.

She dimmed her light and crept slowly into the cave. Messiah was a shaded outline in the dark. He was holding a torch, which he had focused on Mrs Tank, making her a green luminous monster sitting on the Mrs Cox rock. As she was facing Cat, she might have seen Cat's movements in the dark, but she didn't give any indication of it. Cat heard Messiah's voice speaking slowly, almost intoning the words as though they were a prayer.

'I know you are Lady Bumstead. I know you killed my mother. Are you going to admit you also killed Mrs Cox? I know now she was the foreman of the jury who convicted you. Indeed, without her, they were going to let you off. Without her, you would have been found innocent.'

'Just as well I wasn't,' snapped Mrs Tank, 'otherwise you'd have been after me earlier. In this case my prison was my protection.' She snorted. 'What are you going to do, Harry, or is it Messiah? Murder me? I'm an innocent victim, and, although your mother was killed by the CIA, I'm not going to debate it now. We can do that later since I'm clearly going to be taken back to the UK by those tiresome detectives. But I want to set you straight about Mrs Cox. I did not kill her. I didn't even hit her on the head as her husband is claiming. Why would I? Go on, tell me that. Yes, she was the foreman but did she really convince the entire jury that I was guilty? If you believe that, you're seriously underestimating the stubborn British character. You can lead them but you can't push, and Mrs Cox was clearly a pusher. Not a leader.

'If the jury had believed I was innocent, they would have stuck with it, no matter what that silly self-aggrandising woman said. Believe me, it was the barrister for the prosecution that I would like to garrotte, not that bumptious baby. You're looking in the wrong place for Mrs Cox's murderer.'

Cat realised that Lady Bumstead was talking to her as well as Messiah. However, Cat, unlike Messiah, knew she was right and she now knew who had killed Mrs Cox, although she might find it hard to prove. She spoke quietly. 'Messiah.'

Messiah jumped as though a ghost had spoken and the knife slipped from his hand and clattered onto the floor.

'Messiah,' said Cat again, not moving towards the knife or indeed even mentioning it: it would be too easy for him to push Lady Bumstead into the hole. A tiny woman like Lady B would have no defence against such a large man. Cat's only hope was words.

'Don't do this, Messiah. You're the one who'll suffer if you kill her. One more death on top of the others will not help anyone.'

She paused, waiting for this to sink in. Messiah didn't move, either to get the knife or to sit back. It was almost as though he hadn't heard Cat, but she knew he had.

The three of them stayed there for so long Cat worried Cyril and Sandy might burst in and make the situation worse. But they didn't.

After a long silence, Cat said, 'She didn't kill Mrs Cox. Someone else did. If you make Lady Bumstead the scapegoat, the perpetrator will get away with her death.'

There was another long silence then Messiah sighed. 'Will she get a proper punishment this time? The proper punishment for killing my mother?'

Cat gave a sigh of relief, which she hastily suppressed. He was engaging. That was a step forward.

'Yes, after this she will be put in a proper prison. The

mere fact the government cares enough to send Miranda and me out here to bring the absconders back shows she won't be returned to her gilded prison. No amount of money will compensate for British justice being made a mockery of.'

She desperately hoped he didn't know they'd only been sent here to look for Bella Chantry, not Lady Bumstead.

'Why should I believe you?' he said, and Cat saw him moving his right foot in the dark, searching for the knife. 'Why?'

'Because I know who killed Mrs Cox and it wasn't Lady Bumstead,' Cat repeated. 'You can help me, if you will.'

His right foot stopped searching and he sat solidly still. The tension in the cave increased. 'Why do you think I can help?'

'Because you have lulled the real killer into a false sense of security. Everyone back at the hotel thinks Mrs Tank is the murderer, so the perpetrator's relaxed and will be talking. Talking often leads to slips.'

Messiah sat. Then with a quick movement he bent down and picked up the knife. Cat gave an inward groan.

'It's no good,' he said. 'I no longer believe in British justice.'

Cat was silent. The tension returned and no one spoke.

And then, in the gloaming behind her, Cat sensed movement: Cyril and Sandy. The young ones, unable to stay outside for another moment, were quietly making their way into the cave, inching round the back, aiming to get between Mrs Tank and Messiah.

Cat turned off her light completely, hoping they would take that as a sign. But neither of them stopped moving.

Damn, she thought, *everyone wants to be a home-grown hero!*

Messiah suddenly sensed the movement to his right.

'What?' He swung his torch and caught Sandy in the light. 'Sandy?'

Sandy was caught in a crouch creeping towards him. Her hands flew to her eyes to protect them from the light. Then putting one hand down and pressing on the rock, she straightened up.

'Yes, sorry, Messiah,' she said, her young voice vibrating around the cave. 'I don't think murder is ever justified. It's God's right to take away life, not man's. Killing a single person without reason is as bad as killing the whole of humanity. Whoever saves the life of a single person is considered to have saved the life of all mankind.'

Messiah made a strange noise, then he stood up. 'OK,' he said, 'let's go.'

Cat could hardly believe it. How did that happen?

Sandy could have a brilliant future in negotiating.

As Messiah turned towards the mouth of the cave, leaving Lady Bumstead in the darkness, Cat heard Cyril whisper to Sandy, 'Is that a quote from the Quran?'

'Yes,' she whispered back. 'I told you I did lots of research before coming out. I found a short version on the internet and that was one of the quotes.'

'Marry me, Sandy.'

She laughed softly but Cat saw her put her hand on the boy's arm and blow him a kiss.

Cat moved over towards Lady Bumstead. 'How are you? Can you walk back to the donkeys?'

She snorted. 'It's quite horrible to think I must thank you for helping me, but I do. And yes, of course I can walk back to the donkey, but what I'm really looking forward to is a hot bath and a late lunch.'

Cat shook her head and gave Lady Bumstead her arm. 'Let's go.'

When they joined Miranda, down at the donkeys' cave, Cat said, 'Cyril, can you drive back in our car? Take Lady Bumstead and Sandy and we'll follow you in the van. I want to talk to Messiah.'

'Sure,' he said, 'and when they pull us over at the check-points, I'll mention we're together and you are behind, and they probably won't stop you.'

'Oh my God!' said Lady Bumstead. 'Don't say I'm going to have to be a chaperone to the lovers. Really.'

Cat bit her lip. 'You can tell them about your book. Sandy's a writer too.'

Lady Bumstead huffed. 'I need a nap.'

CHAPTER 40
WE HAVE ONE MOUTH AND TWO EARS: WE NEED TO LISTEN MORE, SPEAK LESS

Abbey stared at her phone hoping she might get a message, but, as ever, no one thought about communicating with her. That flipping Sandy had been blogging madly but when it came to telling Abbey what was happening, no one cared. Young people nowadays! And that Cat should know better. Rushing off with all the available transport and leaving her here to deal with the police and the guests. It was outside of enough. And as for this keeping a watch on Roxy and taking away her chair. Why? No one thought to give her reasons; it was just do this, do that, and off they go without a word of explanation. Anyone would think that Cat was the group leader and she was just the handmaiden.

Abbey had told the guests that the detectives had gone to apprehend Mrs Tank and Harry, who, it was believed, had driven to Petra, and although they all seemed a bit puzzled, they were very happy to go to lunch and discuss the possibilities with each other. Mavis, she noticed, was now keeping a tight hold on her handbag.

At lunch, Mr Jarvis came to sit beside her. 'The detectives,' he said, 'left here at 2 p.m. It is a minimum three-hour drive to Petra, assuming no delays and they don't get lost, so they should arrive there at 5 p.m. Now, I'm being generous here, because it isn't impossible at this time of year that a sandstorm might blow up, and then one mustn't forget all the police checks and the sleeping policemen slowing the traffic at the villages.' He took a sip of his water. 'So, let's say they arrive at the donkey stand by 5.30 p.m. It gets dark at 5.37 p.m., so the donkey boys will have gone home. That means the detectives will have to walk up to the cave, if that's where they are going. Well, that will take an hour. That little round one isn't fit. The tall red-haired one might manage it quicker but I assume she will wait for her friend. So they won't catch up with Harry and Mrs Tank until 6.30 p.m., and again I'm being generous. And then, of course, they may not find our fugitives, which may mean more time spent looking. However, I will still err on the generous side and assume a fast turnaround. So they are unlikely to return here before 10 p.m.'

'Probably,' said Abbey, trying to be polite but imagining giving Mr Jarvis a quick bonk on the head to relieve her feelings.

'In which case, I shall take Mavis shopping after lunch. Jolly and Spice have just reported an excellent experience in West Amman that I'm happy to replicate with my daughter.'

'Oh, right.'

He got up and moved over to the buffet to get fortified for his afternoon of shopping.

Later in the afternoon, two policemen returned Jade to the hotel. Abbey noticed the officers looked tired and wondered if Jade had been difficult.

'Where are Detectives Cat and Miranda?' the more senior policeman asked.

Abbey took him into the drawing room where she explained all the movements of the day. He looked confused and said if things were not sorted soon, they would be charging Adam, and possibly Jade as his accomplice. However, he did agree to have a check of passengers leaving the airport and border crossings.

Several of the policemen had been through the guests' hotel rooms, both at Petra and in the hotel at Amman. They had also been through the rubbish at both hotels and had a small bag of things they wished to leave for Cat and Miranda.

Looking apologetically at Abbey, since their actions seemed to suggest she could not be trusted to take the bag, the senior policeman told her the bag had been put in the hotel safe and the manager had the key.

When the policemen had left, Jade came in smoking one of Adam's roll-your-owns.

'What's going on, Miss Abbey? There's lots of chatting in cliques and everyone shuts up when I get close, except Jolly and Spice who keep giggling and poking each other.'

Abbey turned to her, biting her cheek in exasperation. Why hadn't those blooming detectives told everyone what was really happening before they left? Now she was left trying to appease the group, who were all making up their own stories, a lot of which appeared to be related to Bulgarians who had trafficked girls in Britain. Did they *really* imagine Mrs Tank was about to be trafficked?

And what was she supposed to tell Jade?

'How is Adam?'

'Miserable but he keeps telling me he had no choice; it was a family decision. I don't think we understand in the

West how strong family ties are out here, but I'm learning. Mind you,' she added smiling thoughtfully, 'I'm keen to explore the idea of family ties.'

She took a long drag on her fag, and a sharp smell of old hay filled the room. Abbey coughed and indicated the *No Smoking* sign. Jade walked over to it, lifted her rollie and scrunched its last remnants on the *No*. She watched, amused, as the fag end slid across the N and part of the O and dropped to the floor.

'Provided we find out who killed Mrs Cox, I'm optimistic I'll be able to do a deal,' she said, lighting another cigarette.

Abbey stopped coughing and stared at her. 'A deal? What do you mean? With the police... the government?'

'Yes, of course. All life is business or, as we say now, *transactional*! I'd have thought you've lived long enough to know that. How long before the detectives return?'

'Probably about 10 p.m.,' said Abbey, thinking about Mr Jarvis and wondering if he was right or would they still be waiting at midnight?

'OK. I can wait.'

CHAPTER 41

WHERE OTHERS SEE BLUR,
YOU SEE LIGHT

As Cat and Miranda drove back down the dark desert highway, Miranda's phone bleeped.

'Interesting news from Stevie,' she said, looking up from the screen and wondering if they could speak in front of Messiah.

'OK,' said Cat, who was presumably thinking the same. 'Anything you can tell me?'

'Yes. They've got the results of the analysis of everything we collected in the cave. There's no trace of digoxin in any of the things, including the little plastic dispenser you found.'

'Oh.'

'However, the dispenser had remaining traces of amiodarone in it. And it itself was one of those dispensers that give ultra-quick medicine. Do you understand what she means?'

'Yes,' said Cat. 'Something you would use in an emergency. Can you check the autopsy report to see if there's any mention of amiodarone in Mrs Cox's body?'

Miranda got the report up on her phone. 'I hope we

don't get pulled over in a police check. How am I going to explain this list? Oh yes, officer, I always carry a list of poisons suitable for murdering old women. So useful if I come across an old friend.'

'Get on with it.'

Miranda scrolled through the report. 'It isn't that easy to understand but it does mention amiodarone, only it says traces found but, as amiodarone remains in the body for months after delivery, this may be a historic drug. Ha ha, a historic drug, does that mean the Nabateans had it?'

Cat snorted. 'Very funny. Did Mr Jarvis mention any other drugs in Mavis's handbag that you can remember?'

'No.'

'So, I wonder where it came from.'

'Mrs Williams carries amitriptyline with her for her fibromyalgia,' said Messiah. 'Old people often carry drugs that they don't declare. Given that most of the tourists are elderly and wheelchair bound I imagine they all have something with them.'

'Yes, good point,' said Cat, 'and I do remember someone mentioning they had amiodarone with them. Messiah, you can help us prove who did it.'

Mr Jarvis's most generous calculation was too kind and the detectives and the others finally got back to the hotel in Amman at midnight.

All the guests had gone to bed except Miss Abbey and Jade. Miss Abbey was pacing up and down in the foyer, while Jade smoked one cigarette after another until the *No Smoking* sign was completely covered with soggy grey ash. When Jade saw Mrs Tank hobbling in, she dropped the remains of her fag and flew over, hugging her tightly.

'Oh! You're OK. Thank heavens.'

'Jade, Jade, really,' said Mrs Tank, extracting herself but smiling. 'No PDAs, please.'

'PDAs?' asked Sandy curiously.

'Public displays of affection,' Cyril told her. 'Like kissing me in the cave!'

He winked at her and she blushed. 'Mean!'

'So,' said Jade, 'what's the answer? What happened?'

Mrs Tank gave a body-wracking sigh. 'Frankly, it's all too much and I don't care. I'm off to bed. Those SeeMs women want to take me back into custody, tiresome people. But don't worry, I didn't kill the old fool in the cave.'

'No,' said Jade, 'of course not. I never thought you did. Why would you?'

As they walked away, Miss Abbey came up to Cat. 'Are we any closer to the truth?'

'Yes, but since everyone has gone to bed it will have to wait until the morning. Did the police leave anything for me?'

'There's a bag in the safe. The manager has the key.'

Cat nodded at Miranda who went off to get it.

'As Jade is here, I assume the police have finished with her?'

'For the moment. One of the British consular secretaries came over to talk to you, Cat, but he said it would wait until tomorrow. He left a card and asked you to ring him. It has a mobile number on the back.'

Cat took the card. 'Thanks. I'll ring him in the morning. I was a bit surprised they hadn't been in touch earlier.'

Miss Abbey raised an eyebrow, wondering why on earth Cat would expect to be contacted. 'Governments work at their own pace,' she said. 'Were you hoping for something special?'

Cat gave a vague smile and moved towards the lift. 'Goodnight.'

CHAPTER 42

IF SOMEONE HAS A HEAD WOUND THEY KEEP TOUCHING IT

After returning from Petra, Sandy and Cyril were too wired to sleep so they sat in the vestibule in the middle of the hotel, talking and laughing at the events of the evening.

'Would you like a drink, Sandy? I see Faisal coming our way.'

She looked over and saw the man walking their way pushing something.

'Excuse me, Miss Sandy, but we have had a delivery for Roxanna Victory and she asked if you could bring it up to her room.'

'Oh,' said Sandy, 'yes, of course. Cyril, can you order me a milky coffee and I'll just pop this up to Roxy's room?'

He nodded and walked to the bar while she went up to Roxy's room with the bulky package to which Faisal had kindly attached wheels.

The coffees had already arrived when Sandy got back.

'What was it? An early Christmas gift?'

She laughed. 'No, a new chair. She told me she was so

fed up with the ones provided by WWH that she was going to order her own. Pity it only arrived just in time for us to go home. It's a wonderful chair. I opened it for her and she was delighted with it. It's electric, so it's quite heavy but she said it was much better than anything she's had before.'

'I'm glad she likes something. She's an abrupt woman. Was she OK with you?'

'Most of the time, but she had some interesting moods...'

'Tell me.'

Sandy proceeded to do so but sighed to herself. Cyril was probably the only person who took her opinions seriously but he was out of her league, even though he did seem to like her. And then there was Elsa, whom he obviously adored. And who adored him. She forced herself to make light conversation.

'What was it like going to school here?' she asked.

He rubbed his palm with his thumb. 'It was fabulous, so free. The only problem was when we went back to England, somehow I didn't fit in there. I was too foreign. And even my European bits were too French. I made myself into someone they could cope with, but I couldn't be myself and the other kids didn't really like me.'

Sandy moued. She understood that too well. She had never fitted in; she was always Sandra Dee to her contemporaries.

He shrugged. 'But then the good thing there was that Elsa and I became, if anything, even closer. We—'

'Elsa?'

'Elsa. My sister. You know Elsa, you see her every day.'

'She's your sister? Your sister?' Sandy started to laugh. 'Elsa's your sister!'

For a moment he looked puzzled, then he laughed too.

'Oh my God! You thought... I thought you knew. Oh, Sandy... Oh, Sandy!'

Sandy felt as though she could ride a thousand camels and never notice the wobbles.

'So you were waiting for her to come to Camel Rock? It was her puffer.'

'No. It was her puffer but I was waiting for you. I... er... I thought you seemed nice, different... I... er... wanted to get to know you.'

'Ah! Wow.'

They had been chatting and laughing for what seemed like just minutes when Sandy noticed the waiter behind Cyril looking rather weary. She looked at her watch.

'Hey, it's three o'clock! If Cat and Miranda are going to tell us who killed Mrs Cox tomorrow, we'd better not sleep through it.'

'OK. As long as you promise we'll keep meeting at home and don't shut me out of your life.' His face was serious and he even looked slightly worried.

She grinned. 'I promise. Although you may change your mind after you've met my brother.'

He laughed. 'I don't think so. Compared to our experience these last two weeks, he's going to seem like an angel.'

As they stood waiting for the lift, reliving incidents of the evening, all of which now seemed incredibly funny, the doors opened. An elderly Indian woman in an elegant silk sari wheeled herself expertly out of the lift in a sporty-looking chair hung with ornaments. She smiled at them.

'Good morning, children,' she said. 'Or is it goodnight to you?' She laughed. 'May you both achieve success in your lives and may they be long and happy.'

'Thank you.'

The woman passed, her ornaments clattering against

the metal of the chair and Sandy looked at Cyril, raising her eyebrows. 'Is that a typical Indian saying or something?'

'I don't know, but we can take it as a good omen.'

Allowing their hands to brush as they pushed the lift buttons, they entered it and parted on the third floor, going to their separate rooms to dream of a beautiful future.

The Indian woman wheeled on to the reception. 'Good morning, Faisal. I apologise for being so early but could you get me a taxi to the airport? I have a very early flight.'

'Of course, lady. Ahmed is outside, he'll take you. Will that be Air India?'

She smiled. 'It will.'

Only a few hours later the guests started to come down for breakfast. Sandy and Cyril were both late. Jade and Mrs Tank had left early to go to the embassy, and Roxy had sent a WhatsApp to Miss Abbey saying she would be delayed with a small but unimportant medical emergency and that there was no need to return her chair until she messaged again.

Miss Abbey, relieved not to have to worry about Roxy for a while, spoke to the remaining guests in a subdued voice, almost as though she felt loud noises might upset them.

'The detectives want to have a brief word with you this morning. I hope that suits you all.' She smiled brightly but her ravaged face showed how little sleep she had had, and how much she longed to get home to reset her own future. 'So, perhaps we can move to the drawing room where we will be private.'

'Mrs Poirot found out who killed my wife yet?' shouted Mr Cox, who clearly wasn't bothered about other guests' nerves. 'It was that Tank woman, wasn't it? I always knew she was a killer, especially after I saw her hit my darling Ophelia. And now she's made a getaway! You let her go!'

'Please, Mr Cox...' Miss Abbey began wearily. 'She is at the embassy and there is a police presence there. She will not be allowed to move anywhere without supervision.'

Elsa took the handles of Mr Cox's chair and firmly wheeled him into the drawing room, while the others followed more slowly.

Before long, Cat walked breezily into the room followed by Miranda, who was talking to a beautiful young man in a Savile Row suit, and behind them two men wearing the uniform of the PSD. The guests watched the policemen, nervously eyeing up their guns as though fearful the police might suddenly turn into terrorists. Just behind the group, Sandy and Cyril rushed into the room mouthing apologies and slipping into the nearest seats.

'Good morning, ladies and gentlemen, thank you so much for coming,' said Cat. 'I won't keep you long. Please may I introduce Mr Fliter from the consul. He's here to sort out all your travel needs and any other problems.'

The guests looked pleased but Harry said, 'And, Mrs Cat, before we leave, could you tell us what happened to Mrs Cox?'

'I can,' said Cat, getting immediate silence. 'Firstly, I'd like to show you two things the police found when they searched your rooms.'

She opened the police evidence bag and pulled out a pair of pliers and a daily pill dispensing tray.

Holding up the pliers, she said, 'We believe these pliers were used to cut the brakes on Mr Cox's chair. Does anyone remember seeing them before?'

Sandy gasped. 'Yes, I do. Did they find them in my room? In my suitcase?'

All eyes swung in her direction. None of them had thought of Sandy as a killer, but now it seemed she not only had (possibly) a clue to the murder, in her suitcase, but was admitting it.

'Where did they come from?'

'Er,' said Sandy. She knew, of course, that they were the pliers Mavis had given her, but she didn't want to say so in case it sounded as though she was implicating the girl. 'Um. They were found in the Amman amphitheatre. Someone had clearly dropped them.'

'And you found them?'

'No. But... are they important? I mean, they're just pliers.'

'Yes,' said Cat, 'but we think they may have been used to cut Mr Cox's brake cable when he was in the amphitheatre.'

'You're not suggesting that Sandy cut Mr Cox's brake cable, are you?' said Cyril, standing up protectively as though to shield Sandy from the detective's innuendo. He looked down at her. 'Do you know anything about mechanics, Sandy?'

'Oh yes,' she said blithely, 'my mother had a wheelchair at the end of her life. I used to fix the brakes when they went wrong. I know I tried to push Roxy's chair with the brakes connected but that was just nerves. I do really know how it all works.'

'I gave them to Sandy,' said Mavis, and everyone jumped. Her voice was stronger and clearer than before and even her father looked at her puzzled. 'I found them at the base of one of the trees in the amphitheatre. Looked like someone had thrown them there.'

She grinned at Sandy, looking rather pleased with herself. 'I'll save you, Sandy,' she mouthed.

Sandy tried not to laugh, but mouthed back, 'Thank you.'

'OK,' said Cat. 'They could have been thrown there by anyone. Did anyone see anything being thrown?'

Everyone shook their heads except Jolly, who said, 'Oh, that's what it was? I thought it was a cigarette. Do you remember, Spice? I said to you how disgusting to be throwing cigarettes into the trees and you laughed and said, "But that one's not a smoker!"'

Spice giggled. 'I do, Jolly, I do. And then later at Jerash when there was all that hoo-ha over the oleander we said it again.'

'We did, Spice, we did.'

'Hang on,' said Cyril. 'Mr Cox didn't cascade down the amphitheatre steps because of a worn brake cable. It still hadn't broken when we changed his chair... it may have looked bad but it didn't actually cause any problems.'

'Yes,' said Cat, 'I know and we'll come back to the pliers. I feel we're drifting from the point.' She held up the plastic tray. 'Does anyone recognise this?'

'Yes,' said Elsa, 'it's a pill dispenser. Older people often have them because they tend to forget whether they've taken their daily medication. Most places will give them to older patients now, as there were too many incidences of them taking all their medication on the first day it was given.'

'Thank you, Elsa,' said Cat. 'This was found in your rubbish bin. It was bagged up with a couple of empty pill vials, which included digoxin and beta blockers.'

There was a collective glance as all the guests took in what Cat had said.

'Elsa!' said someone.

'Well,' whispered Jolly to Spice, 'who'd have thought?'

'She never…' said Mr Cox angrily. 'She's a doctor…'

'But why…?' said Spice to Jolly. 'Why would…?'

Cat put her hand out for silence and returned to Elsa. 'You said you only carried medicine if you were on duty, and that you were currently on holiday. This doesn't seem consistent with the things found in your bin at the hotel in Petra. When did you throw these away?'

Cyril jumped up from his seat beside Sandy and hurried towards Elsa. 'Are you accusing my sister…?'

'Your sister?' said Miss Abbey. 'Now you know that's not allowed…'

'Please,' said Cat, holding out her hand for silence. 'Elsa, can you explain?'

Elsa was frowning. 'No. I… I don't know. Could the maid have put someone else's rubbish in my room? I certainly haven't used the pill dispenser myself. I suppose I might have taken someone else's rubbish in if they needed help and gave me it… but… a lot has happened recently and thinking about rubbish doesn't come high on my agenda.'

'Yes, that's true,' said Cat. 'In fact, we've had the dispenser checked for fingerprints and yours were not on it, although there were some other people's.'

Elsa nodded and moved over so her brother could sit next to her. Over the other side of the room, Sandy was looking at them with such a huge smile on her face that if she'd had a flashing display it would have shown *YOUR SISTER* in huge capitals. Yes, she heard it last night, but now it was confirmed: Elsa was Cyril's sister.

'So,' Cat continued, 'this pill dispenser belonged to Mrs Cox. It has both her name on it and instructions for its use. It's dated for the week leading up to her death. It's empty, but we sent it for analysis along with all the detritus we found in the cave. Interestingly, although it's labelled *Beta*

Blockers, every other day the beta blockers have been replaced with digoxin. This is an unhealthy combination in itself, but not unusual, although both medications slow the heart rate. However, in Mrs Cox's case she had been given a warning that she should not mix her beta blockers with any other medication as it could have fatal consequences.'

She paused and the guests looked at each other, surprised.

Jolly whispered to Spice, 'Was she committing suicide, you think?'

Spice giggled. 'I might if I was married to Mr Cox.'

They sniggered.

Cat said, 'In the cave we also found a crushed ampoule that on analysis proved to have contained amiodarone. Amiodarone, when combined with digoxin and beta blockers, would be fatal to Mrs Cox.'

A sudden tension filled the room as though the listeners were contaminating the air with their fear. Cat thought of the phrase *you could cut the atmosphere with a knife*.

'Someone gave Mrs Cox a lethal dose of amiodarone in the cave, with almost instant results. It seems she was able to stagger to the flat rock after the amiodarone was administered and died there. Then, as Elsa suggested earlier, when rigor mortis kicked in, she fell off the rock and into the hole.'

'There!' said Mr Cox. 'I knew it! It was that Roxy... She was the only one close enough to inject her.' He looked around the room. 'And she ain't here. She's done a bunk. You let her get away.'

'Please, Mr Cox,' said Miss Abbey. 'She's upstairs as she's not feeling very well.'

'Oh yes! How convenient!'

Cat suddenly felt nervous and glanced at Miranda but she was watching Harry.

'But that's ridiculous,' said Harry. 'If Roxy did it, she would have to know that Ophelia was taking beta blockers, and she would have to substitute the digoxin in her dispenser. How would she have got access to Mrs Cox's room? Indeed, how many people did have access to her pills? That person would have to be regularly in her room, like a maid or someone close to her.'

'Or,' screamed Mr Cox, 'Roxy disguised as a maid... You women with your make-up. You can look like anyone, can't you?'

Harry swung around to face him. 'She's in a wheelchair. How many maids are in wheelchairs?'

'Precisely,' said Cat. 'It could be someone in a wheelchair, certainly, but only if they were close to Mrs Cox and could be in her room regularly without surprising her.'

The information echoed slowly around the room as each person understood the implication of what she was saying. Almost imperceptibly, chairs began to be edged away.

'And,' said Cat, 'someone whose fingerprints were on the pill dispenser as well as his wife's.'

'What!' shouted Mr Cox. 'You're accusing me? What rubbish! That's slander. You're saying everything points to me. You are making aspersions. Of course my fingerprints were on the pill dispenser; I helped her with it. But in the cave I wasn't anywhere near my wife. I couldn't have given her a dose of amiodarone or digoxin or anything else. I was too far away. Everyone knows that, we proved it.'

'But you weren't,' said Elsa slowly. 'You patted her hand as she went past to sit on the rock. I remember thinking it was rather sweet of you. I thought you were trying to reassure her, but in fact, you were killing her. You were the only person who knew she was taking beta blockers. You were the only person who could have substituted them with digoxin. And you were the only person who could have added the amiodarone. Oh, Charlie!'

The old man's face crumpled in. 'I did it for you, Elsa. I'm free now. We could be together forever. It was for you. I love you. She was dying anyway, I just sped it up.'

Elsa stared at him, her mouth open, and her hand flew to her cheek. 'But I'm already married,' she murmured. 'So sorry... I had no idea... I didn't... I thought I was being helpful and kind.'

'What?' he said. 'You flirt! You were leading me on!'

Cyril put his arm around Elsa. 'My sister's only twenty-eight. How old are you? Seventy? Seventy-seven? Are you serious?'

'Yeah,' said Mavis from the back, 'course he was, he's got EMS – elder man syndrome – makes you blind to every-thing except the girl you want!' She laughed.

'That's enough, Mavis!' said Mr Jarvis.

'And the pliers?' asked the consul, now interested in the detection. 'What did they have to do with anything?'

'We think,' said Cat, watching the police wheeling Mr Cox out of the room. 'That Mr Cox used the pliers on his own wheels. Because the WWH chairs were very old they had cables instead of levers for the brakes. At the top of the stairs in the amphitheatre, he was gently working away with the end of the pliers, aiming to break the cable so he would cannon down the steps. Mr Cox has been in a chair for many years and he can judge when a slope is likely to turn over the chair or not. In the amphitheatre the steps from the entrance have a fairly shallow slope, unlikely to upset a chair. His plan was to cut the brake cable, then edge himself over the first step and catapult onto the bottom. However, before he could fully cut the cable, his wife called him a rude word and he was so incensed he leant back and hit her on the head, forgetting he was still holding the pliers. She fell over, her head cut by the tool, and as she went, she pushed the wheelchair and sent him sailing down the stairs anyway. At the same time, he chucked the pliers into the nearest tree base.'

'But why? Why would he want to fly down the steps like that?'

'Because he wanted it to look like someone was trying to kill him. Then, he reasoned, when she died instead of him, it would either look as though someone had meant to kill him, not her, or he would be thought of as another victim rather than the murderer. He was making provision for when that moment arose.

'He has a very good insurance policy out on his wife, and he has for some time been trying to get rid of her by feeding her digoxin along with her beta blockers – a slow but fatal combination that was weakening her system but could be put down to natural causes.

'However, when he met Elsa and convinced himself she was interested in him, he thought he would speed up the process. He already knew that Mavis would have digoxin for her condition – that's his job, he makes these chemicals – so he looked in her handbag, found some and took half. That way, if digoxin was found in his wife's system, it would be easy to throw the blame elsewhere.

'He started carrying his amiodarone with him, waiting for the moment when he could end his wife's life. Then Adam provided the moment, and Mrs Cox's fate was sealed.'

Lucky Jade wasn't there or she would have objected to Adam's name being used, thought Cat.

'Why does Mr Cox carry amiodarone?'

'He has atrial fibrillation. He carries it in case his heart needs a little jolt.'

The consul nodded. 'These guests seem like a walking hospital,' he said drily.

Cat frowned. 'Except not walking.'

He blushed. 'Oh yes, sorry. It's just an expression. I meant they carry a lot of drugs between them and very few seem to have bothered bringing the paperwork.'

CHAPTER 43
IT IS A GOAT, EVEN IF IT FLIES

After the police had taken Mr Cox away, Cat introduced Mr Fliter, the consul, again. He explained they could leave on the next flight home but suggested it was better for them to do a daytime flight, as night flights were now diverted south because of the increasing insurrection in the region and took much longer. Slowly, he went around the guests, finding out their needs and writing everything down on his tablet for his assistant. Some people were so keen to get home they were prepared for the longer journey at night, but most preferred to wait for a day flight.

In the early afternoon, Mr Fliter came back to the hotel and found Cat. 'The flights are going well. Nothing is full and we are progressing nicely. However, Mrs Cat, there is still one person missing and I can't find her anywhere. She will, of course, also need a flight home.'

Cat felt a sudden cold lump in her stomach. 'And that is... who... whom?'

'Miss Roxanna Victory. I did ask one of the maids to pop up to her room in case she had fallen asleep but she said the room was empty although all her clothes and her suitcase are still there.'

'I'll go and have a look,' Cat said. 'Miranda, can you get hold of Stevie and see if anything has happened on Bella's email?'

As she ran up the stairs to Roxy's room, she thought how lucky it was that Stevie, as an ex-girlfriend of Bella Chantry's, had all the woman's email login details, which Bella hadn't changed since they broke up.

Miranda smiled at the consul, who was looking puzzled, but before he could ask anything, a WhatsApp came in from Stevie. Miranda opened it. *Just had a quick look at Bella's emails and she has received a visa to India in the name of Renee Singh. Incidentally, Renee means reborn.*

'Oh no,' said Miranda.

Cat came downstairs shaking her head. 'She's left everything, even her passport, which is out on the table. Maybe she just went shopping.'

'Without a chair?' said Miranda. 'I haven't seen her since last night, have you? Look at Stevie's WhatsApp.'

Cat read it, biting her lip. She walked to the outside door where the doorman was guarding the scanner.

'Hello, lady,' he saluted her, smiling.

'Hello, Kalipha, did an Indian lady in a wheelchair come out any time recently?'

Kalipha thought about it. 'Not since I've been on, but I could ask the night doorman.'

'Please do.'

Cat felt even worse. It was getting towards late afternoon. If Roxy had done a bunk yesterday, OMG they were idiots. She had told Miss Abbey to take away Roxy's chair but it never occurred to her that Roxy might have got another one.

Roxy had even insisted that Mrs Tank was her, the absconder. Why did they not realise that once she saw Mrs Tank had been revealed as Lady Bumstead and not Bella Chantry, she would make her escape?

It took some time before Faisal, who had been on night doorman duty, arrived from his quarters and by then Cat had started pacing the reception, making Kalipha so anxious he offered her a cup of tea.

'Camomile tea,' he said, 'very calming.'

Eventually, a tired Faisal arrived. 'Yes, indeed,' he said, 'an elderly Indian lady came out very early this morning. She apologised for the inconvenience but said she had to catch an early flight. The hotel taxi took her to the airport. The driver was Ahmed, shall I call him?'

'Please. That would be very kind.'

Ahmed confirmed he had taken the nice, friendly woman to the airport. She had given him a big tip and told him her name was Renee Singh. She was laughing when she said it. 'A very charming woman,' he said.

'Thank you. Did she have any luggage?'

'Just a handbag when she got into the car. She asked me to take her somewhere she could buy a suitcase and a few basics. She said hers got wet and were ruined.'

'In the middle of the night?'

Ahmed looked apologetic. 'I have friends. They opened their shop for her... she paid well.'

Cat nodded her head ruefully. Yes, of course she paid well.

'Thank you, Ahmed.'

Cat walked back to Miranda and the consul, who had

now been filled in on the events. He frowned when Cat arrived.

'Well, that was unfortunate,' he said, his voice peevish. 'Your job was to find and apprehend Bella Chantry, not to apprehend killers and help with negotiations. This obsession with detecting has lost us Ms Chantry. You were distracted by Mrs Cox's murder and forgot your main job. Now we're going to have to find her, *again*.'

'Yes,' said Cat. She felt guilty. They knew what Bella Chantry was like. She should have left Miranda here to keep an eye on her while she went chasing after Lady Bumstead and Messiah. Now she could be in India, or that might be a diversion. She could go via India and on to somewhere else. She brought her mind back to the consul who was still talking.

'Well,' he said, 'luckily we were checking the airports, and I believe she has been seen there. You'd better go after her. If she has a visa, we can easily discover which airport she is flying to. I'll have her tracked from there and see where she goes.' He gave a rather strained laugh. 'Shouldn't be so difficult. It's only the largest populated country in the world with the largest number of undocumented people living on the streets!' He gave a long-suffering sigh.

'Assuming you do find her, keep hold of her this time until you've escorted her back to the UK. Do not get sidetracked again.'

Cat bit her lip. It appeared they were being given a second chance.

'Hmm,' Miranda said, 'you don't seem very surprised that she left.'

The consul gave her a long look, then said, 'To be honest, Mrs Miranda, it suits our purpose. We had been informed she came here to meet someone. We were told it was Lady Bumstead, and, since she too had left the UK without permission, that seemed very possible. Our sources told us that Miss Victory was hoping to kill Lady Bumstead and take her place in society. Lady Bumstead's home would be a very comfortable hideout for Bella Chantry.'

'Oh. So, was there an arrangement to meet?' asked Miranda.

'No. Now we think not. Current feeling is that Lady Bumstead, who clearly thinks herself above authority, just felt like a holiday. A completely illogical woman.'

He shook his head, sighing at the incomprehensibility of the opposite sex. 'Clearly, Miss Victory had not envisaged the appearance of Messiah and his longing for revenge. We think his presence meant she changed her plans.'

He looked at the detectives. 'OK, your new job is to follow her, see what she is doing in India. As long as we know where she is, we can always bring her in, but we would rather discover why she broke out of prison, who she wants to meet, and why.'

'So,' said Miranda, grinning impishly, 'it wasn't Indiana Jones's treasure but instead something more sinister?'

He smiled politely. 'I'll get your tickets and visas.'

When he moved off to talk to Miss Abbey, Miranda said to Cat, twisting her lips, 'The government is using us! We thought we were just searching for Bella Chantry and bringing her home but there's more involved here.'

'Yes,' said Cat, feeling cheered. She'd always wanted to visit India. 'But could this be Bella teasing us? She might not be meeting anyone. This could just be her humour to have the UK law and us detectives chasing her around the world.'

Miranda shrugged. 'Who knows? However, one thing is certain – travel costs money and someone is paying. Who?'

So, thought Cat, they hadn't failed, they just hadn't had a

complete briefing. She walked up to the desk to tell the clerk they would be checking out.

'Mrs Cat?'

'Yes.'

'I have a message for you. It was left with the maid.'

Cat sighed. No prizes for guessing who that was from. 'Thank you.'

She took it and walked back to Miranda, opening the envelope Kalipha had given her. The message said:

Too slow, darling. I even warned you, and still I proved too clever for you. See you in India! And, just to help you on the way, I'm going to visit Teresa Bojaxhiu's grave. Tell Stevie you'll never find me unless she comes too!

'Who is Teresa Bojaxhiu?' asked Miranda.

'Mother Teresa,' said Cat. 'We are going to Kolkata.'

As Mr Fliter came back to say goodbye, Jade entered the hotel lobby.

'Come to pick up our things,' she said, smiling at the consul and the detectives. 'We're off soon, but I didn't want to go without saying goodbye to Sandy and thanking her for saving my grandmother.'

Sandy heard her name and came into the hall with Cyril. They were both laughing about something, grinning while trying to keep Elsa included. 'Thank you, Jade, that was nice of you: my dreams of being a hero never encompassed quoting the Quran in a cave in Petra.'

She gave Jade a hug, which the girl accepted awkwardly.

'Come and have a coffee with Cyril and Elsa.'

As they moved away, Cat turned to Mr Fliter and asked quietly, 'What will happen to Adam now? Will he be returned to Egypt?'

The consul looked surprised. 'Oh, sorry, I thought you knew.'

'Knew what?'

Mr Fliter made a self-deprecating smile. 'Yes, I think we have sorted that out rather successfully. A bit of a coup. In fact, Lady Bumstead and her granddaughter have been very helpful in this matter, something that won't go unnoticed when she goes to further sentence resolution.'

Cat tried not to groan. Poor Messiah.

'Jade and Adam got married in the British embassy this morning. It's not normally allowed unless you both live in Jordan but they got a special dispensation. Adam can now start the process to become a British citizen and he will be treated as such.'

'Married!' said Cat. 'So Jade did do a deal.'

Jade, who had stopped when she heard Cat talking about her, came back. She raised a cynical eyebrow at the group. 'You may not like it, Mrs Cat, but believe me, this is the best way. I want him. Jordan doesn't and Egypt doesn't either. Win–win. And I have friends who do archaeology in other countries. I can find him a job. In fact, I envisage him becoming the chief trainer of our new archaeology department in Underdog, the charity I'm running. Sometimes the people know best! Marrying in the British embassy was definitely the best way.'

Cyril laughed and dropped down onto one knee. 'Would you like to marry me in the embassy, Sandy?'

She blushed and then giggled. 'Yes... But not in the embassy. How embarrassing. But... oh heck! Let's go back to Britain and get to know each other. I *do* now know Elsa is your sister, but I still don't know why you carry baby wipes in your pocket.'

Elsa and Cyril laughed too, and he kissed Sandy's hand.

'Elsa is two months pregnant; I thought it as well to be prepared!'

Sandy nearly doubled up with uncontrollable giggles. 'Planning ahead or what! In that case I'm worried you're interested in me for the half a million blog followers who will be with me shortly.'

He got up and stroked her cheek. 'I love you, Sandy. We belong together!'

ACKNOWLEDGMENTS

Acknowledgements

Thanks to Sean McHale and Janie Grant for their medical expertise. Jenny Mackness for her hugely insightful blogs on wheelchair travel and her knowledge on the difficulties of wheelchair travel

My writing group for their support and encouragement and Jenny Bardwell for her help with the blurb.

Abbie Rutherford for editing, Lorna Hinde for proofreading and Kari Brownlie for yet another amazing cover

I also wanted to thank all the wonderful readers who have given me helpful reviews and been instrumental in improving my writing and my stories.

ABOUT THE AUTHOR

About the Author

Like many authors Gina has had a lot of different jobs and careers. She has been a physiotherapist, a flying instructor and pilot, a dog breeder, and a journalist. This is her sixth book in the SeeMs Detective series: the agency that looks behind what seems to be true.

Gina had two periods when she was in a wheelchair (after a car crash and a helicopter accident) and having experienced the difficulties of wheel chair travel first hand she wanted to write a book that showed the challenges for wheelchair users when travelling: not just steps and narrow doorways for example, but unexpected things like the difficulties of traversing cobbles.

When not writing or travelling Gina lives in Sussex with her husband and dogs.

If you feel like writing a review of this or any other of the Gina Cheyne books on Amazon or Goodreads it would be wonderful. Thank you.

For more information about Gina and her stories see:
www.ginacheyne.com

ALSO BY GINA CHEYNE

In the same series:

Book 1 The Mystery of the Lost Husbands

Book 2 Murder in the Cards

Book 3 The Mystery of the Homeless Man

Book 4 The Chameleon Killer Mystery

Book 5 After the Husbands

Under the name of Georgina Hunter-Jones

Atlantic Warriors

Peckham Diamonds

Comic books

The Twerple with Too Many Brains

Ronald the Postage Stamp

Wicked Wheeze

Nola the Rhinoceros

Biscuit and Oscar Learn to Fly

Pugwash Runs Away to Sea

NEXT IN THE SERIES

Death of a Tourist

Chapter One

The catalyst for the chaos was the fire in the substation at Heathrow, but the effect, which caught up 291,001 people and stopped 1,347 flights, also killed John Thomas Lang.

John Thomas Lang was one of the 291,001 passengers on their way to Heathrow, in his case from his holiday in India, and he was on the 10.50 flight out of Delhi.

Sitting in the departure lounge an hour after the flight should have been called John Thomas Lang wondered for the first time if there was a problem.

John Thomas was not a big reader of newspapers or even social media. He liked computer games, although not all the time, and, occasionally, he read paperbacks, but most of all he preferred colouring books. He was not one of those anxious men in suits worrying about timetables or one of the beautiful women abusing the ground staff. He was quite content sitting, gently colouring, and observing the chaos.

Finally, one of the harassed BA ground crew made an announcement. The flight was cancelled, all passengers would be reimbursed. First though, they must reverse their passage through security and departures to collect their luggage, then they would be allotted hotels in order of their status, starting with first class and progressing down to the *good value* seats.

John Thomas Lang was on a cheap flight.

After a long wait, standing on the tarmac and fighting for the few shady areas, John Thomas and his fellow 300 passengers were taken by bus to a hotel in the centre of Delhi. Once there they all moaned a bit and then enjoyed the fully paid for lunch and shared a beer or two (not courtesy of BA) in the shady garden. Then John Thomas fell asleep.

When JT awoke he found his drinking companions had gone and it was now evening. Bored of the hotel, but pleased about the extra two days of holiday from his supermarket job, he decided to go for a walk in Old Delhi. As he left the hotel one of the other BA refugees caught up with him and they agreed to share a taxi downtown. The taxi driver dropped them outside the old mosque.

JT's body was found next day in an ally in Chandni Chowk area where old Delhi and New Delhi meet. Not far from the famous Red Fort, which sadly he had omitted to visit.

www.ingramcontent.com/pod-product-compliance
Lightning Source LLC
Chambersburg PA
CBHW050604190726
48283CB00007B/2272